PIE  RATS

THE TROPHY OF CHAMPIONS

Cyclone Sea

Western Passage

DRUMSTICK ISLAND

THE CRESCENT SEA

PHOENIX ISLAND

Devil's Cliffs

SEA SHANTY ISLAND

RUINED CITADEL

Silver Falls

King River

West

Eastern River

ISLAND OF KINGS

Southern Passage

QUEEN ISLAND

CLAW'S REACH

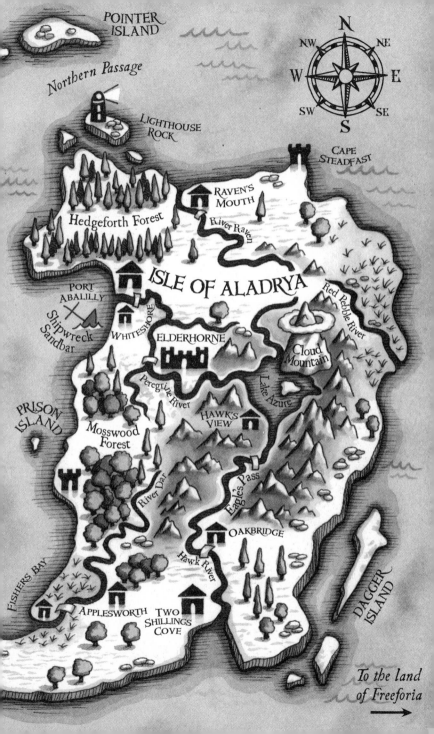

PIE 🐀 RATS

THE TROPHY OF CHAMPIONS

CAMERON STELZER

Illustrations by the Author

DAYDREAM
PRESS

*For my sister, Lauren,
the little champion.*

*Thank you to Tyson, Rachael, Sarah
and Jenny for their input into this story. C.S.*

First published by Daydream Press, Brisbane, Australia, 2015
Text and illustrations copyright © Dr Cameron Stelzer 2015
Illustrations are watercolour and pen on paper

National Library of Australia Cataloguing-in-Publication Entry
Creator: Stelzer, Cameron, 1977 – author, illustrator.
Title: The Trophy of Champions / by Cameron Stelzer
ISBN: 978 0 9874615 3 7 (paperback)
Series: Stelzer, Cameron, 1977 – Pie Rats; bk. 4.
Target audience: For primary school age.
Subjects: Rats – Juvenile fiction. Pirates – Juvenile fiction.
Dewey number: A823.4

Printed in China by Everbest Printing Co Ltd

When victory appears unattainable,
true champions rise to the challenge.

The Book of Knowledge

A Dark Descent

The small, hooded creature moved swiftly through the shadowy undergrowth of the forest. Rust-coloured strips of bark, dry and flaking, lay strewn across his path. To his left and right, the slender trunks of grey gums rose majestically into the air, their uppermost branches swaying rhythmically in the overhead wind. Each falling leaf sparkled like gold in the flickering rays of the dying summer sun.

With urgency and purpose, he leapt over crumbling logs and bounded through patches of sprawling lantana, his tiny feet barely touching the ground. His cloak caught on prickly burrs and his fur snagged on sharp twigs, but he tore himself free, never slowing his frantic pace.

Reaching the edge of a small gully, he suddenly halted and threw back his hood. The heavy aroma of eucalyptus oil filled his nostrils. It masked any scents of lurking predators, but the awkward twitch in his tail told him he wasn't alone.

Cautiously, he began creeping past blackened stumps and withered shrubs, towards a dry riverbed at the foot of the gully. He knew if he could reach the riverbed unseen, he still had a chance.

Rivers lead to the sea, he told himself. *And the sea is where I'll find them ...*

The sun vanished from sight as he moved deeper into the gully. Fine webs of silk hung motionless between dead branches. Oily red sap oozed from the sides of pale trunks. The entire place sent a shiver down his tail.

Something's here, he trembled. *I know it ...*

In trepidation, he moved forward, barely daring to breathe. He was quiet – but not silent.

The first blast echoed over his left shoulder, shattering the stillness. He threw himself headfirst into a pile of leaves as a huge shape crashed into a tree above him.

Rolling clear of the avalanche of falling debris, he heard a second ear-splitting *BOOM!* The riverbank in front of him exploded, sending pebbles and bark ricocheting in all directions. He ducked to his right to evade a flying stone, somersaulted over a gnarled tree root and took off through the undergrowth.

With the roar of cannons in his ears, he clawed his way through the dense vegetation lining the riverbank. Dark shapes hurtled overhead, crashing into the furrowed trunks of ironbark trees, sending jagged splinters raining down around him.

There was no thought of stopping.

The river turned south-west and the rough slopes of the gully transformed into sandstone cliffs. Avoiding the *easy* route through the open riverbed, he began scaling a rocky cliff to higher ground. He moved stealthily over the rocks, his agile tail aiding his ascent, his dusty, grey cloak camouflaging his body.

Reaching the top of the cliff, with no sign of his pursuers, he began his descent past young saplings and spindly paperbarks. Behind him, a dusty amber glow lingered in the western sky. The first evening stars twinkled high overhead. Peering through the gaps in the foliage, he saw the riverbed snaking east to the shoreline.

I can be there before darkness sets in, he thought. *If I hurry.*

With blue eyes fixed on the river mouth, he took a step forward – and stopped. Cocking his head to one side, he squinted into the distance to where a shadowy black shape moved across the waves.

There was a mighty gust of wind and the swaying branches blocked his vision. When the leaves had stopped quivering, the black shape was gone.

Puzzled, he pushed his way through the trees to a rocky outcrop, hoping for a clearer view. From the edge of the plateau, he could see the entire eastern ocean spreading out in front of him, empty and still. As he reached down for a small spyglass tucked in his drawstring bag, he felt something brush past his whiskers.

He had just enough time to glimpse a long, straight shaft whizzing through the air before it disappeared into the undergrowth.

'Arrows!' he hissed, throwing himself to the ground. *They've found me ... and they're close.*

Flattening his body against the rock, he scanned the ridge for an escape route. The quickest way down was directly in front of him: a steep, gravelly slope, descending almost all the way to the ocean. With a cliff on one side and sparse vegetation to the other, the slope was even more exposed than the riverbed.

One clean shot and I'm done, he told himself.

He glanced to his right, searching for another option.

Nearby, the trunk of an enormous grey gum rose from the plateau. Where its bark had fallen away, huge orange sections covered its trunk. Thick strips of reddish-tinged bark lay in a pile at its base. As the bark had dried, it had curved inwards to form long canoe-like shapes.

A canoe needs water, he thought hopelessly ... *or does it?*

With the sound of approaching footsteps, he knew he must act fast. Slithering across the ground like a snake, he moved towards the foot of the tree, searching for the perfect piece of bark: medium length, flat bottom, curved sides, raised front ...

He found it just in time.

There was a loud *STOMP* directly behind him. Grabbing the edges of the bark with both paws, he raised it like a shield and ran towards the slope.

He felt a sudden jolt as an arrow grazed the side of the bark, throwing him off balance. He half-leapt, half-fell over the edge, throwing the makeshift sled beneath him. The bark hit the slope at speed and his chest slammed down on top of it. Head lowered and body rigid, he held on for dear life.

He'd only travelled a few metres when he heard the faint twang of a bow string and knew a second arrow was already on its way.

Taking evasive action, he threw his entire body to the left, catapulting the right edge of the sled into the air. The arrow bounced harmlessly off the high bark wall, but the craft veered dangerously close to the edge of the cliff.

Panic-stricken, he hurled his body to the opposite side of the sled to counteract the momentum. For a moment he was skidding precariously along the very edge of the cliff.

Then, with the pull of his weight, the sled began to right its course.

With a breath of relief, he lifted his head and scanned the sky for further arrows. The air was clear, but the slope ahead revealed something far worse: an entire line of egg-shaped rocks.

He let out a horrified gasp. There was no way around.

Without brakes, he acted daringly and decisively. Leaping to the very back of the sled, he grabbed the upper edges of the bark with both paws and slowly stood up. As the lichen-covered rocks came into range, he leant back as far as he could and raised the front half of the sled off the ground.

There was a sickening *SCREEECH* as the bottom of the bark collided with the rocks, almost throwing him free. The next moment, the sled was airborne, soaring high over the stones and gravel like a strange, wingless bird – surrounded by stars, held up by the wind. Then it was falling, plummeting down towards the barren slope.

The back of the sled hit first, gouging into the ground. Its passenger lost his grip and sprawled face-down in the centre of the sled. He dug his claws into the bark to steady himself, as his tail and legs bounced uncontrollably behind him.

When he finally managed to regain his balance and clamber to his knees, the sled was already speeding down the final section of the hill.

The gravelly slope levelled out into a grassy meadow extending to the sandy dunes of the coastline. The battered sled skidded to a halt at the foot of a small banksia shrub and its shaken passenger scrambled out.

There's still time, he told himself, fixing his sights on a dune near the river mouth. *But only just …*

With the last hint of colour fading from the sky, he set off across the gently swaying field of redgrass. Parched by a long, hot summer, the grass was thin and dry. Withered stalks crunched under his feet. Straw-like stems rustled beside him.

As he crossed the darkening field, he noticed other sounds: the soft swish of the wind; the gentle rumble of breaking waves … and something else.

Standing on the tips of his toes, he peered above the surrounding seed heads. To his right, not far from the riverbed, he saw movement in the tallest stalks of grass.

At first he mistook it for the wind, but as he looked closer, he realised the grass was parting to form a path – a path headed in his direction.

His heart beating fast, he turned on his heel and ran. Tall stalks of grass battered his face and eyes. The sharp edges of leaves sliced past him like knives, cutting his feet and paws.

Ignoring the pain, he kept on running, tearing through the field like a flame in straw.

He heard scampering footsteps on either side of him and knew his pursuers were close. The next moment, an arrow raced past him, clipping the sleeve of his coat.

Head down, he ducked and wove through the thinning grass, not daring to stop. There was no thought of hiding – movement was his only defence.

He rolled, dived and twisted like an eel, changing direction with every step. The steady stream of arrows missed their mark and the sound of footsteps slowly faded to other parts of the field.

When he finally ventured to raise his head, the dune

was right in front of him. Smooth, white and pure, it beckoned him closer.

With aching limbs he began his ascent. The fine grains of sand felt warm beneath his paws and the salty air of the sea tingled on the back of his throat. He took a deep, calming breath.

At last, he thought. *I'm here.*

Exhausted, he reached the crest of the dune. Behind him the field of grass lay silent and still. In front of him, in silhouette against the deep blue of the twilight sky, stood three rats.

They took one look at him, drew their weapons and charged.

TWO

Familiar Faces

T hree rats …

The words echoed through his mind, awakening a memory. For a moment he was somewhere else. He was standing on a sundrenched beach surrounded by three familiar faces. A deep yearning filled his heart as he pictured them standing beside him – his mother, his father, his sister. He wished they were with him now …

With a small sigh, he was back on the dune and the advancing figures began to grow clearer.

The first rat was dressed in a red and black long-sleeve sports top with a golden rat insignia across the chest. On his head, he wore a stately black captain's hat. He whispered a hasty command to his companions before raising a strange scissor-shaped sword above his head.

The second rat, dressed in a similar sports uniform, grunted a response and aimed a giant fork at the stranger. This rat was huge and hunched and towered above the dune like a misshapen piece of driftwood. His oversized chef's hat flapped in the wind, his safety pin earring swayed back and forth, and his monstrous left eye stared down like a full moon on a cloudless night.

There was a soft *swish* of sand as the third rat

approached, balancing on the tip of his wooden pencil leg. As his bony frame drew closer, a strange ticking sound resonated from a small object in his paw. He sniffed the air with his long, crooked nose and narrowed his pink albino eyes at the stranger in the cloak.

The stranger looked from one hostile rat to the next and then slowly removed his hood. As the folds of fabric dropped lightly to his shoulders, the unruly fur on the top of his head sprang up like the leaves of a pineapple, revealing his true identity.

The three rats stopped dead in their tracks.

'Oh my precious paws!' exclaimed the rat with the pencil leg. 'It's you, *Whisker*. We weren't expecting you for another twenty minutes.'

'Hi, Pete,' Whisker squeaked. 'Better early than late.'

As the other rats slowly lowered their weapons, Pencil Leg Pete held out a shiny brass pocket watch and pointed to the minute hand.

'Take a look at your time, young apprentice,' he said excitedly. 'No one has completed the Treasure Hunt training course in less than ninety minutes, let alone seventy.'

Before Whisker could reply, the giant rat stepped forward, grabbed him by the collar and hoisted him into the air.

'Bravo, Whisker,' he grunted, giving the small rat a crushing bear hug. 'You're a champion.'

'Steady – on – Fred –' Whisker gasped, struggling for air. 'I couldn't have done it without all the unexpected encouragement.'

The rat in the captain's hat laughed out loud and clapped Pencil Leg Pete on the back. 'Did you hear that?

Encouragement indeed. That's the politest description of a surprise cannon attack I've heard in years.'

'Aye, Captain,' Pete said, deadpan. 'But I'm sure he wouldn't be as complimentary if he arrived back with half his leg missing.'

Whisker stared down at Pete's pencil leg and gulped.

'Don't worry, Whisker,' the Captain said in a deep, reassuring voice. 'I'm sure none of the cannons were actually aimed at you.'

'You might be right about the cannons,' Whisker conceded, 'but the arrows were awfully accurate.'

The Captain let out a long sigh, 'That sounds like my dear niece, Ruby. Always the perfectionist.'

'In my defence,' cried a voice from the field, 'they weren't technically arrows and I didn't actually hit anyone.'

Whisker looked down to see the immaculately presented Ruby Rat striding towards the dune. She carried a silver bow over one shoulder and a quiver of arrows over the other. Her crimson eye patch framed her stern yet attractive face and her green eye sparkled up at him like an emerald.

Before Whisker knew what was happening, Ruby had plucked a long, slim shaft from her quiver and was aiming it directly at him.

'Do you have a problem with my archery, apprentice?' she asked, twitching her fingers on the string.

'N-no,' Whisker stammered. 'I'd just prefer if you pointed that thing somewhere else.'

Ruby shrugged. 'Sure thing, Whisker.'

Without warning, she spun the bow to her left and released the string. The arrow sped through the air, striking the backside of a short rat staggering out of the grass.

'Shiver me britches!' he yelled, tumbling to the ground. 'We're under attack. Raise the alarm!'

Ruby ignored the theatrical display and began marching up the dune. She gave Whisker a sly wink as she passed. 'It's about time I hit something …'

Whisker glanced uneasily at the small rat, rolling around in the grass.

'Will Horace be alright …?' he began.

With an annoyed huff, Ruby pulled another arrow from her quiver and thrust it at Whisker.

'Hollow-stemmed bulrush,' she said abruptly. 'I took the liberty of removing the spiky tip. I doubt it could hurt a fly.'

There was an agitated buzz of wings from the Captain's shoulder and a large green blowfly raised four tiny fists in the air as if to say, *don't you even try it.*

'Steady on, Smudge,' the Captain said calmly. 'I'm sure Ruby has no intention of harming our official mascot.'

Smudge lowered his fists and settled back on his perch. Whisker turned his attention to the bulrush and ran his fingers over its spongy, sausage-shaped end.

'So much for impenetrable bark,' he thought aloud. 'It's no wonder the arrows simply bounced off.'

'They can still bruise a backside,' Hook Hand Horace called out, rubbing his rear end with his golden hook. 'My sensitive skin is sixteen times softer than gnarled old tree bark.'

Ruby rolled her eye. 'Save the science for the scientists, Horace.'

'Rotten pies to scientists!' Horace shot back. 'I know what I'm talking about. You can look it up in that dusty old book if you don't believe me.'

Fish Eye Fred

Captain Black Rat

Pencil Leg Pete

TEAM
PIE RATS

Whisker

Smudge

Hook Hand Horace

Ruby Rat

'Shh,' the Captain hissed. 'The Book of Knowledge is not something to be discussed in public.'

The Captain glanced around suspiciously and lowered his voice. 'I can't stress to you enough the importance of secrecy when it comes to that item – especially here. The Pirate Cup gathers the vilest of villains and rottenest of rogues together in one location. Regardless of how private your conversations may appear, there is always someone listening. Is that understood?'

'Aye aye, Captain,' Horace sighed. 'I won't mention you-know-what again.'

'Good,' the Captain said. 'Given the right situation, the information contained in that book could give us a superior tactical advantage over our competitors. It may sound a tad academic, but *brains* are just as important as *brawn* in the Pirate Cup. Now, if we have concluded the science lesson, I suggest we get a move on. The opening ceremony commences at midnight tonight, and I am yet to introduce you to our new head coach.'

Pete's ears pricked up. 'Head coach? Who? Why wasn't I consulted about this?'

'It was a last minute decision,' the Captain replied flatly, 'and one made in the best interests of the crew.'

Pete held his ground, ready to mount a challenge.

The Captain let out a troubled groan and tried to explain. 'As you are aware, our entire campaign had been funded by Madam Pearl, our gracious benefactor. It is also no secret that she expects a winning result. You might assume we can simply sail away with a second place and try our luck elsewhere. But the fact remains that as soon as Madam Pearl's assistance runs out, we find ourselves stone broke. The *Apple Pie* is in desperate need of repair, we have a growing number of mouths to feed and, with the entire Aladryan navy breathing down our necks, our future pirating prospects look even slimmer than our bank balance! It pains me to admit it, but the competition prize money may be our sole means of staying afloat.'

'I hear you. I hear you,' Pete snorted. 'We win or we starve. My only hope is that this mysterious coach of yours is some kind of gold-medal guru. I doubt we can win one bloodthirsty event on our own, let alone the entire tournament.'

The Captain managed a wry smile. 'Let's just say I've enlisted the services of someone highly *motivational ...*'

The return trek through the forest was pleasantly uneventful. Whisker led the march up the dry riverbed, with Ruby and Horace keeping pace beside him. Only a tiny sliver of the moon was visible in the western sky and Horace carried a flaming torch in his hook, illuminating the way.

'You're taking this Pirate Cup thing pretty seriously, Whisker,' Horace panted, struggling to keep up with the energetic rat. 'I mean, I've wanted to win since I was a kid and I know how much is at stake for the Captain, but you've taken things to a whole new level. My mind boggles at how much training you can fit into one day.' He peered across at Ruby and cautiously added, 'And here I was thinking *Little Miss Archery* was the competitive one. She's always got something to prove.'

Lost in her own thoughts, Ruby said nothing. Whisker simply shrugged and increased his pace. Deep down inside he knew that it wasn't his desire to win the cup that spurred him on. It was the training itself. The long, gruelling days of running, sailing and diving had given him a new focus. Each hour of training had taken his mind off the one thing he was powerless to control: finding his family.

In the rare stillness of the evening, his mind drifted back to the moment he first glimpsed his father's boat, repaired and restored by Rat Bait after the terrible cyclone. There had been no sign of Whisker's family when Rat Bait purchased the dilapidated vessel on Drumstick Island and, after much questioning, the only useful information the old rogue could share was: *'I be buyin' the boat from a trader. Strange fellow he was, a fox with no name, wearin' a long black coat ...'*

As a gesture of goodwill, Rat Bait offered Whisker the restored boat: the *Golden Anchor*. Whisker resolved that he would only accept the vessel after he had found his family.

In days that followed, the Pie Rats had searched every small island in the Cyclone Sea, following a map from the newly acquired Book of Knowledge. Although the islands were close to where Whisker's family had disappeared, his heart was never fully in the search. He knew what they would discover before they even started looking.

Empty handed, they had sailed east to Drumstick Island, where Whisker hoped to locate the mysterious fox. To his dismay, the elusive trader had vanished without a trace, leaving no clue as to who he was or where he was headed.

Now, walking through the dark forest on Dagger Island, Whisker's heart was heavy. He was no closer to finding his parents and sister than he was when the Pie Rats first plucked him from the stormy ocean many weeks earlier.

Refusing to wallow in his own misery, he tried to focus on the days ahead, hoping the thrill of the Centenary Games would somehow fill the void in his heart. Images of cheering spectators, last minute goals and victory parades filled his mind. He even pictured himself holding up the famed *Trophy of Champions* – a dream shared by Ruby and Horace. But as hard as he tried, the emptiness remained.

'Whisker?' Ruby said, breaking his concentration.

'Yeah,' he mumbled, his head still in a dark cloud.

'There's something I've been puzzling over,' she said softly.

Whisker turned to look at her. In the flickering light of Horace's torch he could see her staring straight at him, as if reading his thoughts.

'When we first arrived here,' she continued, 'Rat Bait told me that *everyone who's anyone* will be at these games.'

'Everyone?' he repeated.

'Well, not technically everyone,' Horace butted in. 'I doubt General Thunderclaw and his Blue Claw buddies got an official invite. And Mr Tribble and the twins aren't coming, not with school starting back in Oakbridge. And it's too risky for our fugitive sponsor Madam Pearl to make an appearance …'

'That's not what I meant, Horace,' Ruby snapped. 'Rat Bait was referring to every scoundrel and villain of importance. You know, the kingpins of the smuggling world and the godfathers of piracy.'

'Not my godfather,' Horace said. 'He has a weak bladder and doesn't travel well … although my Mama, Papa and sisters are coming, and my Papa Niko is a big shot in the

25

Death Ball world – he coached the Freeforian Firetails to three consecutive inter-island championships.'

'Thank you for that highly relevant information,' Ruby said sarcastically. 'I'll make sure I ask your papa for some little league tips if I run into him.' Frowning, she turned back to Whisker. 'Where was I?'

'Scoundrels and villains,' Whisker replied.

'Oh, yes,' Ruby said, collecting her thoughts. 'According to Rat Bait, the Pirate Cup doubles as a lucrative business opportunity for underworld figures. Its secret location is the perfect place to cut a deal, plan a heist or –' she paused for impact, 'offload a shipment of stolen goods without the authorities knowing.'

'I'm not quite following you,' Whisker said quizzically. 'Is there something on the black market you want to buy?'

Ruby shook her head. 'It's not the goods I'm talking about, it's the shady characters selling them.'

'Traders,' Whisker gasped, suddenly understanding.

'Exactly,' Ruby said. 'Items sold during the games often fetch top dollar. When the money is flowing, the traders swoop like vultures. If your nameless fox has something valuable to trade, he'll make an appearance sooner or later.'

Whisker felt a wave of excitement race up his tail. He couldn't believe what he was hearing. Instead of searching the vast oceans for the mysterious trader, all he had to do was wait for the fox to come to him.

'Oh, one other thing,' Ruby added. 'Spectators always spend more money when they're being entertained.'

'And how do we do that?' Horace asked, re-joining the conversation. 'Comedic routines? Death defying stunts?'

'That's easy,' Ruby grinned. 'We win in style!'

26

THREE

Suitcases

The athletes' village of the 25th Pirate Cup was a hive of activity. Teepees, tents and primitive bark huts covered almost every inch of the grassy clearing. Dozens of small iron braziers burned freely, spreading a warm orange glow over the entire campsite. Feathered, furred and scaly creatures bustled to and fro in the firelight, polishing weapons and adding the final touches to their team uniforms.

Doubling as a spectators' resort, the village had it all: souvenir stands, food stalls, betting parlours and the glorious Champions Tavern. Covered by a huge canvas roof, the tavern was the social heart of the games. Long planks of freshly-cut timber, raised on tree stumps, ran the entire length of the expanse to form enormous tabletops. Huge barrels of Apple Fizz, Hot Chilli Cola and Blackberry Surprise lined the back wall, waiting for thirsty competitors to flood in after a gruelling day's events.

Situated on the western side of the island, a short walk from the marina berths, the village provided easy access to the nearby waterhole and the outlying Death Ball arena. Further to the south, a cleared strip of land served as the cannon firing range.

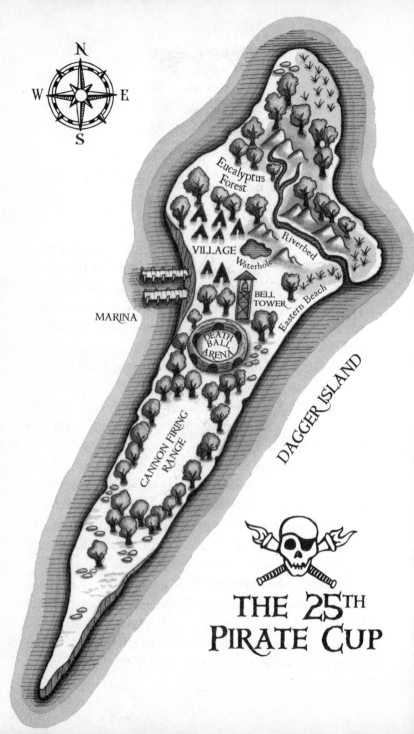

Whisker arrived back at the bustling village to see dozens of noisy spectators pouring through a ticket booth. His eyes darted from animal to animal, hoping for a glimpse of orange fur or a flash of black fabric.

Be patient, he told himself. *Your trader will come.*

'Has your mother turned up with our spare uniforms yet, Horace?' the Captain asked, lowering a small map of the island and peering around the crowd.

'Not yet, Captain,' Horace squeaked, trying to blow out his torch without singeing his whiskers. 'She's arriving on the last ferry from Freeforia.' He raised his flaming torch and looked in the direction of the marina. 'I think they've just docked. I recognise some of the ...'

With a loud *CRACKLE*, Horace's whiskers caught alight. He threw his hook in the air and let out a panicked *'SQUEAK!'*

Fred gave the torch an enormous puff, extinguishing the flames and sending Horace's oversized purple hat flying through the open window of a tent.

There was a terrible screech from inside and a wrinkly old rat poked her head through the doorway. Horace's hat sat sideways across her head.

'Which one of you despicable, low-life drongos threw this lice-infested hat at me?' she yelled, throwing the hat to the ground.

'It was the wind,' Horace coughed through the cloud of smoke. 'A big gust of wind.'

The old rat glared at Horace, unconvinced.

The Captain took a hasty step forward before things got out of control.

'I think a few introductions are in order,' he said, helping the furious old rat out of the tent. 'Crew, may I present to you Granny Rat, my beloved mother and your new head coach.'

The unexpected announcement caught the crew by surprise. Horace's jaw dropped open, Whisker's tail went into a spasm and Pete almost broke a lead. Fred, in his usual gentle manner, began a polite round of applause. Granny Rat ignored all four of them and took a step towards Ruby.

Ruby crossed her arms and scowled, clearly displeased with her uncle's surprise choice of coach.

'And how's my favourite granddaughter?' Granny Rat asked, brushing a fleck of dust off Ruby's scarlet vest.

'*Only* granddaughter,' Ruby corrected, gruffly.

'Yes, well, it's good to find you in a presentable state for a change,' Granny Rat said, ignoring Ruby's hostile demeanour. 'I may have failed in preventing you from becoming a lawless pirate, but at least I gave you a firm grounding in how to be a stylish one.'

'My cabin's not filled with pretty little skull-and-cross-bones dresses if that's what you're implying,' Ruby huffed.

'No,' Granny Rat murmured, locking eyes with her headstrong granddaughter. 'That would be too much to expect …' She sighed to herself then resumed her small talk as if the two rats were best friends. 'So, have you met any respectable cabin boys yet?'

Ruby mumbled something inaudible and Whisker looked awkwardly at his toes.

'Chin up, Sonny,' Granny Rat snapped, whipping her head in his direction. 'You won't win the Pirate Cup staring at the ground.'

Startled, Whisker leapt to attention like a soldier on parade. Granny Rat hobbled over to him with an expression that was anything but granny-like. Her ageing body was slight and frail, but her mind was sharper than a razor. It wasn't hard for Whisker to see why she'd been recruited as the head coach.

What Granny Rat wants, Granny Rat gets, he thought to himself.

'You must be the new apprentice,' she said, eyeing him suspiciously. '*Wafer* or whatever your name is.'

'It's Whisker, actually,' Whisker replied.

'Well, Wafer,' she continued, 'I've heard you're quite the adventurer. My dear fool of a husband, the Hermit, hasn't stopped gabbling on about you since he returned from his island hiatus. From what I've deciphered from his ramblings, you've already passed four apprenticeship tests and are on track to becoming a capable young Pie Rat. I personally can't see any of that by looking at you and you're yet to pass the all-important *Pie Rat Sailing Test*, but if you combed your pirate fur and learnt to control that fidgeting tail of yours, you might just win us a medal.'

She leant closer to Whisker and whispered with minty breath, 'I'll have you know that this isn't the first time I've coached a team in the Pirate Cup, but unlike my previous team's pathetic performance, I intend to leave these games as a victor. Understand?'

'Yes, coach,' Whisker replied, straightening his messy fringe with his trembling tail. 'I won't let you down.'

Granny Rat relaxed a few wrinkles and turned to the hulking figure of Fred and the miniscule body of Horace.

'As for you two …' she began.

While the newly appointed head coach gave Horace and Fred a pep talk on personal hygiene and team etiquette, a wiry rat wearing a baggy tracksuit approached the tent. He dropped two large suitcases on the ground and crumpled over in exhaustion.

'Hermit not used to girls' suitcases, no, no,' he panted. 'Girls bring half a house with them.'

'Don't ye be complainin',' puffed a portly rat behind him, carrying an even larger suitcase. 'Me case be three times the size o' yers.' He straightened his back and began fanning himself with his tattered blue captain's hat.

Granny Rat   Rat Bait   The Hermit

'I'm too old to be carryin' damsel's bags, especially with me injury,' he said, pointing to a large, purple circle around his left eye. 'This bruise be growin' bigger by the minute –'

Before he could continue, there were several high-pitched squeals from a nearby ticket booth.

'Over there,' cried an excited voice. 'It's Horace … near the tent.'

'Are you sure?' shrilled another. 'He looks shorter.'

'It's him alright,' exclaimed a third. 'Look at those legs. He always was the runt of the litter!'

Horace stuck his head in his hook and whispered, 'Save me, Whisker. I'm trapped between a maniac coach who wants to bathe me in bleach and three squealing sisters who think I'm a suckling pig.'

As the three overdressed rats pranced towards the pile of suitcases, Whisker wondered if he was looking at the right sisters. Each girl was tall, slender and elegantly presented – a stark contrast to Horace's stocky frame and ill-fitting pirate attire. With fine features and perfectly straight teeth, the sisters could easily be mistaken for fashion models or pageant queens.

The tallest of the three rats addressed Horace in a patronising tone. 'Hello, *big* brother. We almost didn't recognise you. It's been such a long time …'

'Hi, Hera,' Horace replied, gazing up at her. 'Still growing I see.'

'Perhaps,' she said with a bored shrug. 'Or perhaps you're just shrinking –'

Horace shot Whisker a look that said, *see what I mean.*

The second sister lowered the novel she was reading and gave Whisker a flirtatious wink through a pair of red spectacles.

Aphrodite   *Hera*   *Athena*

'So, Brother,' she said, not taking her eyes off Whisker, 'when are you going to introduce us to your handsome friend?'

'Oh,' Horace said. 'Of course, Athena. How remiss of me.' He cleared his throat and waved his hook in a circle around his companion. 'This, my dear sisters, is Whisker, master escape artist and apprentice extraordinaire.'

The three girls batted their eyelashes and curtseyed in unison. 'Hi, Whisker.'

Whisker suddenly felt like a deer in lamplights. His tail coiled around his leg. Death-defying escapes were one thing, but girls had never been one of his strong points.

Horace continued, 'And these are my three sisters, Hera, Athena and Aphrodite – equally famous for their beauty as they are for their bickering.'

'Bickering?' exclaimed the youngest and prettiest rat, almost dropping her small pocket mirror. 'Since when? Everyone knows I'm perfectly agreeable all of the time …'

'Put a sock in it, Aphrodite,' Hera broke in. 'You and Athena spend more time arguing than you do looking in the mirror. Now, if you simply learnt to do what you were told …'

As the sisters continued their petty quarrelling, an extremely short rat, wearing a Pie Rat supporter's cap, staggered into view. He carried a suitcase and was clearly struggling to keep it from dragging on the ground. A plump, jolly-faced rat in a golden shawl walked beside him, clutching a basket of fresh chillies. When she saw Horace, she immediately dropped her basket and rushed over to him, smothering him in hugs and kisses.

'My darling Horace,' she laughed in a rich, velvety accent. 'It is so good to see you.'

'You too, Mama Kolina,' Horace said warmly, hugging her back. 'Look, here's my friend, Whisker.'

'Ah, Whisker,' Mama Kolina exclaimed, releasing Horace and throwing her arms around the startled onlooker.

Mama Kolina kissed Whisker on both cheeks and then placed her paws on his shoulders.

Papa Niko   *Mama Kolina*

'You need anything, you ask Mama Kolina,' she said with a wide grin. 'I cook chilli pies, I mend uniforms, I run errands, I polish boots ...'

'Yes, Mama,' Horace said, his ears turning red with embarrassment. 'He gets the idea.'

Horace directed Whisker over to his father, still struggling with the suitcase.

'And this is my Papa Niko,' Horace said proudly.

Papa Niko lowered his bags and shook Whisker's paw.

'That's a mighty strong striker's grip you've got there,'

he said, clutching Whisker's right arm. 'I take it you've played some Death Ball?'

'A little,' Whisker replied.

'It's a great game, Death Ball,' Papa Niko said, with a broad smile. 'Why, it was just the other day I was talking to Frankie Belorio about that very thing.'

'Frankie Belorio?' Whisker said, trying to place the name.

'You know,' Papa Niko went on. 'Frankie *the flame*, the *Big B*, Super Slammer of '86, the fastest Bilby in the Aladryan league, world record holder for the most goals scored in consecutive games ...'

'Yes, of course,' Whisker said, still drawing a blank, '*him*.'

'Do you want his autograph?' Papa Niko asked. 'I can get it for you – no sweat. I know he's a big celebrity and all but he's on a promotional tour in Two Shillings Cove, not far from here, and he owes me a favour.'

'Gee, thanks,' Whisker mumbled.

'Speaking of all things Frankie,' Papa Niko continued, 'I've got an inside scoop – straight from the Bilby's mouth. I'm yet to learn the details, but Frankie's working on a new set play for the winter season.' He beckoned for Whisker and Horace to move closer and whispered, 'It's called the *Double Decoy – Centre Steal*. Pretty amazing, hey? You should see his set plays from last season – unbelievable! I'll show you sometime. When's your next training session?'

'Err ... I'm not exactly sure,' Whisker replied, 'but right now we need to get ready for the opening ceremony.'

'Of course you do,' Papa Niko laughed. 'Hey, that reminds me, I saw some of the other teams down at the marina – big strong brutes, all of them. Boy oh boy, it's going to be a fierce competition.'

The Centenary Games

D ressed in their official team colours of red, black and gold, the Pie Rats stood in the shadows of the dark tunnel, awaiting their entry cue. Large sheets of bark curved over their heads, supported by a framework of sticks and rope. Through small cracks in the bark, Whisker could see the flickering light of hundreds of flaming torches in the grandstands above him. The dull stomping of feet and the muffled shouts of excited spectators reverberated through the roof.

Clearly visible at the end of the tunnel was the glorious Death Ball arena, a dusty circle of earth where challengers would battle for victory in the days to come.

Joining the Pie Rats in the tunnel were their team officials: Granny Rat (Head Coach), the Hermit (Team Trainer) and Rat Bait (Chief of Security). The noticeable absentees were Madam Pearl (Team Sponsor) and the three mice. With an enormous bounty on her head, the fugitive white weasel had decided it was safer not to attend the games, while Mr Tribble, Eaton and Emmie were forced to return to Oakbridge Primary School for the start of the autumn term.

Whisker was glad to have Rat Bait as a valued member

of the team. The reformed scoundrel had found a new lease on life since landing on the island and he seemed determined to prove his loyalty to the Pie Rats. Wearing a black shirt marked *SECURITY,* he appeared to know more than anyone about the evening's proceedings, and it came as no surprise to Whisker to learn that Rat Bait and the Hermit were both members of Granny Rat's original Pirate Cup team.

'Any moment now,' Rat Bait whispered to Whisker, as the sound of the crowd grew louder. 'It's always the same. As soon as the mysterious organiser appears, the teams'll parade out.' He gave his swollen eye a quick rub. 'Tell me when we're up, lad, me vision's still a bit hazy.'

Whisker looked cagily at Rat Bait's black eye.

'Did you get that in the line of duty, sir?' he asked.

'Err, not exactly,' Rat Bait answered sheepishly. 'It be more a matter o' someone settlin' an old score.' He shot Granny a quick glance and whispered. 'Best ye be followin' yer coach's instructions, young Whisker.'

'Aye,' Whisker said, with wide eyes.

There was a loud fanfare of trumpets and the entire crowd fell silent. Whisker saw a tall white rabbit in a purple coat and a top hat hopping into view. With several graceful bounds, he reached the centre of the arena and raised a funnel-shaped bullhorn to his mouth.

'Ladies and gentlemen,' he began in a thick accent, 'it is a great pleasure to velcome you to ze twenty-fifth Pirate Cup. As you know, zis spectacular event is held once every four years, making zis year's tournament ze Centenary Games. I am Baron Gustave, otherwise known as 'G', your games organiser.'

There was an enthusiastic round of applause.

Baron Gustave

Horace nudged Whisker with his hook. 'I thought I recognised him. Baron Gustave owns the Gunpowder Galleria on Sea Shanty Island.'

'Remind me to thank him sometime,' Whisker murmured. 'That Gourmet Gunpowder really packs a punch.'

The sound of the crowd died down and Gustave continued, 'As you are avare, ze authorities have gone out of zeir vay to stop zese games. Rest assured, no Pirate Cup has ever been cancelled. Nor vill it be. Zis year's entries may be small, but ze talent is enormous.'

The crowd roared and Gustave pointed to a tunnel on

the opposite side of the arena.

'Presenting ze first challengers. From ze icy waters of Antarctica, I give you ze Penguin Pirates!'

There was a cacophony of squawks and hoots as six identical fairy penguins waddled out. Each wore a checked bandanna and a navy blue singlet with the monogram *PP* emblazoned across the chest. A flag bearer at the front of the procession carried an enormous navy and white flag.

'Me old employers from the south,' Rat Bait laughed. 'Not the fastest bunch o' birds in a footrace, but they're as quick as fish in the water.'

Gustave pointed to a second tunnel and continued his introductions. 'From ze west coast of Aladrya, I present to you ze Cane Toad River Pirates!'

With loud *CROAKS* and *RIBBITS,* six large cane toads hopped into the arena. Their puffed-up leader carried a mustard-coloured flag with two crossed cane stalks. The all-girl crew behind her wore matching sports dresses. On closer inspection, Whisker noticed their warty faces were smothered in brightly coloured mascara, eyeliner and lipstick.

Horace winced. 'And I thought my sisters overdid the makeup.'

'*POND SCUM,*' the Captain said, reading the large, green letters on the flag bearer's shirt. 'Penelope Pond Scum to be precise. She's the poison-spitting captain of the *Leaping Lily,* and her slippery gang consists of her five *enchanting* daughters.' He gave Horace a look of concern. 'Despite what the fairy tales may say, Horace, I would not recommend kissing any of these toads.'

'Advice taken, Captain,' Horace gulped. 'I'll stick to girls of a less warty appearance.'

The third team was now making its way into the stadium. Even with a bullhorn, Baron Gustave was drowned out by the deafening howls and barks of adoring fans dressed in blue and white.

'There's no mistaking that reception,' Pete muttered, twitching his pencil leg uncomfortably. 'Those rough-as-guts Sea Dogs always get the crowd support – especially when they're throwing innocent rats into shark-infested waters.'

Horace gave Pete's pencil leg a hard tap with his hook. 'I thought a small fish nibbled your leg off?'

Pete screwed up his nose. 'That's beside the point. I'd still have both legs if those bottom-sniffing canines showed some chivalry and left me on dry land.'

'Well, I doubt you'll get an apology,' Horace said, gesturing to a commotion at the end of the tunnel. 'Bartholomew Brawl and his howlers don't appear to have attended any doggy obedience classes lately.'

Horace was right. On their march into the arena, two poodles and a bulldog had already bumped over several Penguin Pirates, and were currently heckling a cane toad named Sugar about her choice of blue eye shadow.

Unimpressed, Gustave shook his ears and gestured for the Pie Rats to proceed up the tunnel.

'And now, dear spectators,' he boomed through the bullhorn, 'I present to you, ze most appetising team in ze competition, ze delicious Pie Rats!'

There was a mixture of laughs and jeers as Fred raised the *Jolly Rat* high into the air and proudly led the Pie Rats onto the field.

As Whisker left the safety of the tunnel and stepped into the bright lights of the stadium, he felt his tail pulsing with energy. All around him, the mighty grandstands rose to the tops of the tallest trees to create a cauldron-like atmosphere. Ecstatic spectators crammed into every available seat and dangled precariously from overhanging branches. The stadium was a waterfall of moving bodies, louder and larger than any circus audience he'd ever seen.

Whisker knew that Papa Niko and the others were cheering him on from the stands, but it was impossible to make out their faces amidst the screaming mammals, birds and amphibians.

Who else is hidden in that crowd? he asked himself.

Mesmerised by the sights and sounds, he stumbled around the arena in a bewildered daze, almost running into a three-legged pug with a biscuit peg leg. Acting ignorant, Whisker gave the snarling dog a friendly wave and pretended to be listening to Baron Gustave's next introduction.

'... Ze fifth team of participants is ze always enthusiastic royal family from ze Island of Kings, ze Marvellous Marmosets.'

A pompous parade of crown-wearing monkeys with white ear tufts and long, banded tails marched out of the closest tunnel. A cross-eyed marmoset in a jester's hat led the procession, followed by a knight in a rusty metal helmet.

'Rotten pies to show ponies,' Horace groaned, trying to hide behind his hook. 'Since when were they eligible to enter? I'd hardly call jungle kidnapping an act of piracy.'

King Marvownion's eyes lit up when he spotted Captain Black Rat in the centre of the arena.

'Great goslings in gumtrees!' he exclaimed, almost losing his oversized crown. 'Isn't this a remarkable coincidence? My old buddies the Pie Rats are here for a rematch.'

The Captain tipped his hat and replied with a pained smile, 'I'm sure we can squeeze another victory into our tight schedule, Marvownion.'

King Marvownion opened his mouth to object, but Baron Gustave was already introducing the sixth team, his words echoing around the stadium.

'Our final team is a last minute entry. I have no doubt zey vill bring much excitement to zis tournament.'

There was a startled gasp from the crowd as the team came into view. Whisker's heart skipped a beat.

'Ladies and gentlemen,' Gustave cried, 'I give you ze dreaded Cat Fish!'

The entire audience watched in fearful silence as Captain Sabre, the formidable orange and black Bengal, led the Cat Fish into the arena.

Brimming with confidence, he pranced into the centre of the field, scanning the trembling faces of his opponents. At the sight of the young Pie Rat apprentice, standing rigid with his teammates, Sabre's face suddenly turned sour.

'Dirty little rat,' he hissed, throwing his flag to the ground. 'Crawled out of your dingy cave, did you?'

Overcome with terror, Whisker took a stumbling step backwards. Sabre drew his cheese knife and prowled closer, with a look of pure contempt in his eyes.

'That's right,' Sabre scowled, slashing his knife through the air. 'Run away, little apprentice. You're not so tough without your pet bear, are you?'

Whisker bit his tongue and held his ground, hoping his trembling legs weren't about to collapse beneath him. Out of the corner of his eye, he noticed Ruby edging closer, with her paws on the handles of her two scarlet scissor swords. Horace was right beside her.

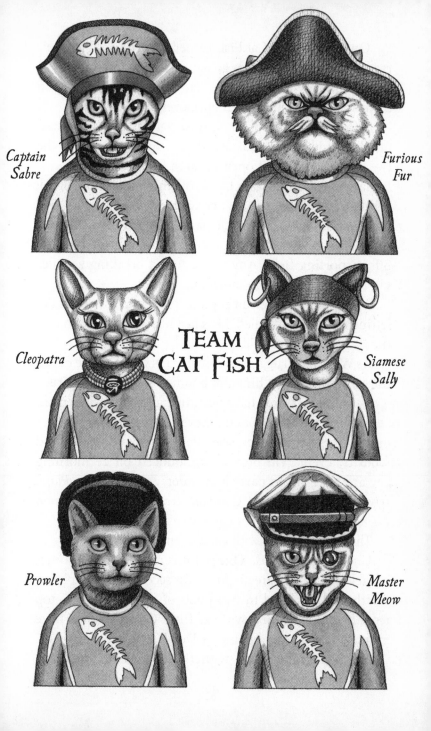

Captain Sabre

Furious Fur

TEAM CAT FISH

Cleopatra

Siamese Sally

Prowler

Master Meow

One by one, the Cat Fish gathered around Sabre, their razor-sharp cheese knives glistening in the torchlight.

'Just like the good ol' days,' Horace gulped, putting on a brave face. 'Outnumbered but never outdone ...'

Before the 'reunion' could turn ugly, there was a flash of white and Baron Gustave threw himself between the two teams, waving an open scroll in his paw.

Sabre took one look at the scroll and pulled away. Ruby slowly released the grip on her swords.

'A reminder to all participants,' Gustave said firmly, 'according to ze code of ze games, zere is to be no fighting off ze sporting field. Any teams found breaking ze rules vill be expelled from ze tournament.'

'Well, that's a welcome piece of news,' Horace said, letting out a sigh of relief. 'Let's just hope we don't run into the Cat Fish *on* the field.'

As Whisker struggled to calm his nerves, Gustave raised the scroll in front of him and boomed into the bullhorn.

'Now zat ze teams have been introduced, I vill explain ze events for zis year's cup. Seven events vill be held – one for each of ze seven seas. For reasons of secrecy and security, events vill only be announced on ze morning zey are held. In no particular order, ze events are: *Plank Diving, Hand-to-Hand Combat, Treasure Hunt, Cannon Firing, Sea Race, Mystery Challenge* and *Death Ball.*'

The crowd roared with excitement.

Gustave continued, 'One point is avorded to ze vinner of each event. Zere are no points for second or third places. Death Ball is played in two pools of three teams. Ze top team from each pool plays in ze final. Only ze vinner of ze grand final receives a point for Death Ball –'

He tapped the scroll with the end of his bullhorn.

'However, ze rules state zat if two teams are tied on equal points at ze end of ze tournament, ze team vith ze most Death Ball victories vill be declared ze champions.' There was a dull murmur of approval from the crowd. Gustave began rolling up the scroll. 'And now, gallant competitors, I vill show you vot you are competing for.'

A line of youthful white rabbits wearing matching purple coats marched out of a tunnel carrying three large open chests. Each chest overflowed with sparkling gold coins. As alluring as the treasure was, all eyes were fixed on the rabbit at the end of the line. In his paws he clutched an enormous two-handled cup. A line of precious jewels ran in a circle around its base. Etched into the side of the cup was an elaborate skull and two crossed torches. Cast from solid gold, the Trophy of Champions was truly magnificent.

The athletes watched, spellbound, as the rabbit placed the glittering object on a velvet-covered pedestal. Without a word, another white rabbit hopped out of the tunnel, carrying a flaming torch. When he neared the trophy he took a single graceful leap into the air and thrust the end of the torch over the rim of the giant cup. With a hiss of bright violet flames, the trophy blazed to life.

The arena erupted in spontaneous applause.

'Zis sacred purple fire vill burn until ze Centenary Games have concluded,' Gustave stated. 'To celebrate one hundred years of athletic achievement, I have one final event to announce.' He waited for total silence. 'Zis trophy vill remain in public sight at all times. You may see it on ze island, or you may see it on my ship, ze *Velvet Wave*. Ze first team zat can touch zis trophy before ze end of ze last event vill receive one bonus point.'

There was a murmur of curious interest from the athletes.

'Piece of cake,' croaked one of the toads. 'That's easier than catching a cane beetle stuck on its back.' She gave her hind legs a mighty kick and launched herself high into the air.

With lightening quick reflexes, the surrounding rabbits whipped out an arsenal of pea shooters and slingshots from their coats and peppered the unsuspecting toad with purple paint pellets. She crashed to the ground, dripping in sticky purple liquid.

'The colour suits you, Sugar!' barked one of the poodles.

Gingerly, she picked herself up and limped back to her team, while the audience roared with laughter.

'I failed to mention zat my twelve sons vill be keeping a close eye on ze trophy,' Gustave chuckled. 'A single spot of paint on any team member vill rule out ze entire team from ze bonus event.' He frowned sympathetically at the paint-splattered toad. 'I'm afraid to say, zat includes you, Miss Sugar.'

Ignoring the croaking protests of the toads, Gustave gestured to a square-sided tower rising high above the trees. It was constructed from rough planks of timber and topped with a bark roof. A large bronze bell hung at the top, accessed by a rickety rope ladder. The entire tower appeared to be leaning precariously to the right.

'Ze first event vill commence tomorrow morning,' Gustave announced. 'You vill hear ze bell toll vhen it is time to assemble. I bid you all goodnight.'

'What about the Death Ball pools?' Bartholomew Brawl barked. 'Aren't you gonna tell us who we're fightin'?'

'No,' Gustave replied bluntly. 'Zat vould spoil ze surprise – and surprises are vot zese games are about.'

FIVE

The Bells of Autumn

The stars were still shining in the indigo sky when the bell rang out across the sleepy island. Whisker opened his bleary eyes and stared at the roof of the tent. Troubled thoughts of the Cat Fish had plagued his mind for most of the night.

Every crash and clang from the bustling Champions Tavern had woken him with a fright. Every snarl, sneeze, sigh and snore that echoed through the campsite had set his nerves on edge. In the dark hours of the morning he'd almost convinced himself Sabre was lurking outside his tent, waiting to pounce. Whisker longed for the quiet sanctuary of the ocean, where the dull murmur of the wind and the rhythm of the waves gently rocked him to sleep.

'Couldn't they wait till sunrise to ring that blasted bell?' Horace moaned, covering his ears with his pillow. 'Professional athletes deserve their rest.'

Fred opened his enormous eye and blinked at his two tent-mates.

'No time for a cooked breakfast,' he grunted, clambering out of his sleeping bag. 'Cold pies on the run – again.'

Nibbling on a slice of stale apricot pie, Whisker followed

the rest of the crew towards the lookout tower. The sky was slowly lightening in the east, revealing the black silhouettes of the forest trees high above them.

'How's my precious granddaughter this morning?' Granny Rat asked as Ruby begrudgingly guided her along the uneven track. 'Ready to show those vile thugs what we girls are made of?'

'Sure, Gran,' Ruby muttered, 'as soon as we know what event we're in.'

'It will be Death Ball,' Granny replied confidently, 'mark my words. I've seen enough of these barbaric games to know how it works. No organiser would be daft enough to start with a *soft* event like Plank Diving. The spectators would tear him to shreds.'

As the line of sleepy animals neared the wooden tower, the chimes of the bell were replaced by the booming voice of Baron Gustave.

'Please proceed to ze Death Ball arena immediately,' he shouted from the top of the swaying tower. 'All ticket holders are asked to take zeir allocated seats in ze grandstands. Sea Dogs and Pie Rats are to report to ze dressing rooms at once. Ze first pool game will commence in thirty minutes.'

Granny Rat grinned with satisfaction. 'Told you so …'

The southern dressing room of the Death Ball arena was nothing more than a rectangular hole dug under the grandstands. Several frosted glass lanterns hung from the roof, providing dim light for the competitors. The Pie Rats sat on a long bench against one wall, watching their coach hobbling around the centre of the room. Rat Bait stood with his arms crossed and his back to a closed door.

'Here,' Horace whispered, passing Whisker a small yellow card. 'You might want to brush up on your Death Ball rules.'

THE PIRATE CUP
RULES OF DEATH BALL

- One point is scored when the ball is kicked or hit under the crossbar between two posts.

- The ball may be carried, thrown, kicked or passed from one side of the field to the other.

- A player possessing the ball may be tackled, tripped or wrestled until they release the ball.

- Players not involved in a tackle are limited to shoulder contact only.

- Infringements attract a penalty shot at goal.

- Spectators are entitled to return out-of-bounds balls to any player of their choosing.

- The ball is bounced in the centre circle at the beginning of each half and after each goal.

- Each half runs for thirty minutes.

- Teams change directions after a fifteen-minute half-time break.

- No more than five players from each team are to be on the field at any one time.

- Drawn games are decided by a penalty shootout.

'You'll notice a few differences to the jungle version of the game,' Horace explained as Whisker ran his eye down the list, 'most noticeably the length of matches. Each half runs for thirty minutes and is measured by an hourglass – not a sundial. Due to the brutality of the matches, penalty shootouts replace any extra time.'

'Sixty minutes is still a long time to survive a Sea Dog pounding,' Pete grimaced.

'Speaking of those slobber-ridden dogs,' Granny Rat said, 'do we have any inside information on them?'

'They be the reignin' Cup champions an' competition favourites,' Rat Bait replied, avoiding eye contact with the fiery coach. 'More bark than bite if ye ask me. Them two poodles, Tuffy an' Fluffy, will only pick on smaller folk than themselves.'

'Like me,' Horace muttered, attaching a tightly strung racket to the end of his golden stump.

'Err … I s'pose,' Rat Bait mumbled. 'That wee terrier's a harmless ball o' fur, though. They call him *The Kid*. And the three-legged Pug, Biscuit, he's a pushover. As for the Beagle, Scallywag Sam, well, he's only interested in entertainin' the crowd.'

Granny rat hobbled over to the wall and drew a large circle with a piece of chalk.

'Those despicable dogs will get most of the crowd balls,' she said, filling the circle with names and symbols. 'Make it your priority to keep the ball in play. Your opposition will be good for short bursts but they'll tire by the end of each half. Run them ragged if you can and then strike when their tongues are dragging on the ground.'

She turned and studied the faces of the Pie Rat team, paying particular attention to Horace and Whisker.

TEAM
SEA DOGS

Bartholomew
Brawl

Scallywag
Sam

Fluffy

The Kid

Tuffy

Biscuit

'This might seem like a warm-up game for some of you,' she scoffed, 'but I can't stress enough the importance of Death Ball victories in the bigger scheme of things. A pool-game victory is worth nearly as much as an event win if two teams are tied at the end of the tournament.'

She glared in Rat Bait's direction. 'My first Pirate Cup team lost their opening pool game and it cost them the competition. If I'm to have any hope of winning the cup this time around, I'll need a strong start from every one of you the moment you step onto that field.'

'Talk about pressure,' Horace whispered to Whisker. 'It's hard enough living up to the expectations of three perfect sisters without adding Granny Rat to the mix.'

Whisker let out a deep sigh. 'Welcome to the Pirate Cup.'

There was a muffled trumpet blast from outside.

'That's your cue,' Granny Rat exclaimed. 'Now get out there and do us proud!'

Surrounded by an ocean of blue and white-clad supporters, the Pie Rats made their way onto the field. Huge, striped flags fluttered in the morning breeze like the sails of a racing regatta. Spectators jeered and hissed, pelting the rats with half-chewed pie crusts and soggy dog biscuits.

Shielding his head from the flying projectiles, Whisker glimpsed Horace's family sitting directly behind the reserve bench dressed in red, black and gold.

'Hi, Whisker,' chimed the three sisters, waving gold handkerchiefs and blowing kisses.

Whisker gave them an awkward wave and tried not to blush.

'*Groupies* …' Ruby muttered, pushing past him to the centre of the field.

From a velvet-seated commentary box in the first row, Baron Gustave introduced a large blue-and-yellow Macaw named Chatterbeak as the game's official commentator. The flamboyant parrot puffed up his feathers and squawked excitedly, 'Madness, madness, hold onto your hats, here come the reigning Cup champions …'

Chatterbeak

The reception for the Sea Dogs was almost deafening. Energised by the welcome, the dogs bounded out of the tunnel and sprinted around the perimeter of the field, sparking a Mexican wave.

After several whistles from a white rabbit in a striped referee's shirt, the dogs finally stopped their frivolous display and trotted over to the reserve bench. Panting and slobbering, they gulped down great mouthfuls of water from a line of blue water bowls.

An angry-looking poodle with a bone through her nose and a mohawk shaved into her head made her way towards Whisker on the left wing. Judging by her rough appearance and skull-and-crossbones tattoos, Whisker guessed she was Tuffy.

'You're mincemeat,' she growled, taking her place opposite him.

Whisker decided it was safest not to respond and waited for the opening bounce. The referee brought the hard rubber ball forward, and with the flip of an hourglass, the game was underway.

'Caw, caw,' Chatterbeak squawked. 'Look at that leap! The Kid out-jumps Ruby for the ball and the dogs have first possession … Right step, left step. Smokin' jalapenos he's quick … Here comes Fish Eye Fred with a flying tackle – and crunch time, The Kid goes down …

There was a loud *BOO* from the crowd.

'Skraww, skraww,' Chatterbeak shrilled, flapping his feathers excitedly. 'Whisker scoops up the ball in his tail and passes to Horace on the right wing. *WHAM BAM*! What a racket pass to full forward … Captain Black Rat makes contact with his foot … The ball is on its way … Fluffy soars through the air … Dog and ball collide …

Coooeee! It's a fluff-fest. The goal is saved by a perm.'

The spectators roared with delight. Fluffy hurled the ball into the crowd before the Captain could attempt a second shot.

'... And the ball is back in play,' Chatterbeak screeched. 'Bartholomew Brawl receives a short pass from Sam and takes off down the centre of the field ... Wait a minute, folks. Something is happening. I haven't seen this before, but Brawl is wedging the ball into his ... *mouth?*'

There was a startled gasp from the crowd.

Ruby threw her paws in the air and howled in protest, 'It's a penalty offence. Send the cheat off!'

The referee, as equally baffled as the spectators, looked to Gustave for a response. Gustave gestured to an extended list of rules on the commentary table.

'Brittle birdseed!' Chatterbeak exclaimed, peering down at the list. 'According to the rules, it's perfectly legal for players to carry the ball in their mouths, as long as it remains visible at all times.' He pointed his wing at Brawl's powerful jaws. 'With chompers like those, I doubt anyone will get the ball out!'

Ruby stamped her foot in frustration. Bartholomew Brawl growled with satisfaction and took off towards the goal. With his four legs free for running, he barged through Whisker and Horace like a runaway stagecoach.

The Sea Dog captain continued his charge, colliding with Fred in the goal box. As the two of them tumbled to the ground, Brawl spat out the ball and Scallywag Sam sent it spinning through the goal.

The crowd leapt to their feet and cheered in jubilation.

'One-nil,' Chatterbeak announced. 'The Sea Dogs take the early lead.'

The rest of the first half continued in a similar fashion. The Sea Dogs used their strong jaws to carry the ball from one end of the field to the other and, despite their determined efforts, the Pie Rats were unable to wrench it free. Frustrated to be cursed with such insignificant jaws, incapable of holding even the smallest of Death Balls, the rats had to wait until late in the period before they could mount a comeback.

Winning the centre bounce, Ruby ran in circles around the tired dogs and eventually passed the ball to the Captain, who scored in the top right corner of the goal. When the half-time whistle sounded moments later, the Pie Rats were down five goals to one.

Snapping and snarling at their opposition, the thirsty dogs trotted over to their water bowls and quickly drained the contents. The Pie Rats trudged off the field with slumped shoulders and downcast frowns and sat in a sombre line on the bench.

'Not the start we were looking for,' Horace said gloomily, lowering his water flask. 'We're helpless against Bartholomew *make-up-your-own-rules* Brawl. He's got the jaws of a crocodile and the ferocity of a charging rhino.'

Granny Rat looked down the line of long faces and pointed to her bonnet. 'Use your brains, you thick-skulled sardines. Fight fire with fire! If Brawl's twisting the rules then twist them back again. Surely one of you nincompoops can think up a cunning plan to get us out of this mess.'

In unison, all eyes flashed to Whisker, the go-to rat in desperate situations. With his water flask to his lips, Whisker almost choked on a mouthful of water.

He coughed and spluttered for some time before

pointing to the water dribbling down the side of his mouth.

'Granny's right,' he gasped. 'We'll have to fight fire with fire …'

'What on earth are you talking about?' Pete exclaimed. 'You're not a lava spitting dragon!'

Wasting no time on an explanation, Whisker turned to the row of spectators behind the reserve bench. Horace's three sisters fluttered their eyelashes and puckered their lips, trying to win his attention. Whisker smiled politely and forced himself to stay focused.

'Mama Kolina,' he said with an air of urgency, 'I have a small favour to ask.'

'Yes, of course, my dear boy,' she replied. 'What can I do for you?'

'If it's not too much trouble,' Whisker said, removing a gold coin from his drawstring bag. 'I'd like to order some half-time refreshments for our thirsty opponents.' He leant closer, handing the coin to Mama Kolina and whispered his request in her ear.

'Certainly, Whisker,' Mama Kolina said with a broad grin. 'I'll rustle up your order at once. Is there anything else you require?'

Whisker glanced across at the Sea Dog's bench.

'Well,' he said, a little embarrassed, 'there is one other thing we could use: a charming young waitress – preferably dressed in blue.'

'Of course,' Mama Kolina laughed, putting her arm around her youngest daughter. 'My charming Aphrodite looks fabulous in blue and she has packed every dress she owns.'

SIX

Old Dogs, New Tricks

As the half-time break drew to a close, Mama Kolina shuffled into the stadium with the rest of the spectators. Slightly out of breath, she squeezed into her seat and handed Whisker a small wicker basket.

'Thanks,' he whispered, peering over the rim at six tiny red pods.

'The rest of the refreshments are on their way,' she panted. 'The line at the tavern was so long I thought we would miss the second half.'

As Whisker handed each of his teammates one of the red pods, he noticed Aphrodite moving down an aisle with a large wooden bucket in her paws. She looked prettier than ever in her sky-blue dress, white apron and elegant drop earrings, and it was no surprise that wolf-whistles echoed from both sides of the crowd.

She reached the dogs' reserve bench as the last grains of sand fell through the half-time hourglass.

'Yoo hoo, Mr Brawl,' she called out in an innocent voice. 'I'm such a huge fan. Have you got a moment?'

The Sea Dogs were already making their way onto the field, but Bartholomew Brawl stopped in his tracks when he heard her sweet voice.

'Hello, li'l lady!' he exclaimed, wagging his tail excitedly. 'I'd love to chat with an adoring fan, but I'm kinda busy winnin' right now.'

'Oh,' she said. 'Of course you are. I don't mean to hold you up, but I noticed your drinking bowls are all empty.' She held up her bucket. 'It would be an honour to fill them up for you. I'd hate for you to be thirsty during the second half.'

'Mighty kind of you, luv,' Brawl replied. 'You can fill up my bowl any time you want.'

Aphrodite giggled. 'Good luck, Mr Brawl, I hope you have a *scorching* second half.'

Lingering on the Pie Rats' bench, Whisker was glad Bartholomew Brawl hadn't picked up Aphrodite's cryptic message or noticed the Pie Rats smearing their paws with sticky red juice and tiny white seeds.

'Are we all set?' Granny Rat asked impatiently as Aphrodite finished filling up the bowls.

'Aye, Mother,' the Captain said, throwing the remains of his pod under the bench. 'Thanks to our bright young apprentice, we might just pull off the biggest upset in Death Ball history.'

The whistle blew and the second half action commenced.

'Caw, caw,' Chatterbeak squawked, 'here we go again. Ruby wins first possession with a well-timed leap and the Pie Rats have the ball in the midfield ... She plays it safe and passes back to Whisker. Whisker spins the ball to Horace. Horace throws a high lob to Fred. Now Black Rat's got a piece of it – miles from his goal. Tickle me tail feathers, folks. The Pie Rats are really sharing the ball around.'

There were shouts of 'boring' and 'hurry up and smash 'em' from several Sea Dog supporters in the crowd.

'Patience, patience! Here's a chance for the Sea Dogs,'

Chatterbeak chirped. 'The Captain is sandwiched between Tuffy and Sam and the ball flies free. Tuffy scoops up the ball in her mouth and dashes down the sideline … Wait a minute, folks. She's dropped the ball cold.'

Tuffy let out an enormous howl and made a beeline for the reserve bench. Scallywag Sam picked up the ball in his mouth but dropped it before he'd even taken his first step. With similar yelps and howls, he followed Tuffy in the direction of the drinking bowls.

'… And The Kid is on the charge,' Chatterbeak screeched. 'He sidesteps Ruby … Slippery sardines! He's dropped the ball as well … Oh no! He's frothing at the mouth … He's calling for a substitute. Poor Biscuit doesn't know who to replace.'

While the rest of the dogs fell like flies, the enraged Sea Dog captain barged past Ruby and dived on the ball. He only made it as far as the midfield before the ball tumbled from his mouth and he began howling like a hyena.

'Awoo, awoo! It burns, it burns! My tongue is on fire. My mouth is meltin'. Water, I need water!'

He leapt towards the reserve bench and, ignoring the frantic barks from the three other dogs, began guzzling from his water bowl. The whites of his eyes turned redder than an over-ripe tomato.

'AWOOOOOOO!' he bellowed. 'Hot-Chilli Cola! Call the fire brigade, I'm about to ignite …'

With no relief in sight, the four howling dogs dashed out of the stadium in the direction of the waterhole.

'Skraww, skraww!' Chatterbeak prattled as the sound of the dogs died away. 'What a turn of events. But back to the action, folks, the Pie Rats have just scored …'

With only a fluffy white poodle and a three-legged dog

in their way, the Pie Rats scored seven unanswered goals to win the game eight-five.

'As Frankie Belorio always says, *It's a game of two halves,*' Horace declared as the triumphant Pie Rats filed into the dressing room with their small group of supporters.

'A half with red-hot chillies and a half without,' Whisker laughed, brushing the last of the chilli seeds from his paws.

Aphrodite, still wearing her blue dress, rushed over to him and threw her arms around his neck.

'How did I do, Whisker?' she asked, squeezing him tightly.

Overwhelmed by the strong smell of her perfume, Whisker felt his eyes glazing over.

'Say what …?' he answered in a trance.

From across the room, Ruby let out a loud huff and began clanging around with her swords. Aphrodite paid her no attention and nestled her head into Whisker's shoulder.

'We make a great team, don't we, Whisker?' she whispered.

'Sure – Aphrodite,' he replied, gasping for fresh air.

Aphrodite simply hugged him tighter.

'Err – do you mind?' he said, uncomfortably. 'Your earring's digging into my neck.'

'Oh,' she said, pulling away. 'Sorry.' She moved her paw to her diamond-shaped earring and gave it a little flick. The rose-coloured stone sparkled in the lantern light.

'It's a pretty little diamond, isn't it?' she said dreamily.

'Sure,' Whisker replied, his head still spinning, 'but aren't diamonds supposed to be clear?'

'Most diamonds are,' Aphrodite stated, 'but these are rare Freeforian pink diamonds. They once belonged to my grandmother –'

'– and they now belong to me,' Hera snapped. 'You're

only wearing them because of your silly little Death Ball stunt. If you're finished playing half-time heroine, you can hand them back over.'

Aphrodite spun around and glared at her elder sister. 'It's so unfair! You always get the good jewellery. I get nothing but second-rate sapphires and tacky opals ...'

Whisker tuned out as the two sisters began one of their regular arguments. Athena seized her opportunity and jumped in where Aphrodite left off with Whisker.

'As a point of interest,' she said knowledgeably, Freeforia is known as the Diamond Isle. No diamonds have been found there for many years, of course, but that hardly matters, with the new gold mine in operation.' She opened up a small purse and took out a gold coin. Its surface was engraved with two paws surrounded by a diamond.

'Our new currency,' she said, placing it tenderly in his paw.

Whisker nodded in recognition. He'd received three similar coins from Rat Bait following their adventure on the Island of Destiny. They had originally come from the mysterious fox, as part of his trade for Whisker's parent's boat. Whisker had used one of the coins to pay for the half-time refreshments and the other two coins lay at the bottom of his drawstring bag.

As Whisker stared at the coin, Athena adjusted her black-framed glasses and launched into a detailed history lesson.

'Imagine this coin was a map. The four main villages of our island, when joined by straight lines, form a perfect diamond.' She leant across and pointed to the left tip of the diamond. 'Our village is there, in Western Freeforia. The new gold mine is in the volcano region at the centre of the island – where you can see the two paws. The volcano is shared by all four provinces. As our tribal chief, Papa Niko was given one of the first chests of gold six weeks ago, with the promise of more to come ...'

'Hang on,' Whisker broke in, 'Do you mean to say the currency is only six weeks old?'

'That's right,' Athena replied. 'The coins are yet to be in full circulation.'

Whisker took a moment to gather his thoughts. *So the fox must have visited Freeforia sometime after the cyclone. And if he was there, and my parents' boat fell into his possession, then ...*

'Athena,' he exclaimed. 'Have there been any recent sightings of strangers in Freeforia? Three rats. One male and one female and their young daughter. Somewhere near the coast ...'

She shook her head. 'No. The only arrivals in the last few months were mine workers, and none of them were rats.'

'Are you sure?' Whisker gasped. 'What about the other provinces?'

'I-I can't be certain,' she said, fumbling with her glasses. 'Freeforia is a big island.'

Overwhelmed by desperation, Whisker turned to the other sisters. 'What about you, Hera – and you, Aphrodite? Surely you've seen something.'

The two rats stopped their bickering and looked at him with confusion in their eyes.

'TELL ME!' he shouted, suddenly losing control 'You've got to tell me. I have to know. WHERE ARE THEY?'

'Whisker, you're scaring me,' Aphrodite trembled. 'I haven't seen anything. None of us have.'

'But,' Whisker began, 'they have to be …' He felt a firm paw on his shoulder and cut himself short.

'Easy does it, lad,' Rat Bait murmured. 'Yer frightenin' the wee lasses. How 'bout we take a li'l walk while ye calm down?'

Before Whisker could say anything, Rat Bait placed a second paw on his shoulder and began guiding him out of the dressing room. Neither of them spoke as they trudged down the dark tunnel. Ahead of them, the warm morning sunshine streamed through the narrow entrance on the outskirts of the stadium.

The moment Whisker stepped into the light, he felt a wave of exhaustion pass over him. All the sleepless nights, all the gruelling training sessions, all the stress of searching for his family seemed to implode on him at once. Embarrassed and ashamed, he slumped to the ground and closed his eyes.

'I made a fine fool out of myself, didn't I?' he muttered.

'Aye, that ye did,' Rat Bat replied. 'But don't ye be worryin'. It happens to the best o' us. We all know yer heart's in the right place, Whisker, but ye have to be patient.'

'I know,' Whisker said, drawing a deep breath. 'I'm just sick of feeling helpless.'

Rat Bait curled up the corner of this mouth. 'Those be familiar words, me boy. I was a youthful an' headstrong rat just like ye.'

Whisker opened one eye and peered up at the old rogue.

'That's right,' Rat Bait chuckled. 'I was once young – an'

reckless too. I be convinced I could take on the world an' all it could throw at me despite what me elders said.'

'So what did you do?' Whisker asked with sudden interest.

'I said rotten pies to the lot o' them!' Rat Bait exclaimed. 'I sailed an' fought an' conquered an' proved meself to everyone and everythin'...' His voice drifted off and he let out a long sigh. 'The funny thing be, I spent too much time provin' and not enough time carin'. Before I realised the error of me ways, I was an empty shell of a rat – driftin' on a sea of self-pity – a million miles from anywhere that mattered ...'

'But you got a second chance,' Whisker said, '– on the island. You started caring again. We all saw it.'

'Aye,' Rat Bait said pensively. 'That I did. An' it feels good to be among friends again.' He looked Whisker straight in the eye. 'Some things can be salvaged in life, me lad; other things are lost forever. Regardless o' what ye're searchin' for, don't ye forget what ye have right here. They're good folk, all of 'em – yer crew, them Freeforians, the Hermit, even Granny Rat.'

'I won't forget,' Whisker said. 'I promise –'

The conversation was interrupted by a loud squawk, followed by several vicious snarls from the Death Ball arena. Rat Bait twitched his ears and glanced up at the massive structure.

'Sounds like the second pool game's startin',' he murmured.

'Who's playing?' Whisker asked, as a mighty cheer echoed down the tunnel.

'Cat Fish versus Penguin Pirates,' Rat Bait said, pulling Whisker to his feet. 'An' if ye want me honest opinion, them penguins don't stand a chance.'

SEVEN

Gladiators

Day Two of the Centenary Games began under the changing hues of a glorious autumn sky. Orange-rimmed clouds drifted high overhead, merging and separating into new shapes as they moved across the purple heavens.

Whisker reached the newly nicknamed 'leaning tower of pirates,' as Baron Gustave was finishing his announcement.

' ... Due to ze large number of concussions suffered by ze penguins in zeir eighteen-nil defeat to ze Cat Fish, today's event of Hand-to-Hand Combat vill commence at 3 pm. All teams are to nominate two candidates for a gladiator-style contest. Ze goal of zis event is to force ze other fighters out of ze centre circle. Ze last competitor left standing in ze circle vill be ze vinner ...'

Following the announcement, Whisker departed for a much needed bath in the waterhole. Refreshed, he returned to the athletes' village, almost colliding with Mama Kolina and her three daughters outside the supply tent.

'H-hi,' he stammered, skidding to a halt.

Mama Kolina handed him a basket of bread and berries.

'I've brought you breakfast,' she said with a smile. 'I

hope you like raspberries.'

'Sure,' Whisker replied. 'Thanks. They look great ... you really didn't have to.'

Mama Kolina raised her paws to silence him. 'It was no trouble. My daughters and I are always happy to help.'

The three girls nodded affectionately.

'Horace told me all about your family,' Mama Kolina continued. 'I am very sorry. When we return home, Papa Niko will ask the tribal leaders for their assistance. If your parents and sister have landed on our island, we will find them. I give you my word.'

'Thanks,' Whisker said, overwhelmed by her kindness. 'I'm sorry for yesterday. I shouldn't have ...'

'Yesterday is over,' Mama Kolina said. 'Today has its own battles.'

As she turned to leave, Whisker noticed Ruby at the edge of the village, walking towards the tents. When she caught sight of him, surrounded by the three sisters, she abruptly changed direction and headed for the tavern.

After breakfast, the Pie Rats assembled in the supply tent to discuss their nominations for the afternoon's event. Ruby spent the whole time sharpening her swords and refused to make eye contact with Whisker.

'We need candidates who display a good mix of strength and skill,' Granny Rat said. 'If we exclude the pipsqueaks, brittle-bones and tremble-tails of the crew, we're left with our number one swords-rat, Ruby, and our resident giant, Fred. My boy, Black Rat was an option but Fred here is ugly enough to scare half the opponents out of the ring with a single wink of his eye.'

Horace tapped Fred's massive tattooed arm with his hook and whispered, 'She means that in the nicest possible way.'

Fred simply grunted and picked up his huge fighting fork.

'The Hermit and I will be conducting a training session in the forest,' Granny Rat said, addressing the two candidates. 'On the off chance that you're disarmed during the fight, you'll need a few rat-fu moves up your grubby sleeves.'

'Yes, yes,' the Hermit said, striking an elaborate pose. 'Hermit teach you desert island defence strategies.'

'Don't go showing off, dear,' Granny Rat said, ushering him through the doorway. 'You're hardly a black belt.'

Several hours later, when the candidates returned from their training session, it was clear that Ruby's bad mood had only become worse. Granny Rat had suggested a watch-and-wait strategy for the contest and the thought of being a passive bystander during a sword fight grated on Ruby's nerves. She was still fuming at the decision when the twelve combatants assembled inside the large painted circle in the Death Ball arena. Standing back-to-back in a quiet area of the circle. Ruby and Fred watched their adversaries heckling and taunting one another.

The roughest of the rough had been selected to participate and it was no surprise that Captain Sabre and Furious Fur took centre stage. Opposite the knife-wielding cats stood Bartholomew Brawl and Tuffy. Red-raw around their mouths from the hot chilli episode, the two dogs held club-like bones in their paws and growled menacingly at the cats.

Two toads in uniforms reading *WART FACE* and *ALGAE ANN* hopped around on their back legs, clutching long stalks of cane and croaking, 'Prepare to be *toad-ally* annihilated!'

The most theatrical display came from the Marvellous Marmosets.

Sir Mecks and Jester Mimp

Sir Mecks sat squarely on the back of Jester Mimp and charged around the circle like a knight on horseback. Hanging from the end of his gold striped lance, the royal flag fluttered majestically in the light breeze. The jingling of Mimp's bells gave the whole event a strange festive appeal.

The fairy penguins appeared to be the least threatening of the competitors. Covered in bandages from their Death Ball defeat, they had considerable difficulty stopping their icicle swords from melting in the warm sun.

'I'll give them penguins thirty seconds, tops,' Rat Bait whispered to Whisker as they watched from the grandstand. 'They'd fare much better in the winter games.'

'Attention, attention!' Chatterbeak squawked, raising his wings into the air. 'Competitors who are about to lose a limb, we salute you! Weapons at the ready and let the battle begin.'

With a flash of steel and the glimmer of gold, the fight was on. It took Sir Mecks less than ten seconds to bundle the first penguin out of the circle with a well-aimed prod to the backside. The toads took care of the second penguin by shattering his icicle and sliding him through the puddle it left on the ground.

In the centre of the circle, the dogs and the cats traded blow for blow. Bones and blades sliced through the air. Snarls and barks rang out. Well clear of the action, Ruby and Fred inched behind the cats, sheltering their bodies from the charging marmosets.

Clinging tightly to Mimp's fur, Sir Mecks collected Wart Face squarely in the chest and sent her hurtling into the fourth row of the grandstand.

Algae Ann, standing in readiness, swung her stalk through the air as Sir Mecks passed, clobbering the back of his rusty helmet. He tried to keep his balance but dropped his lance and rolled to one side, landing on top of Tuffy.

As the furious poodle and the semi-dazed knight began wrestling on the ground, Furious Fur joined forces with Sabre to drive Bartholomew Brawl towards the sideline.

Close by, Algae Ann leapt onto Jester Mimp's shoulders, smothering his face with her webbed feet. With Ann holding on for dear life, Mimp stumbled around blindly, searching for the fallen lance. He eventually picked it up with his left foot and began waving it wildly through the air, while hopping on his right foot. His uncontrolled movements snagged the royal flag on Brawl's studded dog collar and, with a hard kick from Sabre, the three tangled animals sprawled in a heap outside the circle.

As Sabre and Furious Fur stood gloating on the very edge of the circle, Ruby made her move.

She broke away from Fred with lightning-fast speed, her eyes locked on the cats. Nearing her target, the wrestling bodies of Mimp and Tuffy suddenly rolled into her path. Unable to stop, her boot collided with Sir Mecks' helmet and her upper body flew forward. Thudding to the ground, her swords bounced free.

In the split-second that followed, Sabre pounced. Throwing his cheese knife aside, he grabbed Ruby like a ragdoll and charged straight at Fred.

The startled rat had just enough time to lower his fork before Ruby's slender torso crashed into his massive stomach. He tried to hold his ground, but the momentum forced him backwards. In three stumbling steps he was out of the circle, with Ruby pinned to his chest and Sabre snarling triumphantly behind her.

Back in the circle, Furious Fur grabbed Tuffy and Sir Mecks by their ankles and dragged their stunned bodies over the sideline. He took one look around the empty battlefield and raised two triumphant paws in the air.

'Coooeee!' Chatterbeak squawked. 'The fight is over in record time. The Cat Fish are the champions.'

PIRATE CUP LEADER BOARD

DAY: 2   POINTS REMAINING: 7

PLACE	TEAM	POINTS	DEATH BALL VICTORIES
1ST	CAT FiSH	1	1
2ND	PiE RATS	0	1
3RD	MARMOSETS	0	0
4TH	CANE TOADS	0	0
5TH	SEA DOGS	0	0
6TH	PENGUINS	0	0

A few hours later, six sombre rats and a blowfly sat on a high branch overlooking the marina. It was early evening and the crescent moon hung directly overhead, its pale light barely penetrating the wispy clouds that drifted across the sky. Leaves rustled softly in the breeze. The calm waves of the ocean gently rumbled in to shore.

The surveillance party was there on direct orders from the head coach, while the team officials enjoyed a relaxing dinner in the Champions Tavern.

Pete was still grumbling about the team's defeat and how it could have been prevented. Fred wouldn't stop apologising for stepping out of the circle, and Ruby refused to speak to any of them.

The object of their attention was Baron Gustave's lavish three-masted ship, the *Velvet Wave*. Anchored a short distance beyond the northern pier, its six purple sails, carved mahogany railing and three-tiered deck set it apart from the cruder pirate ships of the marina. Between the foremast and the mainmast of the lower deck was a small raised cabin. Wide double doors hung open on its port and starboard sides. In the centre of the cabin, surrounded by lush velvet curtains, stood the Trophy of Champions, its purple flames clearly visible through an open trapdoor in the roof. An eerie glow radiated upwards, illuminating the edges of furled sails and the tips of the masts.

'There it is,' Horace whispered from the end of the branch. 'Now how do we get to it?'

'With great difficulty,' Pete murmured. 'Have you counted all those guards?'

Whisker moved his paw to his drawstring bag and pulled out a tiny golden spyglass, one of many useful items Madam Pearl had supplied for the games. Extending the spyglass to its full length, he scanned the ship for signs of Gustave's twelve sons.

He easily spotted two of them standing outside the starboard doors of the trophy room and another two guarding the port side. There was one on the middle deck and two on the helm. Two rabbits watched from the bow of the ship and one crouched in the crow's-nest.

That makes ten, Whisker said to himself. *Now where are the other two?*

He lowered the spyglass to the northern pier. Between Rat Bait's boat, the *Golden Anchor,* and the Sea Dogs' vessel, the *Blood an' Bones,* lay a row of open crates. Each crate was marked with a large purple G and filled with a variety of foodstuffs. One white rabbit was inspecting the contents of the crates while another used a hand-operated wharf crane to lower the crates into a small rowboat.

'They're thorough,' Horace whispered, pointing to the rabbits with his hook. 'I doubt we could smuggle our way on board.'

THE VELVET WAVE

'So how do we get across?' Pete sniffled.

'Oh, there are many ways,' the Captain answered casually, staring through his own spyglass. 'Take a look – starboard side, behind the rudder. The entire royal family is bobbing around down there.'

Whisker trained his spyglass on a green and brown patch in the water, not far from the *Velvet Wave*. King Marvownion, Queen Marmalade and their two children, Prince Marcabio and Princess Mayenya, were paddling towards the ship with long strands of seaweed draped over their heads.

On the opposite side of the rudder, Whisker noticed a large piece of driftwood moving steadily through the waves. There was no mistaking the soggy white poodles clinging to its side.

'Double trouble!' Horace gasped. 'We can't just sit here while another team gets the bonus point –'

'Hold your horses,' Pete cut in. 'I think the bumbling buffoons have just spotted each other.'

The monkeys were too far away to be heard, but their angry paw gestures made it perfectly clear they had sighted the dogs. The dogs responded by lowering their heads and paddling even faster towards the ship.

Unbeknown to the pirates, four rabbits lined the back railing of the ship. Whisker watched, transfixed, as the expert marksmen aimed their paint-pellet rifles at the animals and opened fire with four loud *CRACKS*.

Startled howls and barks echoed across the marina. King Marvownion thrashed around dramatically in a pool of bright purple seaweed and bellowed at the top of his lungs, 'Great grape-flavoured gumballs! Call the coastguard. I've been hit …'

*King
Marvownion*

With the evening's entertainment drawing to a close, the Pie Rats scampered down the tree.

'That was far better than a dreary old dinner in the tavern,' Horace chuckled, reaching the ground. 'Three teams down and three to go.'

'It would be better if the Cat Fish were out of the running for the bonus point,' Pete muttered. 'They're cunning – and we're yet to come up with a plan.'

Whisker sighed. 'Believe me. I'm working on it…'

EIGHT

Bullseye!

The third event of the Centenary Games was the much-loved Cannon Firing contest. Mid-morning, six teams and their supporters assembled at the firing range to the south of the Death Ball arena. It was a dreary, overcast day and many of the well-to-do spectators carried large umbrellas in anticipation of a passing autumn shower or two.

Six large circular targets were lined up in a straight row at the far end of the flat plain. Each target was marked with a red bullseye and a white outer ring. Six iron cannons were positioned at the closest end, surrounded by representatives from each team. A crowd of spectators watched from either side of the range. Much to Whisker's disappointment, no fox was among them.

In accordance with Baron Gustave's instructions, each team was required to shoot five projectiles of their choosing. Two nominated team members took turns shooting the first four shots, with the final shot being fired by either member. Shots that touched the bullseye scored two Cannon Firing points. Shots that hit the outer ring scored one point. If two or more teams were tied in first place at the end of five rounds, a shoot-off would be used to determine the winner. The winning team received one championship point.

Horace and Pete had been selected to represent the Pie Rats and stood in readiness with a pile of Whisker's finned pies. As the inventor of the *three-finned projectile*, Whisker acted as an assistant coach, while Granny Rat watched from the safety of the sidelines.

'Ridiculously ridiculous!' Horace exclaimed as Prince Marcabio inserted a gold-plated Death Ball into his cannon. 'It's supposed to be a shooting competition – not a flying art show.'

'And you don't think our pie projectiles look a tad *abstract?*' Pete muttered.

'They're an engineering masterpiece,' Horace exclaimed, tapping a pastry fin with his hook. 'Cooked to *pie*fection! They're faster than the cats' flaming fur-balls, more accurate than the toads' poison blobs and far less temperamental than the Sea Dog's biscuit bones.'

'I admit we have the aerodynamic edge,' Pete said cautiously, 'but the wind will still be a determining factor. It appears to be blowing from several directions at once.'

'Leave it to me,' Horace said, inserting the first pie into the cannon. 'Bullseye, here I come.'

'Let the first round begin,' Gustave shouted from the sidelines. 'FIRE WHEN READY!'

Horace made his final adjustments and lit the fuse. A moment later, the cannon roared to life with an enormous *KABOOM!*

The pie rocketed into the air, veering hard to the left. It continued its wayward journey across the field before crashing ungraciously into the grass beside the Sea Dogs' target.

'Nice shootin', pie-brain!' Bartholomew Brawl howled. 'Hit our target next time and we'll claim your points.'

Pete gave Horace a firm prod with his pencil. 'What the flaming rat's tail just happened? That was the worst shot I've ever seen. Even the penguins hit something with their melting ice cubes.'

'H-how could that happen …' Horace gabbled, staring into the distance. 'I did everything right, honestly. It's not like a fin fell off or anything …'

At the end of the field, the penguins, toads and marmosets had clipped the edges of their targets to claim one point each, while the Sea Dogs and Cat Fish had both hit bullseyes. Whisker had his doubts about the accuracy of the cats' shot. With their entire target on fire it was impossible to prove exactly where their flaming fur ball had landed.

'I wish it would pour,' Horace sulked, watching the misty patches of drizzle blow across the field. 'Or better still, I wish it would hail. That would put a damper on the cats' flaming start.'

'You still need to hit something,' Pete said, preparing his first shot. 'All the storms in the world won't steal you a victory.'

Minutes later, Pete's first shot hit the bullseye.

'That's how it's done,' he gloated, tapping the base of the cannon with his pencil. 'Go easy on the blast and you'll get a straighter launch.'

'Alright, Professor Perfect,' Horace said through gritted teeth. 'I'll cut back on the gunpowder next time.'

The Pie Rats watched anxiously as the other teams completed their second-round shots. The toads and penguins missed their targets altogether and the Sea Dogs' flying biscuit bone disintegrated in the air. The marmosets and Cat Fish managed to hit bullseyes, moving them to three and four points respectively.

'Oh swell,' Horace muttered, fumbling with a pie. 'What are the cats' chances of missing the next three shots?'

Whisker took a look through his spyglass. 'The targets appear awfully soggy from all this drizzle,' he said. 'It might put an end to their easy run.'

'Three perfect shots and we're still in the hunt,' Horace said, managing a small grin. 'Okay, wish me luck.'

Horace's second shot was neither lucky nor was it accurate. From the moment the pie left the cannon, there was no doubt where it was headed. It curved in a wide, wayward arc and landed at the foot of a gum tree.

'Rotten pies to rotten pies!' Horace exclaimed, tearing out his fur with his hook. 'I can't catch a break. If the blasted thing isn't pulling left, it's pulling right.'

Pete wiped the droplets of water from his nose and flicked them at Horace. 'You're as inaccurate as you are incompetent –'

'Ahem,' Whisker said, interrupting Pete mid-insult. 'I've got good news and bad news. The good news is the Cat Fish didn't hit a flaming bullseye. The bad news is they did score a steaming one-pointer. They're on five points, the same as the marmosets, who managed to pull off another perfect shot.'

'And we're on two lousy points with two shots remaining.' Pete added, scratching numbers in the dirt with his pencil leg. 'You don't need to be a mathematician to know there's very little chance we can win from here.'

Horace pulled his purple hat over his face to hide his disappointment. 'Granny Rat is going to skin us alive ...'

As the fourth round commenced, the wind increased in intensity, driving the drizzle away. Pete made several last minute adjustments to the cannon and took his shot.

The pie hit the target, dead centre.

It was a stark contrast to the other performances of the round. The marmosets and the Cat Fish barely registered a point to remain tied in first place. The toads and penguins both missed their targets and the Sea Dogs' biscuit bone exploded as it left the cannon, showering the crowd with brown crumbs. Furious at wasting yet another shot, Bartholomew Brawl began howling insults at his crew.

'Which one of you slobberin' sausage dogs drooled on our ammunition?' he barked, holding up a corner of a blue tarpaulin. 'Every last biscuit bone is soaked through – even under this waterproof tarp. It's no wonder they're crumblin' like cupcakes.' He looked suspiciously at Biscuit and The Kid, hiding behind the cannon.

'It wasn't me, boss,' Biscuit yapped. 'The humidity did it.'

'Yeah,' The Kid agreed, poking his head out. 'Wot he said.'

Brawl punched his paws together. 'Is that so? *Humidity*, did you say? Well, if I lay eyes on this Humidity fellow, he's history!'

Pete screwed up his nose and snorted, 'Humidity and Horace. The two biggest excuses of the day.'

Spitefully, he pushed past Horace to get to the last remaining pie. With a grunt, he raised the heavy object off the ground and inserted it into the cannon.

'At least I can end this with some dignity,' he muttered. 'A bullseye is enough to clinch a shoot-off for first place – presuming the marmosets and Cat Fish both miss their targets …'

The sun appeared from behind a cloud, illuminating the

six targets at the end of the field. Prince Marcabio struck a match and looked across at Master Meow. The cocky First Mate of the Cat Fish gave the young marmoset a confident grin and purred, 'May the best *cat* win.'

Baron Gustave gave the order and six cannons exploded in unison.

To anyone watching, the final round was quite a spectacle. The toads' poison blob stuck to the sides of the cannon and went nowhere. The penguins' ice cube melted in the sunshine before it reached its target. The Sea Dogs' biscuit bone made it halfway down the field before breaking into pieces. The gold plating of the marmosets' Death Ball tore in mid-air and trailed behind it like the tail of a comet. Losing altitude, the ball crashed to the ground at the foot of the target.

The worst shot of the day was reserved for Pete. His pie flew sideways across the field and disappeared over the trees, in the direction of the western ocean.

The enraged quartermaster stamped his pencil in frustration. 'I never shoot like that,' he roared. 'And I mean never!'

The only competitors that managed to hit anything were the Cat Fish. Their flaming fur ball soared effortlessly through the air, colliding with the sunlit target in a spectacular display of sparks and smoke. In moments, the entire target was ablaze.

Baron Gustave checked the final score with the game's three adjudicators and made his official announcement: 'Ze Cat Fish maintain zeir unbeaten vecord at zese games vith another vin,' he said. 'At zis rate ve vill have our tournament champions by day five.'

The crowd cheered and chanted, the Cat Fish blew kisses

to each other, and several Sea Dog supporters threw their blue and white jerseys at the flaming target in disgust.

Pete stuck his head into the barrel of the cannon.

'Don't you dare say anything,' he sniffled as Whisker and Horace crowded around him. 'I'm not in the mood.'

'Err, is something wrong with the cannon?' Horace asked, unable to keep his mouth shut.

'No!' Pete snapped, pulling his ash-covered nose from the barrel. 'But something is definitely *wrong*.' He lowered his voice to a whisper. 'I've got a theory – a rather disturbing theory. I can't prove it yet but I believe our precious pies are not what they seem.'

Standing on the edge of the deserted field, the three rats examined the splattered remains of a fruit salad pie.

'Look carefully,' Pete said, brushing aside a piece of crumbling pastry with the tip of his pencil. 'There! Between the rotten apple and the mouldy mango. What can you see?'

'A squashed plum,' Horace replied.

'No!' Whisker exclaimed. 'A weight – a circular measuring weight.'

'Exactly,' Pete agreed.

'Since when did Fred start using measuring weights?' Horace asked with a puzzled shrug. 'He's more of a *make-it-up-as-you-go* kind of chef.'

Pete stamped his pencil leg in exasperation. 'He didn't, you overcooked omelette! And this is no kitchen accident. It is my hypothesis that this weight and three others like it were inserted into the bottom of three separate pies to shift the centre of gravity. The resulting destabilisation threw the pies off course – it's basic physics.'

'Basic sabotage more like it,' Horace gasped. 'I'm not quite up to speed with the science lingo, but it sounds like someone's added some deadweight to our perfectly aligned projectiles.'

'I noticed some extra weight when I picked up the last pie,' Pete explained. 'At the time it seemed inconsequential, but now it makes perfect sense.'

'So every second pie was sabotaged,' Whisker surmised. 'Horace fired the first two – which were all the same weight – and you fired the last one.'

'Correct,' Pete said.

'Can I have my apology now?' Horace asked.

'For what?' Pete snorted. 'There's still no proof you would have actually hit anything.'

'Fine,' Horace mumbled, 'I'll get my apology from the culprit – whoever they are.' He trudged sulkily down the field. 'Come on, Whisker. All we need are a few more clues.'

Nearing the line of targets, Whisker caught sight of a gold plated Death Ball lying on the ground. He picked it up and studied it closely. A thin layer of gold had torn off during the flight and a perfectly straight line separated the gold plating from the section that had come adrift.

'Anything of interest?' Pete asked, clomping up behind him.

'Further evidence of foul play,' Whisker replied. 'This line is far too precise to be the result of a cannon explosion. It appears to have been pre-cut.'

Pete nodded. 'So we weren't the only ones targeted. I'd bet a packet of soggy biscuits that someone tipped a bucket of water over the Sea Dog's biscuit bones as well.'

'Last night,' Whisker gasped. 'It had to be last night.

The dogs and marmosets were out raiding the *Velvet Wave* and we were stuck up a tree.'

'You might be onto something there,' Pete said in agreement. 'It's a pity our Chief of Security was frolicking in the tavern with Granny instead of watching the tents.'

'Can we demand a rematch?' Whisker said. 'Or call for an enquiry?'

Pete sighed. 'That's not how it works, Whisker. This is the Pirate Cup, not the *Honesty Games*. Once the organiser declares a winner, there's no going back. It stands to reason that Sabre and his conniving cats are behind this. But even if we had the evidence to prove their guilt, the result would stay the same.'

'There is one thing we can do,' Horace said, walking over to them with a second weight in his paw. 'Gossip spreads like an out-of-control bushfire in the Champions Tavern and I'm sure Bartholomew Brawl and King Marvownion would love to hear what Sabre's been up to.'

PIRATE CUP LEADER BOARD
DAY: **3**   POINTS REMAINING: **6**

PLACE	TEAM	POINTS	DEATH BALL VICTORIES
1ST	CAT FISH	2	1
2ND	PIE RATS	0	1
3RD	MARMOSETS	0	0
4TH	CANE TOADS	0	0
5TH	SEA DOGS	0	0
6TH	PENGUINS	0	0

NINE

Belly flops and Bomb Dives

B y the morning of Day Four, the entire athlete's village knew about the deception at the firing range. The no-fighting policy stopped at least one heated discussion between the dogs and the cats from turning into an all-in brawl, and there were rumours the marmosets were saving their revenge for the Death Ball arena.

Not everyone seemed to have a problem with the cats' actions, and a large number of disgruntled Sea Dog supporters began wearing Cat Fish jerseys in the hope their new favourite team could cheat their way to Pirate Cup glory.

The schedule for Day Four included two pool matches of Death Ball. At the announcement of the first game between the Cane Toads and the Sea Dogs, the Pie Rats learnt two important things: one, their next opponents would be the toads, and, two, they wouldn't be competing that day. Granny Rat's orders were to study the Cane Toads closely in anticipation of their final pool game.

The toads used a similar strategy to the Pie Rats to keep the ball out of the dogs' mouths. But instead of hot chillies, they smeared the ball with the milky-white poison from the glands on their backs. They also sprayed poison into the mouths and eyes of the dogs whenever they were tackled. It was no surprise that the tournament's medics worked overtime to stop the Sea Dogs from going into cardiac arrest.

The Pie Rats' surveillance was temporarily distracted when six purple penguins waddled into the grandstand after their failed half-time raid on the *Velvet Wave*.

'… At least we made it aboard,' one of them squawked. 'That torpedo idea worked a treat – *SPLASH!* Straight out of the water and onto the deck.'

'It's a pity they were waiting for us,' groaned another. 'I copped a paintball to the head and four to the chest before I could surrender. My head's still spinning, and I swear I'll be purple for weeks …'

The rest of the game was a scrappy contest which the toads won four-three, setting up a do-or-die clash with the Pie Rats for a grand final berth.

After the match, Whisker was instructed to return to the supply tent to search for information on cane toads. He found a sunny spot in the corner of the tent and removed the Book of Knowledge from Pete's impenetrable iron chest – a self-locking stronghold housing Pete's rarest collection of books. Whisker had only just sat down on a stump with Anso's book in his paws when Horace entered the tent with Athena.

'I come bearing help,' Horace said, leading his sister over to Whisker. 'Athena's a speed reader and, considering our book is written in sun-reactive ink – and contains no index – she's our best chance of finding what we're after.'

'Okay,' Whisker said, giving Athena a grateful smile. 'Pull up a seat in the sun.'

Athena wasted no time in snuggling down next to him.

'Who needs a seat?' she giggled. 'There's plenty of room on this stump for both of us.'

Whisker felt his cheeks flush a bright shade of pink.

'Here's an idea,' Horace said, before Whisker could wiggle his way out of trouble. 'Athena searches the right page, Whisker examines the left and I go and get us all a tasty treat from the tavern.'

'Deal,' Athena said. 'Bring me back a garden salad, – and don't forget one of those souvenir placemats they're giving away this week. I'm collecting the whole set.'

'Sure, sis,' Horace groaned. 'That will be three tasteless salads and three tacky red placemats ...'

'Isn't this cosy, Whisker,' Athena declared as soon as Horace was gone. 'We could start our very own book club – just you and me.'

'Pete loves books, too,' Whisker said hastily. 'I'm sure he'd love to join. Why don't you ask him?'

Athena pretended not to hear him and lowered her golden spectacles to the end of her nose.

'Gracious,' she said, peering down at the sun-drenched book, 'the writing is ever so small.'

'Tell me about it,' Whisker agreed. 'I go cross-eyed after looking at one page. You're lucky you've got reading glasses.'

'These?' Athena laughed, removing the stylish frames from her nose. 'They don't help a bit. Look, the lenses are clear.' She held them up in front of him. 'I only wear them so people appreciate me for my *brains* as well as my *beauty*. You can try them on if you like. I've got dozens of pairs.'

Before Whisker could protest, Athena tucked the arms of the glasses behind his ears and positioned them on his nose.

'What a charmer!' she squealed. 'You look positively dapper.'

There was a rustle of canvas from the entrance to the tent.

Whisker hurriedly tried to remove the glasses from his face.

'T-that was quick, Horace –' he stammered. He stopped when he realised the figure in the doorway wasn't Horace. It was Ruby. She took one look at Whisker and Athena, cuddled up on the stump, grabbed a quiver of arrows and stormed out.

'What's her problem?' Athena said, staring after Ruby. 'She's always so uptight.'

'If you just gave her a chance,' Whisker began, fighting back a wave of guilt, 'you'd find she's really, well …' Athena gave him a bored yawn and Whisker knew it was pointless to continue. 'Let's just focus on these cane toads,' he sighed, returning the glasses to Athena.

The sun-reactive ink of the blank pages grew clear in the morning light and the two rats were soon flicking through detailed sections, searching for information.

Horace returned with their lunch, bearing news that the penguins were being thrashed by the marmosets in the second pool game. He proceeded to offer them his 'expert' assistance, which amounted to a string of loud burps and highly irrelevant comments.

'Listen to this,' he said, reading a caption beside a map:

The three major rivers of Aladrya, the Peregrine River, the Hawk River and the River Raven, flow from Lake Azure in the central mountains. Their names originate from the dreaded birds of prey that inhabit Cloud Mountain. Eagle's Pass is named after the fourth species of mountain bird, the Golden Eagle …

'And how is that relevant, Brother?' Athena interrupted.

'It's not,' Horace replied. 'But the caption goes on to say that the smaller rivers and swamps of Aladrya are discussed on page four hundred and sixty three. I figure that any water-dwelling animals must get a mention sooner or later.'

Athena flicked through the pages until she located the swamp section and began skim-reading the contents.

'Bingo!' she said. 'According to this, *the milky-white secretion from the glands of cane toads is toxic. Care should be taken to avoid contact with the mouth and eyes.*'

'Tell us something we didn't know,' Horace muttered.

Athena continued, '*Toads absorb moisture through their skin. Exposure to large amounts of salt, without access to water, can be fatal.*'

'*Salt,*' Whisker pondered. 'Well, that's an interesting discovery.'

'It's not just interesting,' Horace exclaimed, 'it's inspirational! Fred has a large barrel of salt in the ship's pantry. If we sprinkle ourselves like we're buckets of hot chips, we'll be impenetrable.'

'But what about the poison?' Athena asked. 'The passage doesn't list any preventative measures.'

'I've been thinking about that, Athena,' Whisker said with a sly grin, 'and I think I've got a solution. When the time comes, how would you feel about being our team's official *fashion consultant?*'

The glorious autumn afternoon of Day Five was the perfect time to showcase the Centenary Games' most 'graceful' sport, Plank Diving. Every one of the thirty-six competitors had an opportunity to impress the judges by performing a routine of their choosing. The top four divers would then go into a grand final round.

Unlike other diving competitions, a wide variety of conventional and unconventional techniques were permitted, including: handstands, somersaults, belly flops, bomb dives, face plants and side splats.

'You're in with a good shot, Whisker,' Horace said, as they walked towards the makeshift diving tower on the northern pier. 'Your practice dives were close to perfect.'

'I've had a little more experience in the jumping department, that's all,' Whisker said humbly, recalling the many hours he'd spent on the circus trampoline and flying trapeze.

'Speaking of jumping,' Horace whispered, 'Papa watched some of the other teams practicing this morning. He thinks the toads are the team to beat.'

'That makes sense,' Whisker said. 'They were born in water and spend most of their lives leaping into ponds.'

'Yeah, but those under-sized swimming costumes will hardly win them any points for presentation,' Horace shuddered, pointing his hook at six warty toads posing in front of a sketch artist.

Whisker took one look at their hideous polka dot bikinis and hurried past.

The diving tower was a square wooden structure with a set of stairs twisting up three sides and a bendy plank protruding from the fourth. The plank overhung the ocean to the south, allowing spectators to watch clearly from the nearby southern pier. The three tournament officials (a plump koala, a sleepy turtle and an old hare) sat at a table in front of the crowd with large piles of score cards.

Many of the competitors were already milling around the tower when Whisker and Horace arrived. Through the rowdy taunts of, *'Walk the plank, ye scurvy dog'* and, *'I put the bomb in bomb dive, watch me explode!'* Whisker heard Siamese Sally and Cleopatra protesting to Baron Gustave about the validity of the event.

'… It should have been scrapped a century ago,' Sally hissed. 'Pirates spend all of their time *on* the water, not *in* it.'

While the Cat Fish argued in vain, Whisker noticed Ruby walking over from the far side of the pier. In contrast to the slobbering riffraff around her, she was a sight for toad-scarred eyes. She wore a sleek, red swimming top and a pair of three-quarter black leggings with gold stripes. Her scarlet bandanna was gone, but her crimson eye patch remained firmly fastened across her face.

Whisker suddenly realised how much he missed her. He knew she was only a few feet away, but the gulf between them felt more like a shark-infested ocean than a couple of deck boards. It didn't help that they'd barely spoken in days. Even before the cup, Whisker was so preoccupied with his training that their conversations were few and far between. And when they had spoken, late at night, neither of them said anything that really mattered.

That was before the games, Whisker thought sadly. *Now there are three sisters and a string of failures to complicate things …*

Pulling himself together, he tried to say something sincere. 'Good luck, Ruby. Dive well.'

Without meeting his gaze, Ruby pointed to the southern pier.

'I think that's for you,' she murmured.

Whisker turned his attention to the large crowd

standing along the pier's edge. To the left of the judges hung an enormous red banner. Stretched tightly between two posts, its huge gold letters were as clear as day: *WHISKER RULES THE WAVES.* Standing behind the banner, wearing red, black and gold face paint, were Aphrodite, Athena and Hera. They let out a cheer when they spotted Whisker staring in their direction.

'Shiver me Whisker!' Horace exclaimed. 'Could they make that banner any bigger? Each letter is larger than my entire body.'

'I-I had no idea,' Whisker said, turning back to Ruby. But all he saw was a three-legged pug wearing floaties – Ruby was gone.

The opening round of Plank Diving was a slow and slippery process. Many of the contestants suffered from vertigo when they reached the top of the tower, calling for considerable encouragement from Chatterbeak to coax them down. Despite their thirst for victory, the Cat Fish were afraid to get their paws wet and flatly refused to participate.

The majority of dives followed the predictable pattern of three bounces, an attempted somersault and a splash-landing. There were, however, several failed back flips, an ill-timed synchronised dive by two penguins and the biggest of all bomb dives by Fred, earning him a standing ovation from the soaked supporters and three straight sevens from the judges.

Whisker commenced his campaign with a routine announced eloquently by Chatterbeak as '*a forward dive with two somersaults in a tuck position.*'

Standing on the end of the plank, with the cheering crowd beneath him, Whisker felt like he was back at the circus. He'd never been an official performer in the big top, but he'd swung from the trapeze and somersaulted into the safety net often enough to know what big moments were all about. Today the attention was on him.

He touched the gold anchor pendant hanging around his neck – not for luck, but for memories, and began his approach. With three steps and a leap he was airborne. He tucked his legs close to his body, somersaulted twice and straightened up. His body sliced through the calm surface of the ocean like a pin. Only his tail left the smallest of splashes.

Invigorated by the freshness of the ocean, he kicked his legs and his body rose through a shower of bubbles. He emerged from the surface of the water to see Mama Kolina and Papa Niko applauding and the judges raising score cards of *nine, eight,* and *eight.*

Nothing to brag about, he thought, a little annoyed with his tail. *Let's hope it's enough to get me through …*

With a large number of threes, fours and fives being handed out by the judges, Whisker finished in third place and progressed to the final with two toads and one marmoset. The surprise performer of the event was Jester Mimp. The mumbling marmoset had removed the bells from his jester's hat and tied them to his toes before his dive. The result was a comical musical routine culminating in a triple spin, which earned him the first ten of the event.

Ruby finished in fifth place with a *backwards two-and-a-half somersaults dive.* Her aerial performance was exquisite but she entered the water at a slight angle, losing vital points from two of the judges. Her disappointment, coupled with Whisker's success, did nothing to help their already strained relationship. Whisker made an effort to say something encouraging, but Ruby was whisked away with the other failed competitors before he could get past, 'Fifth is hardly a result to be ashamed of.'

He was left standing on the northern pier, drawing straws with a musical marmoset, a lipstick-smothered toad and her scantily clad mother.

Penelope Pond Scum

Toad-Pole

TEN

Perfect Tens

M ore than any other moment in the Centenary Games, Whisker felt a compelling urge to win. It wasn't so much the thought of glory that spurred him on, it was the prospect of letting down his entire team if he failed.

He had one dive to get it right.

Drawing the longest straw, Whisker had the advantage of watching the other competitors dive first.

Toad-Pole ascended the tower to perform a *triple somersault handstand dive*. She began the dive by standing on her hands at the front of the board, with her legs raised above her. With a mighty flick of her wrists, she launched her body over the edge, and completed two near-perfect somersaults.

On her third somersault, she slightly over-rotated and splashed awkwardly into the water. The judges awarded her two eights and a seven and gave her a stern warning about climbing out of the water with a distasteful wedgie between her warty buttocks.

Following Toad-Pole was Penelope Pond Scum, attempting *four-and-a-half somersaults in the pike position*. As she launched off the board and spun smoothly through the air it seemed she was destined for glory. Reaching her final half-somersault, however, the tops of her feet clipped a passing wave, creating a small splash. The judges awarded her three nines.

'Caw, caw!' Chatterbeak screeched, shaking his blue and yellow wings wildly. 'What a cracking contest this is turning out to be. For his final dive, the unfathomable Jester Mimp will be undertaking a *gizmo gando twooba balooba ringa ring ding dong in the freestyle position.*'

The crowd watched expectantly as Mimp reached the top of the tower and crouched down in a starter's position. With a loud *SQUAWK* from Chatterbeak, Mimp launched himself into action and sprinted down the length of the plank. When he reached the end, he did a half-somersault and bounced off his head. What followed was nothing short of outrageous. There were twists and spins, somersaults and toe-taps, all to the ring of tiny bells. With a face-first dive into the ocean, the spectacular routine was over.

It was impossible to silence the vocal audience as the judges announced their scores. The koala and the hare both awarded Mimp perfect tens for creativity and execution. The turtle revealed a conservative score of nine, citing Mimp's 'lack of traditional diving techniques' as his only criticism.

Standing nervously on the northern pier, Whisker did the maths and realised he needed three perfect tens to win the competition. Fancy freestyle manoeuvres simply wouldn't cut it. For the turtle to award top marks, the dive had to be a flawless demonstration of technique and skill. Whisker's only chance was to perform the most difficult dive in the book, a routine known as *a reverse four-and-a-half somersaults in the pike position*. It was a dive few animals ever attempted and hardly any pulled off.

As Whisker climbed the tower, he felt the pressure mounting. He'd practiced the dive during the training sessions with mixed results. Sometimes his feet had clipped the surface of the water, creating a splash, other times his somersaults were too slow. Today, there was no margin for error. A slight over-rotation meant disaster. A slow take-off would hand victory to Mimp, leaving the Pie Rats with their third straight defeat, and little hope of winning the competition.

It's all in the timing, Whisker told himself, recalling the instructions his father had given him in the big top. *Focus on the routine. Block everything else out.*

He reached the top step and slowly walked onto the plank. Beneath him, the crowd was hushed, watching in anticipation, studying his every move. Above him, the sky was ablaze with colour – gold, peach, purple and blue, the dusk tones reflected in the rippling surface of the darkening sea. The sun hovered low to the west, its ochre rays catching the tips of the tallest trees and illuminating the wavy edges of distant clouds.

The stage was set for a glorious finale.

In the quiet of the moment, Whisker felt a distant memory drifting into his mind. He was no longer standing on a plank overlooking the ocean. He was perched on a trapeze at the very top of the circus tent with his parents and sister willing him on.

Drawing strength from his vision, he fixed his eyes on a spec on the horizon and prepared his take-off.

He jumped once.

He jumped twice.

Then, just as he was about to jump a third time, he

glimpsed a hazy black shape, moving across the waves. He only saw it for a moment before he launched himself into a backwards somersault, but it was enough to break his concentration and send his dive into disarray.

He felt a sickening blow to the back of his skull as his head clipped the edge of the plank.

Stars filled his vision. His arms and legs went limp.

The next thing he knew, he was spinning out of control, tumbling and falling with no sense of up or down.

He saw a dark cloud drawing closer. *Or was it a wave?* He really couldn't tell. There was a hard *THWACK* followed by an enormous *SPLASH* and his eyes filled with salt water. The sea awakened his senses and suddenly he knew where he was and what had just happened.

The bubbles rose around him, growing bigger as they made their way to the surface. Whisker made no attempt to follow them upwards. He knew they would only lead to failure. Instead, he waited until the last bubble had meandered past his nose, and began swimming under the northern pier. He reached the far side and surfaced behind a barnacle-covered pylon, out of sight of the watching crowd.

From the shadowy water he listened to the gasps and murmurs of the startled onlookers as the scores were announced.

'What kind of final was that?' someone groaned. 'Two ones and a zero. That's the lowest score ever recorded at a Pirate Cup.'

'Was that even a *dive*?' someone else asked.

'Where is that disgraceful rodent?' questioned a third. 'Do you think he's drowned? Good riddance I say …'

Treading water, Whisker pressed his back against the

rough post and contemplated swimming to the mainland.

How can I ever show my face again? he thought. *I'm the laughing stock of the games.*

'Caw, caw, he's over here!' screeched a loud voice above him. 'Alive and well it seems, though a little disoriented ...'

Despite Chatterbeak's attempts to coax Whisker from his hiding spot, the water-logged rat waited until the sun had disappeared and the celebrating marmosets had left the marina before he finally clambered onto the deserted pier. The leader board that awaited him did nothing to bolster his spirits.

PIRATE CUP LEADER BOARD
DAY: 5   POINTS REMAINING: 5

PLACE	TEAM	POINTS	DEATH BALL VICTORIES
1ST	CAT FISH	2	1
2ND	MARMOSETS	1	1
3RD	CANE TOADS	0	1
4TH	PIE RATS	0	1
5TH	SEA DOGS	0	0
6TH	PENGUINS	0	0

No one wants to see a pathetic loser, he told himself, sloshing past the diving tower. He heard the sound of footsteps and a short figure appeared at the far end of the marina.

'I've been sent to collect you, Whisker,' Horace called out. 'You're lucky it's me and not Granny Rat. She had intended to drag you out herself, but the pier was far too uneven for her frail legs.'

Whisker trudged down the pier without responding.

'I told Granny the plank was to blame for your mishap,' Horace said, trying to make conversation. 'I think she bought it.'

'It wasn't the plank,' Whisker muttered. 'It was me.'

'You must have a reason though?' Horace said sympathetically. 'You're much too good to simply hit your head and fall.'

'I saw something,' Whisker blurted out, 'but that's no excuse. I should have maintained my concentration.'

'What was it?' Horace asked.

'Nothing, really,' Whisker said, glancing out to sea. 'Just a ship ...'

'I didn't see any ships,' Horace said, perplexed. 'No one on the southern pier did.'

'Of course you didn't,' Whisker moaned. 'You were all watching me make a donkey out of myself.'

'Err, good point,' Horace said, reaching the end of the pier. He stopped to look back at the ocean. 'The ship wasn't a Claw-of-War, was it?'

Whisker shook his head. 'No. It only had three masts, not four, and its sails weren't blue like Aladryan warships. They were black – jet-black.'

Horace gulped. '*Jet-black*. Are you sure?'

'I'm certain,' Whisker said. 'Jet-black sails. Jet-black hull. I've never seen anything like it –' He paused. 'Well, I have seen the ship once before – on the night of the training run.'

The colour drained from Horace's face. 'You're positive it was the same black ship? I mean, there were plenty of other ships on the water that night, with all the spectators arriving.'

'I know what I saw,' Whisker said stubbornly, 'and it wasn't a spectator ferry. Besides, the ship wasn't headed for the island, it was sailing straight past it.'

Horace was unusually quiet as he processed what Whisker had said.

'Two sightings of the black ship in less than a week,' he murmured. 'And no one else saw it ...'

'So?' Whisker blurted out in confusion. 'What does that mean? What's so significant about this ship?'

Without answering, Horace turned around and began walking up the coastal track.

'Come on,' he said, over his shoulder. 'It's time we visited my Mama. She has a few stories you probably should hear.'

Mama Kolina's lavish tent was located on the western outskirts of the village. Whisker could hear her singing to herself as he approached the long, triangular structure. He stopped when he reached the entrance to the tent.

'In you go,' Horace said, hastily pushing Whisker through the open doorway. 'I'll be out here if you need me. Mama Kolina prefers to do these things alone.'

'What *things*?' Whisker whispered. 'I thought we were here for a story.'

'Just tell her what you saw,' Horace said, closing the canvas flaps. 'Don't be shy ...'

Anxiously, Whisker stared around the dimly lit interior of the tent. Five stretcher beds ran in a line along one wall, each covered by a detailed patchwork quilt. Strange runes and symbols criss-crossed the patterned fabric. At the far end of the tent, illuminated by the warm glow of a wood stove, sat Mama Kolina in her golden shawl. She was hunched over a small table, polishing what appeared to be a crystal ball. A large cauldron bubbled on the stove beside her.

Whisker stared at the strange objects around him and a sick feeling of dread grew in his stomach.

Runes, crystal balls and boiling caldrons, he thought in panic. *What have I gotten myself into?*

He considered backing out before Mama Kolina caught sight of him, but her strong voice broke the silence.

'Ah, Whisker,' she said, without looking up. 'Welcome, my dear boy. Do come in. I have been expecting you.'

'R-really?' Whisker stammered. 'You knew I was coming?'

'Why, of course,' she replied. 'Why else would I be waiting here? Now, hurry in before you catch a cursed cold.'

Curses, Whisker thought in horror. *This is getting worse by the minute.*

With his tail trembling uncontrollably behind him, Whisker took a shaky step forward. It was only when he reached the small table and Mama Kolina wrapped a spare blanket around his shoulders that he realised he was wearing nothing but a pair of wet swimmers. Mama Kolina pointed to a folded uniform next to the crystal ball.

'I took the liberty of organising a spare uniform for you,' she said. 'Your old one was torn to shreds by the crowd after your dive. Horace promised to pass on the message – though I half expected him to forget.'

'Oh,' Whisker said, suddenly understanding. 'So that's how you knew I was coming?' He picked up the shirt and moved his eyes to the crystal ball. On closer inspection he realised it was actually a shiny rubber Death Ball.

'Papa Niko won't leave home without his favourite

Death Ball,' Mama Kolina explained, giving the ball a quick rub with a cloth. 'And he hates when it gets dusty.' She picked up a long-handled wooden spoon and stepped towards to the cauldron.

'What's in there?' Whisker asked, shifting his attention to the concoction on the stove.

'Something to curl your whiskers,' Mama Kolina grinned. 'It is a special batch of my famous hot chilli soup. There's plenty to go around if you want to stay for dinner. The others will be back from the waterhole shortly.'

Whisker felt his whole body relaxing. *No magic potions, no crystal balls and definitely no witches.* He even recognised the symbols on the blanket as harmless Freeforian navigation symbols, not mystic runes as he had first thought.

'Mama Kolina,' he said, warming his paws by the fire, 'Horace told me to mention something I saw today.'

'What was it, dear?' she asked, continuing to stir the soup.

'A black ship,' Whisker replied slowly.

Mama Kolina almost dropped her spoon in the pot. 'The black ship!' she gasped. 'You have seen it?'

'Y-yes,' Whisker said in alarm. 'Is something wrong?'

Mama Kolina's eyes grew wide. 'That depends ...'

'On what?' Whisker asked, desperate for an answer.

'Whisker,' she said, trying to calm her voice, 'do you believe in omens?'

'*Omens?*' Whisker repeated, lowering himself onto a tree stump. 'I-I don't think so. I mean, I believe in things that are real, not superstitious signs that something bad is about to happen –' He hesitated. 'Although lately, I've found it safer not to dismiss anything until I fully understand it.'

'A wise answer,' Mama Kolina said, taking a seat next to

107

him. 'And one that will prepare you for what you are about to hear. Listen, I will tell you what I know about the black ship. What you choose to believe is entirely up to you.'

Whisker nodded. 'Where do we begin?'

Mama Kolina leant closer and whispered, 'I have heard rumours of a shadowy, black ship that roams the vast ocean. It moves like the wind – never anchoring, never stopping – vanishing from sight in the blink of an eye.' She gave him a cold stare. 'And there are some that claim the black ship sails without a crew.'

Whisker felt his tail shiver in terror.

'Are you telling me I saw a ghost ship?' he gasped.

'Some may consider it a ghost ship,' Mama Kolina said calmly. 'Others refer to it by a far more sinister name: the *Black Shadow*. Unlike other vessels that announce themselves with thunderous cannon fire, the *Black Shadow* appears and disappears in breathless silence, making it even more terrifying. Rarely is it seen by anyone, and those who do see it count their days as numbered. There are some that believe it is simply a hallucination or a trick of the light. There are others who swear it is real –' She paused. 'Though most of them disappear before they can prove what they have seen …'

'Disappear,' Whisker gasped. 'W-where do they go?'

Mama Kolina stood up and gave the pot another stir.

'That is the real mystery,' she said, throwing a pawful of dried herbs into the soup. 'I have heard they vanish without a trace. My cousin, Thelma, told me about a penniless prospector who wandered into her shop in East Freeforia, begging for supplies. He claimed to have seen the *Black Shadow* while searching for diamonds on the Wild Peninsula. The other customers simply laughed at him and told him he had gone mad from sticking his head in too many dark crevices. Thelma gave him a sack of food and suggested he abandon his futile search for diamonds and try gold panning in the volcano region instead. He left in a huff and returned to the peninsula, never to be seen or heard of again.'

'Maybe he fell down a hole,' Whisker said, searching for an answer. 'Or maybe he's still out there?'

'Perhaps –' Mama Kolina began. She was interrupted by a loud squeal from outside. Whisker spun around to see Rat Bait marching into the tent, dragging Horace by his ear.

'Let me go!' Horace squeaked. 'You've got no right to be holding me captive.'

'Stop yer squirmin', ye little sneak,' Rat Bait said gruffly, dangling him over the pot of chilli soup.

Horace took one look at the boiling liquid and promptly stopped his little performance.

'I be on me security rounds an' caught this wee lad hidin' in the dark listenin' to yer conversation,' Rat Bait explained.

'Is that true, Horace?' Mama Kolina asked in a stern voice.

'Partly,' Horace replied, coyly. 'But it hardly matters. Whisker would have told me everything, anyway.' He poked his hook at Rat Bait. 'What about this one? He was spying, too. I saw him peering straight through a hole in the tent. He only caught me when he stood on my hook, trying to get a better look.'

Rat Bait plonked Horace on the ground and pointed to the white letters on his security shirt.

'I be authorised to be spyin',' he stated. 'It's me job to know what's goin' on. Besides, I know a tale or two 'bout this mysterious black ship.' Ignoring Horace's protests, he lowered his voice and whispered to Whisker, 'I be hearin' about the *Black Shadow* from a retired boatswain on Drumstick Island. His doddery old neighbour saw the dreaded ship one evenin' an' ran back to her bungalow, shriekin' in terror. She be so afraid, she bolted the door and refused to come out for anyone. She's still hauled up in there from what I've been told – if she's still alive …'

Whisker gulped.

'Don't listen to him, Whisker,' Horace said, dismissing the story with a wave of his hook. 'You're not a paranoid pensioner. If you ask me, the *Black Shadow* is nothing more than an oversized fishing boat owned by some grumpy recluse who got so sick of washing his pristine white sails he decided to dye them black to hide the dirt.'

Rat Bait let out a bemused snort.

'What do you think, Mama Kolina?' Whisker asked, hoping for a clearer answer. 'I've seen the ship twice in six days, and on both occasions something disastrous happened. I'd hate to think what would happen if I saw the ship a third time.'

Mama Kolina considered her response carefully.

'There are two ways of looking at this, Whisker,' she said. 'The *Black Shadow* is either an extremely bad omen or it is nothing more than an untimely distraction. Seeing as you don't believe in omens, your answer is clear.'

'Hear, hear!' Horace said, clapping Whisker on the back. 'You've got nothing to worry about. As long as you keep your mind on the job and your eyes off the ocean, no spooky ghost ships will ever trouble you again.'

'Right,' Whisker said, only half convinced. 'But what happens when I'm *on* the ocean?'

ELEVEN

Desert Islands

Whisker decided not to stay for dinner. It wasn't the devilishly hot soup that put him off, it was the thought of facing Horace's entire family after his already taxing day. Failed dives and phantom ships were enough for him to worry about without adding dinnertime squabbles to the mix. With a polite goodbye to Mama Kolina, he slipped out of the tent before the sisters arrived.

Creeping from one shadow to the next, he made his way back to the athletes' corner of the village. As he hurried past rows of tents and teepees, he thought about his current predicament: the fox was yet to make an appearance, his chances of winning the cup were fading fast, and he didn't know how he could face Granny Rat or the rest of the team again. The longer he was on the island, the more he wished he was back on the *Apple Pie*. Life aboard a Pie Rat ship seemed so simple compared to the complexities of the Pirate Cup. On the ship it was just him, the crew and the sea.

As he walked past the Champions Tavern, he heard the loud cheers of the celebrating marmosets and longed for the humble surrounds of the *Apple Pie's* mess room. He stared down the dark path that led to the marina and for a moment considered returning to the ship – at least for the night. He quickly changed his mind when he saw the shadowy outline of a cat slinking through the bushes to the south of the path. Although his fear of the Cat Fish had subsided greatly over the course of the games, he wasn't going to take any chances, and opted to return to his tent instead.

The early night proved to be a fortunate move for Whisker, and he woke to the sound of the bell hours before dawn. Horace, who'd been up late eating copious bowls of hot chilli soup, refused to budge from his bed.

'I can't move a muscle,' he moaned. 'I'm a sick volcano with a bellyful of lava.' He let out a long burp. 'Ooogh! I think I'm about to erupt.'

Pencil Leg Pete stuck his bony white nose through the entrance to the tent and glared at Horace.

'Get up, you lazy lizard!' he hissed, prodding Horace with his pencil leg. 'Baron Gustave wants us on the pier in five minutes.'

'Why?' Horace asked, making no attempt to move. 'Is he re-running the Plank Diving event?'

'Hardly,' Pete replied, giving Whisker a less-than-impressed stare. 'Gustave wants to get today's event underway as soon as possible.'

'What event?' Fred yawned.

'He refused to say,' Pete said, 'which leads me to believe it's the Mystery Challenge.' He lowered his voice. 'But here's some breaking Cat Fish news to get you out of bed: Gustave's boys spotted Prowler on the mainmast of the *Velvet Wave* about to drop in on the trophy. How the Tasmanian devil he got up there is anyone's guess, and

112

how he managed to escape without being hit by a splotch of paint is even more mindboggling. It's a relief to know the trophy remains untouched, even if the cats are still in the running for the bonus point.'

Fred and Whisker hastily clambered to their feet. Horace still refused to budge.

Pete shook his head and pointed to a thick waterproof backpack hanging uncomfortably over his shoulder. 'I took the liberty of packing *you-know-what* for the Mystery Challenge. I might need a packhorse to carry it to the pier. It weighs a ton.'

With a grunt, Fred took the heavy pack from Pete and hoisted it onto his back. Horace let out another nasty burp and pulled the covers over his head.

'Bring the *belching burrito*, too,' Pete murmured to Fred. 'We need every member of the crew, regardless of what state they're in.'

Fred leant down and scooped up Horace under one muscular arm – sleeping bag and all – and carried the worm-like shape out of the tent. Horace seemed quite content with the whole arrangement, and the motion of Fred's lumbering footsteps quickly lulled him back to sleep.

The snoring, burping bundle drew many curious stares as the Pie Rats made their way down the coastal track. The athletes were too busy dishing up caterpillar and worm jokes to remember Whisker's poor performance from the previous day, and he reached the marina without a single insult or scathing remark.

At the end of the northern pier, several of Gustave's sons were attaching mooring ropes to bollards and drawing the *Velvet Wave* closer to the dock. A gangplank was lowered from the port side of the ship and Baron Gustave made an announcement from the helm.

'Please form one orderly line and proceed directly onto my vessel,' he instructed.

No one moved.

'Tell us why?' Prowler hissed. 'I've seen enough of that purple menace to pass on a second round of *target practice.*'

'Hear, hear,' added one of the penguins, pointing a flipper at his stained chest. 'I'll never be the same colour again.'

'I can assure you zere is no ambush,' Gustave chuckled. 'But as for our destination, vell, let's just say ve are going on a little cruise. You may stay here if you vish, but zat vill rule out your entire team from today's event.'

'We're coming,' Sabre snarled, pushing past Prowler to reach the gang plank. He looked back at the athletes and added with a hint of arrogance, 'Another win and the trophy will be as good as ours.'

Taking Sabre's remark as a direct challenge, the other competitors hurried after him. Whisker interpreted Sabre's comment in an entirely different way. For him, it wasn't so much about winning the trophy as merely *touching* it.

He felt a sudden rush of excitement as he scurried up the steep plank. The rabbits were so busy preparing the ship for the voyage that not one of them stood guarding the trophy room.

... *Seven, eight, nine,* Whisker counted, his eyes searching frantically for Gustave's sons.

... *Ten, eleven, twelve.* The coast was finally clear.

At the top of the gangplank, the other pirates turned right and headed towards the stern of the ship, Whisker slipped away to the left and made his way along the bulwark to the trophy room. With a final, cautious glance at the empty crow's-nest, he leapt through the darkened doorway.

For a moment he wondered what he was facing. Then, as his eyes adjusted to the blackness, he realised what he was looking at: an empty room. The darkness itself was a dead giveaway. There were no bright purple flames and there was no trophy.

Where has it gone? Whisker thought in dismay, running his eyes over the crimson curtains in the room. He turned and stared through the open doorway. A faint purple glow lit up the distant sky.

Of course, he gasped, *the bell tower.*

He had the fleeting idea of diving into the water and swimming back to the island but the two rabbits standing watch on the pier convinced him otherwise. In the light of several dock lanterns, he realised they were both holding loaded slingshots, aimed directly at him.

Whisker gave them a friendly wave and exclaimed, 'Whoops! That's not the toilet,' and quickly hurried off to join his teammates.

Despite the disappointment of the trophy room, Whisker was glad to be back at sea. The salty air and icy wind gave him renewed vigour and he stood at the bow of the ship, soaking up the dawn atmosphere.

The *Velvet Wave* sailed south, close to where Whisker had seen the *Black Shadow.* He was strangely comforted to know he was in such despicable company. With six crews of lawless pirates and a dozen trigger-happy rabbits, no ship would be foolish enough to consider an attack.

As the rising sun crept over the horizon, the *Velvet Wave* navigated past a barren, rocky island. The vast majority of the pirates were too engrossed in an all-girls card game between Penelope Pond Scum, Ruby and Tuffy to even notice the scenery.

Whisker's comment of 'Great hand, Ruby,' earned him a filthy stare from the competitive rat, and Tuffy's subsequent remark of 'Go talk to your snoring caterpillar buddy, or else ...' had him quickly retreating to a quiet corner of the ship.

As the card game entered a two-way showdown between Ruby and Tuffy (which Tuffy eventually won by a single card), Baron Gustave altered his course and continued westward across a turbulent stretch of sea. In the distance, Whisker spotted a tiny island with pure white sand and a small jungle of trees. Horace, who'd been asleep the entire journey, suddenly woke up in his sleeping bag, looking extremely ill.

'Shiver me sick buckets,' he groaned, trying to block out the sun with the shaft of his hook. 'Who's shaking the tent?'

'A large wave,' Pete droned.

'What?' Horace cried, rolling out of his sleeping bag. 'Has the athletes' village been hit by a tsunami?'

'No, you bamboozled baboon!' Pete snapped. 'We're on a ship.'

'Oh,' Horace said, tapping the deck with his hook. 'That would explain the hard ground.' He grabbed the side of the bulwark and slowly pulled himself to his feet.

'Nice island,' he said, staring at the approaching landmass. 'Do you think there'll be hula girls ...?'

Horace had to wait until the ship had anchored and the

pirates had all been ferried over to the island before he finally got his answer.

'Ze Mystery Challenge is rather simple,' Gustave said to the assembled teams. 'I am about to sail away, leaving you all marooned on zis deserted island.' There were several gasps and groans – most noticeably from Horace. Gustave stepped into his rowboat and pointed to a small spec of land on the horizon. 'Ze first team zat can reach me on ze neighbouring rocky island vill vin ze event. How you get zere is entirely up to you.'

And without further explanation, he picked up the oars and began rowing back to the *Velvet Wave*.

Wasting no time, the Pie Rats gathered in a small huddle on the beach to discuss tactics.

'Our first task is to build a boat to withstand the turbulent crossing,' the Captain said, taking charge. 'We can be on the rocky island by nightfall if we focus solely on locating the right materials for our escape vessel.'

'That's easier said than done,' Whisker said, glancing across at the small forest. 'The wooden boat I built with my father took months to complete, not hours.'

'What about a raft?' Horace ventured. 'We made a log raft on the Island of Kings and it only took a few minutes to build –'

'– and even less time to fall apart,' Pete muttered.

'Oh, stop it!' Horace scolded. 'The raft was perfectly fine until we ran into a school of fresh water piranhas and then tumbled down a waterfall.' He swept his hook in an arc over the sea. 'I can assure you there is zero chance of that happening here.'

'True,' Pete considered. 'But there are hungry sharks, killer whales and six metre waves to contend with.'

'Rotten pies to rickety rafts,' Horace said, quickly losing his enthusiasm.

'Have you considered page six hundred and seventy-two?' Ruby said abruptly from the outskirts of the group.

Six heads turned to her in surprise.

'What?' she snapped, still fuming over her card game defeat. 'I've done my homework. There's an entire section on easy-to-make fishing vessels in there. I presume one of you packed our *reading material*.'

'Aye,' Pete said in a hushed voice. 'Fred's your rat.'

'Might I suggest we find a more private location to review our options,' the Captain said, gesturing to a clump of palm trees at the end of the beach. 'Smudge, you're on spy duty. Let me know what the other teams are plotting – and stay out of tongue's reach of those toads.'

Smudge gave the Captain a four-armed salute and buzzed off down the beach. The Pie Rats set off in the opposite direction and were soon surrounded by coconut palms, pandanus trees and dense clumps of bamboo. Fred removed the book from his backpack and lay it on a sunny patch of sand.

'Page six hundred and seventy two, was it?' the Captain murmured, opening the book two-thirds of the way through.

In the light of the morning sun, the white pages slowly transformed into a detailed ocean map with the title, *The Crumbling Rock Islands*. The number at the bottom of the page read *660*.

'Close,' the Captain chuckled, flicking forward twelve pages.

The crew were soon staring at a double page of canoes, catamarans and miniature sail boats.

Outrigger

'So, which one do we build?' Horace asked, overwhelmed by the variety of vessels on offer.

Ruby pointed to a sketch of a long canoe with a float attached to one side and a sail raised above it. Its title read *Outrigger*.

'That's our boat,' she said confidently. 'It's quick to assemble, easy to paddle, and the float will help stabilise the hull in rough waters.'

'And I have the perfect sail,' Horace added, holding up the corner of his sleeping bag.

'It's a little on the small side,' Pete said, peering down his nose at the striped fabric. 'But I'm sure we can attach a few T-shirts to increase the surface area.'

Fred wasted no time in removing his huge red shirt

and handed it to Pete. Horace grinned at Whisker, then stripped off his own shirt. Awkwardly, Whisker followed suit.

'Now this is desert island living!' Horace exclaimed, dragging Whisker into the forest. 'Come on. You can help me cut down some bamboo. We'll need a hollow stalk for the floatation device, a straight section for the mast and a couple of shorter lengths for the supports. How sharp is your sword …?'

While Horace and Whisker took care of the bamboo, Ruby, Fred and the Captain went in search of a hollow log for the canoe. Pete stayed near the beach, plaiting stringy pandanus leaves together to form short lengths of rope.

The only suitable log the Pie Rats discovered was located deep in the forest and it took the combined efforts of all six rats to roll it to the beach. On their way back they spotted several cane toads carrying the flimsy base of a raft made from sticks and thin stalks of bamboo.

'I doubt that will survive the crossing,' Pete whispered when the toads were out of earshot. 'The waves will smash it to pieces before they're even past the breakers.'

'I suggest we focus on our own vessel,' the Captain said, straining to get the log through the sand. 'Do we have all the materials we need?'

'Aye, aye, Captain,' Horace replied, struggling to see over the log. 'The bamboo is waiting on the shore.'

'What about the paddles?' Ruby asked. 'Did anyone bother to think about them?'

'I did,' Whisker replied. 'I collected a pile of coconuts after we cut down the bamboo.'

'Coconuts?' Ruby huffed, giving the heavy log a firm kick with her foot. 'I said paddles, not provisions!'

Whisker pretended he hadn't heard her and continued pushing.

'Well, apprentice?' she snapped. 'Are you going to explain yourself or not?'

'Err, sure, Ruby,' he said timidly. 'I was thinking we could cut the coconut shells in half and attached them to the ends of our scissor swords to form cupped paddles. We could drink the coconut milk to stay hydrated and save the rest of the coconut for the crossing.'

'Pure genius,' Horace exclaimed. 'You've thought of everything.'

Ruby softened slightly.

'I could do with a glass of coconut milk,' she said, almost managing a smile. And for a moment, all the hostility, all the angst, and all the awkwardness was gone and Ruby and Whisker were simply two friends on a beach, working side by side to build a boat.

Whisker wished it would stay that way forever.

Do we really have to leave? he thought to himself as he handed Ruby a shell full of coconut milk. *Life here would be so simple – and so safe. We could build a shelter instead of a boat. We could eat bananas and swim and forget everything ...*

But Whisker knew he could never forget – not the cyclone and certainly not his family. Not even the most beautiful paradise would ever feel like home without all the people he cared about by his side. 'Home' meant familiar faces, not perfect places.

As he skewered a coconut shell on the end of a scissor sword, he wished they were with him now – his family, his friends, his paradise.

Strange Vessels

With six sets of paws working harmoniously together, the outrigger progressed at a surprisingly fast pace. As the morning wore on, Smudge returned from his surveillance operation with several interesting developments to report.

The Sea Dogs had left the island some time ago with nothing but a large piece of driftwood, relying solely on paddle power to get them to the neighbouring island. The Cane Toads were currently moving through the breakers, struggling to keep their flimsy raft from falling apart. On the far side of the forest, the marmosets were building an elaborate vessel using bamboo, banana leaves and vines.

The Cat Fish, on the other hand, didn't appear to be making a boat at all, but were weaving a large net from whatever materials they could get their paws on. Smudge had no idea what they were playing at, but informed the crew that Prowler was nowhere in sight.

'That's never a good sign,' Horace muttered, tying his sleeping bag to the mast. 'What about the penguins? I doubt they found an iceberg to sail away on.'

Smudge raised two arms in the air as if to say, *Don't ask me. I couldn't keep an eye on everyone.*

'It's likely they're flaked out in a small cave, suffering from heat exhaustion,' the Captain said, unconcerned. 'For now, the dogs are our main threat. If we get a move on, we can still catch them before they reach the island. Their pace will undoubtedly slow when their legs grow tired.'

'We're almost ready to launch, Captain,' Ruby cried. 'One more shirt and we're set.' She stuck her paw out to Pete. 'If you please?'

'Bother!' Pete muttered, stripping off his top. 'I was hoping you had ample clothing with Fred's XXXL-sized jersey.' He reluctantly passed Ruby his slim-fitting shirt and squinted up at the scorching sun. 'If I get a hint of sunburn, there'll be trouble, do you understand?'

'Relax,' Horace laughed. 'A tan will do you the world of good.'

'I'm an albino,' Pete exclaimed. 'I don't tan. I roast!'

Ruby rolled her eye and began tearing off the bottom half of her shirt. When she was finished, she threw the strip of fabric to Pete. 'Here, use this to cover your shoulders. It will protect you from the worst of the sun.'

'Thanks,' Pete sniffled.

'Don't mention it,' Ruby said, glancing down at her tattered half-shirt. 'I just hope midriffs are back in fashion on the mainland …'

It was a less-than-stylish crew that finally made its way out to sea in a makeshift outrigger. The six rats sat in a tight line in the hollow section of the log and Smudge clung to the top of the bamboo mast. The sail remained tightly rolled up as the Pie Rats paddled through the rough breakers, heading north. Ruby took the front position and set the pace, while Pete sat at the stern of the boat, steering the vessel.

Large waves hammered the small boat as it made its way towards the open sea. If it wasn't for the floatation device, the vessel would have surely capsized. Horace had the job of bailing water using a bamboo hook-attachment and worked overtime during the first part of the journey.

When the Pie Rats were finally past the line of breakers, they raised the sail and harnessed the power of the south-east wind.

It wasn't long before Smudge spotted the Cane Toads' disintegrating raft a short distance away. The toads were taking turns kicking with their back legs, paddling with pieces of bark and re-fastening sticks that had come adrift. Their pace was slow and cumbersome.

As the toad's raft disappeared behind the outrigger, the distant shape of the rocky island grew clearer.

'How's the boat holding up?' the Captain asked, as increasingly larger waves jolted the vessel from side to side.

'The float's still secure,' Pete replied, examining each knot thoroughly, 'though the mast is beginning to loosen.'

'Can you refasten it?' Ruby shouted over the roar of the wind.

'Not without collapsing the entire sail,' Pete called back, 'but I might be able to strengthen it.' He pulled the scrap of fabric off his shoulders and began wrapping it around the base of the mast. 'Phooey to sun protection. My nose is sunburnt anyway.' He tied the ends of the fabric together and gave the mast a quick shake. 'That should hold it – for now.'

'Look!' Horace cried. 'Smudge has spotted something.'

All eyes stared up at the wind-swept mast. Smudge gripped the corner of the sleeping bag with five arms and used his one free arm to point directly behind the boat.

Whisker spun around and gasped. Ploughing through

the ocean and rapidly approaching was a mighty two-hulled catamaran. Constructed from hundreds of pieces of lightweight bamboo, it sat high on the water, gliding effortlessly through the waves. Two enormous banana-leaf sails rose from its hulls. What startled Whisker most was not the vessel's brilliant construction, but its brazen crew of six snarling Cat Fish.

'Ratbeard save us!' the Captain exclaimed. 'The conniving cats have hijacked the marmosets' boat.'

'That explains the net,' Pete groaned. 'The poor monkeys must be tied up in the jungle.'

'Poor us more like it,' Horace cried. 'The cats will overtake us in no time.'

'Not necessarily,' Ruby shouted. 'If the wind drops off closer to the shore, we can still paddle our way to victory.'

'What about the dogs?' Pete hollered. 'Maybe they've already landed.'

Without warning, Fred stood up in his seat, almost capsizing the boat. He gave the ocean a quick scan with his powerful eye and promptly sat down again.

'Sea Dogs, dead ahead,' he grunted. 'Halfway to the island.'

'Marvellous!' Ruby cheered, clearly excited by the challenge. 'We have ourselves a race. All bottoms on seats. And row on my count.'

With all six crew members paddling for their lives, the outrigger moved swiftly through the rough water. For every metre the Pie Rats gained on the Sea Dogs, the Cat Fish crept a metre closer to them. The gap between the three vessels was soon so close that Whisker could hear the other captains shouting orders to their crews.

'… Keep paddling, you lazy mutts,' Bartholomew Brawl barked. 'We're still in the lead.'

'… Starboard side, on the double,' Sabre commanded. 'Prepare to tack.'

The catamaran suddenly changed course and Whisker felt a blast of warm air from the beach. The sail twisted backwards and, with a shuddering *CRACK*, the mast snapped in two. Before the Pie Rats could react, the entire sail had lifted into the air and was skimming over their heads like a magic carpet.

'Sail overboard!' Horace wailed as the sail splashed ungraciously into the waves. 'My precious sleeping bag is lost forever …'

'Pull yourself together,' Ruby snapped. 'And don't stop paddling, any of you.'

'But what about our sail?' Horace moaned. 'We can't out-row a catamaran.'

'We won't have to,' Whisker said, staring at two purple flags on the beach, fluttering in his direction. 'The wind's blowing from the shore. The Cat Fish will have to sail across the beach to get anywhere. It's twice as far to travel. We can still beat the dogs if we paddle straight ahead and ride the perfect wave in.'

'You mean we're going to surf our way to the finish line?' Horace exclaimed, plunging his oar into the water.

'If it gets you rowing, then yes!' the Captain cried. 'It's about time we showed those soggy pups who really rules the waves.'

With an enthusiastic cheer, the Pie Rats charged full steam ahead. Startled by the commotion, the Sea Dogs looked around to see the outrigger drawing level with them. Refusing to go down without a fight, they let out a chorus of howls and kicked their legs even harder. Further along the coastline, the Cat Fish had changed direction and were sailing back in a tight line towards the breakers.

'The best wave will win it,' Ruby shouted over her shoulder. 'See those rocks, Pete?'

'Oh my sunburnt paws,' Pete groaned, his red nose turning ghostly white. 'You can't be serious …'

'Of course I'm serious,' Ruby snapped. 'The bigger the rocks, the bigger the waves. Now steer us in.'

Pete had no choice but to obey, and in seconds the Pie Rats were in the very centre of a rocky obstacle course.

'Here comes the next set,' Ruby hollered. 'Get ready to paddle.'

Whisker had a sinking feeling in his stomach as the water beneath him began to fall. The tips of jagged, black rocks rose from the surface. He glanced behind him to see a monstrous wall of water sucking up everything in its path. It grew larger as it thundered towards the Pie Rats.

'Now,' Ruby shouted, plunging her paddle into the wave. 'ROW! ROW! ROW!'

Whisker rowed harder than he had in his entire life. At first it seemed the boat was going nowhere. Then, with the combined strength of the crew, the outrigger began rising upwards, and suddenly it was airborne, riding high on the foaming crest of the wave.

Horace cheered in triumph, Pete covered his eyes with his paws and the rest of the crew held on for dear life.

To either side of the outrigger, the Sea Dogs and Cat Fish were struggling to catch their own small waves, but they soon vanished in showers of spray as the Pie Rats hurtled towards the shore.

'How do we get off this barrelling behemoth?' Pete cried, peering through his trembling fingers.

'I hadn't thought that far ahead,' Ruby shouted back,

'but we've got about five seconds before we hit the beach.'

'The beach!' Pete screamed in terror. 'What happened to all the water?'

There was a rolling, thumping *KERSPLASH* as the wave belted the rocky beach, sending the outrigger plummeting down. The Pie Rats leapt free as the front of the log ploughed into a patch of pebbly sand and stopped dead.

Sopping wet and covered in grazes, Whisker staggered to his feet. He could see Gustave standing between two purple flags, halfway up the beach. A row of cheering spectators lined the rocks behind him. Glancing over his shoulder, Whisker caught sight of the Sea Dogs scrambling ashore. Hot on their heels, the Cat Fish bounded off the catamaran.

'Hurry!' Whisker yelled to his teammates. 'It's raining cats and dogs.'

Ruby and the Captain were beside him in an instant and racing up the beach. Fred took one look at Horace and Pete, lying in a tangled heap in the sand, and scooped both of them up in his huge arms. With his enormous eye fixed firmly on the finish line, he lumbered after the others.

The flags drew closer. Chatterbeak flapped his wings excitedly from the top of a rock.

'Caw, caw!' he squawked to the crowd. 'Here they come. The Pie Rats are leading the charge but the other teams are right behind them. It's going to be close. Ruby breaks away and the Pie Rats have finished in – in – second place.'

'Second place?' Ruby gasped, falling to her knees across the line. 'But we won.'

'Second place, second place,' Chatterbeak prattled. 'It was definitely second place.'

Rising to her feet, Ruby shook a sandy paw at Chatterbeak

and hollered, 'Look here, bird brain, we were the first team to land on the beach and the first team to reach Gustave. Whichever way you look at it, we were here *first.*'

An awkward murmur swept through the crowd.

'How embarrassing,' giggled a familiar voice from the front row. 'She clearly has no idea …'

'No idea about what?' Ruby snapped.

'I'll take it from here,' Gustave said, approaching Ruby. 'You are right to assume your boat arrived first, my dear, but I am afraid you vere not ze first team to reach me.'

'Are you blind?' Ruby huffed. 'Our closest competitors are still halfway up the beach.'

Sensing there was more to the situation than first met the eye, Whisker turned his attention to six navy and white animals shuffling to the front of the crowd. Water dripped from their feathers as they gave each other triumphant flipper-slaps.

The Penguin Pirates

'Ah, Ruby?' Whisker said, suddenly understanding. 'I think you should take a look at this.'

Ruby spun around and stared wide-eyed at the six celebrating fairy penguins.

'The Penguin Pirates!' she gasped. 'How did they get here?'

'I thought that was obvious,' Pete sniffled, 'they *swam.*'

Ruby kicked the sand in frustration. 'You could have told me that before I made a fool out of myself.'

'No one thinks you're a fool, Ruby,' Whisker said, trying to calm her down.

'Unless you're the fashion police,' giggled another voice from the crowd. 'Since when were midriffs back in vogue?'

'They're not,' laughed a third voice, 'at least not on civilised islands ...'

Ruby crossed her arms over her stomach and glared angrily at the culprits: three pretty young rats. They were hiding behind a large cardboard sign displaying the familiar message: *Whisker Rules the Waves.*

Oh no, Whisker thought in dismay, *can this get any worse?*

Taking one furious look at the sign, Ruby spun on her heel and stormed off down the beach.

'Ruby, wait,' Whisker called out. 'Don't go. Just listen to me.'

Ruby took several stomping steps and, without turning around, hissed, 'Save it for your precious girlfriends, apprentice!'

Speechless, Whisker was left staring after her in shock and confusion.

'Way to go, prince charming,' Horace muttered. 'And

here I was thinking I had the rotten love life.'

'*Love life?*' Whisker gasped. 'I don't have a love life.'

'Exactly,' Horace said. 'And you won't get one the way you're going.'

Before Whisker could respond, he felt the strap of his anchor pendant tightening around his neck.

'Ah ha! Caught you at last, you disgraceful little diving disaster,' came the croaky voice of Granny Rat. 'Don't tell me you're responsible for today's defeat too?'

'N-n-no,' Whisker stammered, 'it was all the penguins, honestly.'

'Humph,' Granny snorted, tightening her grip. 'A likely excuse. Now stop squirming and listen up, Wafer. You've got one final chance to redeem yourself, is that understood?'

'Yes, Coach,' Whisker gulped.

Granny Rat released Whisker's pendant and lowered her voice. 'I've been monitoring the tournament schedule over the past few days. Baron *Predictable* has adhered to the simple pattern of two Death Ball games followed by two events. If he continues in this fashion, your do-or-die showdown with the toads will be held tomorrow.' She gave Whisker a smug smile. 'It has also come to my attention that one of you half-brained baboons has discovered a way to defeat the Cane Toads.'

'It's more of a defence strategy,' Whisker said, trying to downplay the idea.

'Well whatever you call it, you've got until sunrise to have it perfected,' Granny ordered. 'If we lose this match our tournament is as good as over.'

Fashion on the Field

W hen the icy dawn wind howled through the campsite the following morning, Whisker was already dressed and fed and waiting in the supply tent with a barrel of salt, a bundle of reeds and a selection of Athena's personal belongings. On the first chime of the bell, he woke Horace and Fred and set off in the direction of the tower. Unlike the previous evening, there was a distinctive lack of purple in the hazy sky.

'The trophy's gone,' Whisker exclaimed as the dark structure came into view. 'Gustave must have moved it during the night.'

'Another lost opportunity,' Horace shivered. 'A pre-dawn ambush would have been our best hope yet.'

A long-eared silhouette appeared at the top of the tower and the small crowd assembled at its base looked up expectantly.

'Ze remaining pool games of Death Ball vill be held today,' Baron Gustave boomed into his bullhorn. 'Ze action vill commence in thirty minutes vith ze Cane Toads versus ze Pie Rats.'

'Surprise, surprise,' Horace said, hurrying down the track. 'We've got just enough time for a refreshing salt shower.'

'Ruby's not going to like it one bit,' Whisker panted. 'You know how much of a clean freak she is.'

'That's the least of her worries,' Horace scoffed. 'She'll forget all about the salt when she sees the stylish head-gear we've designed for her.'

Ruby did not appreciate the salt. Nor did she enjoy Athena's bright pink glasses being strapped to her head. And she definitely did not approve of the tacky souvenir placemat covering her mouth and nose.

'I carn breaf in dis 'orrible ting!' she gasped though the thick, red fabric.

'That's why you have a snorkel,' Horace said, wedging a piece of hollow reed into the corner of Ruby's mouth.

'Mm mm brr brr,' Ruby protested.

'Don't worry, Ruby,' Horace said, turning cross-eyed through a pair of sparkly silver spectacles. 'We'll be nerdy scuba-diving-bushrangers together.' With a flick of his wrist, he pretended to shoot her with his racket attachment. *'KAPOW!'*

Unimpressed, Ruby stormed off to a dark corner of the dressing room and began hurling a practice ball against the dirt wall. The door creaked open and Rat Bait walked in.

'Avast!' he exclaimed, catching sight of the bespectacled crew. 'Who let the underwater optometrists on the loose?'

'Whisker's the mastermind behind our poison protection strategy,' Horace gurgled through his snorkel.

'Aye,' Rat Bait said, turning his attention to the white flecks on Horace's shoulders. 'But what's with all the dandruff?'

'It's not dandruff,' Horace protested. 'It's salt. Pure,

unadulterated salt. Those warty wenches will think twice about getting up close and personal with Mr Salt Shaker.' He wiggled his hips like a cabaret performer and began a ridiculous little dance. Fine grains of salt sprayed everywhere.

'You'd best be perfectin' that *salt-sa* routine quick smart, me boy,' Rat Bait chuckled. 'The match commences in two minutes' time.'

About two minutes later, the Pie Rats entered the stadium to a chorus of heckles and taunts.

'You've outdone yourselves this time,' hollered an old lizard in the third row. 'It's an *F* for fail in the fashion stakes –'

'– and a *C* for cuckoo in the crazy department!' croaked a fat tree frog.

'Argh, give 'em a break,' shouted an otter in a baggy bandanna. 'With wayward cannon shots, bumbling belly flops an' tantrums galore, they're the most entertainin' team I've seen in years.'

If only entertainment equalled success, Whisker sighed as he took his place on the wing.

If the crowd had come for entertainment, they got what they paid for. From the very first bounce, the battle of the *masked salt bandits* versus the *poison-spitting pond dwellers* was as captivating as it was ridiculous. While the Pie Rats were happy to tackle and tussle with the toads, the salt-loathing amphibians refused to get within arms' distance of their opponents. What resulted was a comedic game of *Catch and Kiss* (minus the kissing).

The toads relied on wide passes and long-range shots at goal to stay in the game, but the Pie Rats defended valiantly and maintained a one goal lead for the entire first half. The toads' best chance to level the score came late in the second half, when Wart Face sprayed an unprotected section of Fred's enormous eye with poison. Fred was taken from the field for precautionary treatment and Pete hobbled on as his replacement in the goal box.

With only minutes remaining, Granny Rat ordered the entire team to fall back in defence. The toads shifted the ball from wing to wing and then attacked with a sweeping lob over the defenders' heads. Just when the ball appeared to be headed for an open corner of the goal, Pete arrived out of nowhere, spinning on his pencil leg and, with a spectacular roundhouse kick, sent the ball hurtling out of the stadium.

By the time Gustave's sons had retrieved the ball from the top of a gum tree, the hourglass had run down and the match was officially over. Whisker threw off his mask and glasses and celebrated with a huge breath of fresh air. Ruby was more interested in washing off the salt and poison than savouring the sticky victory and hurried off to the waterhole without her teammates.

'We did it!' Horace exclaimed, high-fiving Whisker with his racket attachment. 'We made the Death Ball final.'

'Thanks to Pete and Athena,' Whisker said, plonking his weary body onto the bench. 'Don't look now, but I think our new hero has just found himself an admirer.'

The two rats stared across at Pete, still wearing his protective glasses. Athena had her arms wrapped tightly around his waist and was hugging him affectionately. Pete looked utterly bewildered.

'That's beautiful,' Horace sighed. 'Those lovey dovey bookworms can bore each other to death and leave the rest of us exciting folk alone. It's the perfect ending to a glorious morning. I couldn't ask for anything more.'

'How 'bout a relaxin' day off?' Rat Bait said, creeping up beside them.

'Are you serious?' Horace gasped. 'That would be the icing on the chocolate mud cake.'

'Shh,' Rat Bait whispered. 'I be overhearin' Gustave talking to Chatterbeak just now. They're plannin' a rest day startin' at sunset t'day an' finishin' at sunrise the day after termorra. Ol' Gustave said somethin' 'bout keepin' the athletes fresh for the final three events.'

'Fantastic!' Horace squeaked, clapping his paw with his racket. 'That's a day-and-a-half of rest.'

'But what about the trophy?' Whisker asked. 'We'd lose two nights of potential raids.'

'That can't be helped,' Rat Bait said softly. 'Listen, if yer keen to have a crack, ye could always squeeze in an afternoon raid, t'day. They won't be expectin' ye, an' half o' Gustave's sons'll be stuck here refereein' the next match.'

'Maybe,' Whisker considered, 'but it's awfully risky during daylight, and we're yet to come up with a suitable plan.'

'Suit yerself,' Rat Bait said with a shrug. 'Now, speakin' of a plan, what say we take a li'l field trip down to Two Shillin's Cove termorra for some *rest an' refreshments?*'

'I'm up for that,' Horace agreed heartily. 'And while we're there, we can visit Frankie Belorio for an autograph. Papa says he's staying at the Fish 'n Ships Inn – it's where all the celebrities go. What do you say, Whisker?'

'Sure,' Whisker sighed, flicking a sticky, white glob off his poison-stained shirt. 'But first we might need to invest in some new outfits …'

PLACE	TEAM	POINTS	DEATH BALL VICTORIES
1ST	CAT FISH	2	2
2ND	MARMOSETS	1	1
3RD	PENGUINS	1	0
4TH	PIE RATS	0	2
5TH	CANE TOADS	0	1
6TH	SEA DOGS	0	0

The bustling town of Two Shillings Cove was situated at the mouth of the Hawk River in southern Aladrya. Functioning as a major trading centre as well as a popular tourist destination, its elegant, stone buildings and round-towered hotels ran up the side of a steep hill overlooking the sheltered cove.

The Pie Rats sailed into the sunny cove mid-morning and berthed their small vessel on an outer dock. The respectable town was no place for a pirate ship, especially one as peculiar as the *Apple Pie*, and Rat Bait had arranged for a less conspicuous craft to ferry the crew to their destination.

In an attempt to blend in with the crowd, the Pie Rats were dressed in a mish-mash of tacky tourist outfits, while their soiled uniforms soaked in a tub of *Salamander's Stain-Busting Soap Suds.* Joining the day-trippers were Granny Rat and Horace's family. The Hermit, unaccustomed to crowded streets and cramped shops, volunteered to stay back and guard the supply tent with Smudge.

Whisker had spent the entire voyage trapped in a conversation with Papa Niko about his favourite subject, Death Ball. When Papa Niko ran out of Freeforian Firetails stories, he turned to his second favourite topic, Greek mythology.

'Did you know that my three lovely daughters were named after Greek goddesses?' he said to Whisker as they stepped onto the wooden dock.

'I think Horace mentioned that once,' Whisker replied, struggling to attach a slippery mooring rope to a bollard.

'Hera, my eldest daughter, was named after the queen of the gods,' Papa Niko said dreamily. 'In Greek mythology, Athena was the goddess of wisdom and the arts and Aphrodite was the goddess of love and beauty.' He chuckled to himself. 'I think Mama Kolina was accurate with her name choices, don't you think?'

'Extremely,' Whisker replied, glancing up at the three sisters parading down the dock. Aphrodite was staring at herself in a pocket mirror, Athena had her head buried in a guide book and Hera was scolding them both for not watching where they were going.

'Have I told you about my favourite Greek myth yet?' Papa Niko asked, helping Whisker secure the rope. 'It's called the *Trojan Horse*. Between you and me, I think it's the answer to your trophy dilemma.'

'Really?' Whisker said with sudden interest.

Papa Niko waited for the rest of the crew to disembark and then whispered, 'Listen, the story goes like this. According to legend, the mighty Greek army once besieged a heavily fortified city named Troy. After countless failed attempts to penetrate the high walls, the Greeks built a huge, wooden horse and left it at the gates of the city. The Greek army then pretended to sail away and the victorious Trojans pulled the horse into the city. Unbeknownst to the Trojans, a small band of Greek warriors were hidden inside the horse. That evening, the warriors crept out and opened the city gates. The rest of the Greek army sailed back under the cover of darkness and stormed into the city.'

He slashed his paw dramatically through the air. 'In one fell swoop, the Greeks defeated their enemy and won the war! How 'bout that for a stealth operation?'

'It's an impressive story, I agree,' Whisker said, not wanting to dampen Papa Niko's enthusiasm. 'But I doubt Gustave is going to fall for a giant horse.'

Papa Niko sighed. 'Yes, I suppose you're right. A six-metre horse on a pier does seem a little out of place ...' His voice trailed off.

In a rare passage of silence, the two rats followed their companions along the narrow dock until they reached a life-sized cut-out of Frankie Belorio. The painted figure of the famous bilby held a shiny, blue fishing rod in one paw and a small sign in the other. The sign's bright yellow writing read, *If it's not a Rodney's Rod, it's a stick!* A few feet away, a second cut-out was wrapped in thick lengths of rope. Only the bilby's long ears were visible above the coils. A wooden plaque on the dock read, *Champions trust Rodney's Rope to keep their precious assets secure!* A third cut-out of Frankie Belorio was visible, halfway up the steep steps to the town. From a distance, its outline resembled a rabbit or a hare.

'Ah ha!' Papa Niko exclaimed, spotting the wooden figure. 'What about a Trojan *Rabbit?*'

'It makes more sense than a horse, but it's still too suspicious,' Whisker said, racking his brain for a better solution. He thought back to the two rabbits loading cargo onto the *Velvet Wave*. 'What we really need is something large and edible.'

'A Trojan Pie!' Papa Niko gasped. 'Why didn't we think of it sooner?'

'Better still,' Whisker said, growing in excitement, 'what about a Trojan Pasty? It would be far less obvious and we can fill it with turnips and parsnips and all the other vegetables that rabbits love.'

'By Zeus, I think you've got it!' Papa Niko cried.

'And if we made several medium-sized pasties rather than one colossal one,' Whisker continued, 'Horace and I could be smuggled on board in one of Gustave's food crates.'

'You're forgetting one thing,' Pete said, eavesdropping from a few paces ahead of them. 'Once you've penetrated the *Velvet Wave*, how are you going to reach the trophy room undetected? Gustave's goons will paint your pasties purple before you're out the pantry door.'

'Point taken,' Papa Niko sighed. 'We'd be hard pressed to get past a dozen armed guards.'

'It could still work,' Whisker said, refusing to shelve the plan, 'if we had an irresistible distraction.'

'A distraction to get the rest of us covered in purple paint,' Pete sniggered. 'You heard Baron Gustave. One speck and we're history.'

'Okay, then what about this,' Whisker said. 'Suppose *none* of our crew were actually involved?'

'It won't work,' Pete said stubbornly. 'I've read the fine print. It's against the rules to let civilians do our dirty work –'

'I didn't mean civilians,' Whisker cut in. 'I meant *him*.' He pointed to a fourth cut-out of Frankie Belorio, positioned on the balcony of a monumental sandstone hotel. Frankie's arm was raised above him, as if waving to the arriving tourists.

'I'm not quite following you, Whisker,' Pete said, screwing up his nose. 'How will a sponsorship deal for Trojan Pasties get us past an arsenal of paint pellets?'

'The cut-outs aren't for advertising,' Whisker laughed, 'they're for romancing.'

Papa Niko removed his cap and scratched the top of his head. 'Zeus's underpants! I don't remember the Trojan Horse story being this complicated.'

'Hear me out,' Whisker said, his tail shaking excitedly. 'What better way to distract Gustave's boys than with a boat-load of beautiful bunnies. We'd need to give our Frankies a makeover, but with a palette of paint, the right accessories and some romantic moonlight, we'll have the entire crew believing they're in bunny heaven.'

'Mythical maidens ahoy!' Papa Niko cried, clapping Whisker on the back. 'Now that's a plan with *Greek legend* written all over it.'

Pete let out a long, wheezing sigh. 'Is it just me, or does every one of Whisker's plans involve dressing up in ridiculous costumes?'

Eager to share their ideas with the rest of their companions, the three rats caught up with the crew in a small square at the top of the steps. Stately buildings rose around them, curving in a line along a crescent-shaped street. There were boutiques and bakeries, cake shops and clothing stores as far as the eye could see. After 'Mission

Trojan Pasty' was approved by the head coach, the party split into small groups to scrounge up supplies for their elaborate raid.

Mama Kolina and Granny Rat headed for the village market to purchase fresh vegetables and puff pastry. Aphrodite and Hera wandered down the fashion strip on the hunt for feather boas, sequinned tops and posh-looking coats. Pete clomped off in search of a painting supplies shop with the *goddess of the arts,* Athena, chattering away beside him about her love of the great masters de Rattio and van Rodent. Ruby and the Captain departed for the industrial section of town to secure a cart to haul the supplies, and the others were instructed to beg, borrow or barter whatever Frankie cut-outs they could get their paws on.

It took Whisker, Horace and Fred several hours of doorknocking before they found a shopkeeper willing to part with her 'precious Frankies.' The shop in question, *Nana's Knitting,* was a run-down looking store with peeling paint and a musty smell. The old ewe behind the counter complained her cut-outs had done absolutely nothing to boost her sales of wool and knitting needles.

'Death Ball fanatics are hardly the knitting type,' Horace sniggered, as they lugged six cardigan-wearing Frankies out of the shop.

With their official duties taken care of, the three rats made their way to the Fish 'n Ships Inn – the rendezvous point for the crew. The inn was situated on the outskirts of town, halfway up the hill, and backed onto a deserted farm.

On their way up the hill, they passed several information plaques describing the history of the popular inn. Built by a rich merchant mink over a century ago, the building had been constructed to resemble a giant, stone ship. The lower two floors formed the ship's hull, complete with a restaurant, dance floor and gaming rooms. Two large accommodation towers rose from the building like the masts of a ship. The penthouse level of each tower contained an authentic crow's-nest balcony with three-hundred-and-sixty degree views. Billowing blue flags flew from each tower, displaying the golden crest of the inn: three fish in a ship.

In keeping with the nautical theme, the entrance to the inn was accessed via a long, wooden gangplank that led from the cobblestoned street to the first floor.

Waiting at the end of the gangplank, the three rats were soon joined by Papa Niko and Rat Bait, carrying a brightly coloured cut-out. The only Frankie they had managed to source was a paint-splattered, hole-ridden target from the Paint Pellet Parlour.

'We'd best not mention any of these to the real Frankie,' Rat Bait suggested as they stashed the wooden figures in a rocky crevice under the gangplank. 'Do ye think he'll be in?'

'Of course he'll be in,' Papa Niko exclaimed, striding up the plank to the fish-shaped saloon doors. 'It's lunch time, and Frankie never misses lunch.'

FOURTEEN

Frankie Belorio

The stylishly dressed bilby sat on a high-backed bar stool, surrounded by sketch artists, reporters and the usual hangers-on. He slicked back his ears, straightened his long nose and posed for yet another picture. Across the room, Whisker and his companions waited patiently for Frankie to finish his official promotional duties.

'I always eat lunch at the Fish 'n Ships Inn on a Thursday,' they heard him say loudly. 'Where else can you order a bowl of steamin' hot Ship-Shaped Chips covered in the Inn's famous seaweed seasoning?'

On cue, a mink waitress appeared from the kitchen and plonked a large bowl on the bar in front of him.

'Mmm, delicious!' he exclaimed, reaching into the bowl. He pulled out a potato wedge with a toothpick flag and held up the boat-shaped morsel for the entire restaurant to see. 'Now this is premiership-winning material!'

There was a flurry of activity from the tables around the room, as patrons tried to grab the waitresses' attention. 'Yoo hoo, over here … can I add a bowl of chips to my order …? Make that two bowls …'

As the flood of orders were taken, Frankie dropped the

Ship-Shaped Chip into the bowl without tasting it and, with a tired sigh, stood up from his chair. He brushed the sketch artists aside with a flick of his paw and began making his way across the room. He was halfway to an exit door when he noticed the five rats waiting in the corner. His tired eyes lit up with recognition.

Frankie Belorio

'Coach Niko!' he exclaimed, throwing his paws in the air. 'And little Horace. What the exploding artichoke are you doing here?'

'We've come to see you, Frankie,' Papa Niko said, rushing over and giving him a big hug.

Frankie clapped Papa Niko on the back and laughed out loud. 'Well, this is a splendid surprise. I didn't expect to see you until the start of the winter season. You will join me for lunch, won't you? I was gonna order room service, but it's much nicer with guests in the VIP lounge.' He pointed to a small mezzanine level to the side of the restaurant, where velvet-cushioned couches and carved coffee tables overlooked the ocean.

'Of course we'll join you, Frankie,' Horace burst out.

'An' how 'bout we order a few jugs o' berry juice to commemorate this momentous occasion,' Rat Bait added, licking his lips.

Frankie whistled to the waitress behind the bar. 'Hey Delores, tell Chef I need a barrel of raspberry juice and a banquet for six pronto –' He glanced up at the hulking figure of Fred and added, 'On second thoughts, you'd better make that *eight*.'

Whisker had never been in a VIP lounge, and he'd certainly never eaten a five-course banquet of the finest delicacies a restaurant had to offer. Unsure how he should act, he sat nervously to Frankie's left and waited for the bilby's lead. It didn't take long for Whisker to realise that Frankie wasn't a silver-service kind of celebrity. Despite the eight different utensils in front of him, Frankie chose to eat each course with the same fork, freeing up his other paw for expressive paw gestures.

'So, Whisker,' he said, making conversation as they

146

munched on their spinach filo pastries. 'I take it you're some kind of overgrown field mouse?'

'Err, no, Mr Belorio,' Whisker replied awkwardly. 'I'm a rat just like the others – just not as big ... or as small ...'

'Yeah, of course you are,' Frankie said, glancing across at Fred and Horace. 'Sorry, I never was too good at zoology.' He took another bite of his food. 'So, anyway, if you're a rat like the rest of 'em, and you're wearin' the tackiest palm tree tourist shirt I've ever seen, you must be a Pie Rat in disguise, right?'

'Um ...' Whisker began, unsure how he should respond.

'Don't worry,' Frankie whispered. 'I know all about the Pie Rats and the Pirate Cup. If Death Ball's involved, I'm onto it. Believe me, I'd be there cheerin' you on if I didn't have my squeaky clean reputation to uphold. I'd lose my sponsors in an instant if they heard I'd been hangin' with a horde of bloodthirsty bandits – present company excepted. So, tell me, kid, who's the team to beat?'

Whisker gulped down a buttery slab of pastry. 'That would be the Cat Fish. The *bloodthirstiest* crew of them all.'

'And we're facing them in the grand final,' Horace added, crumbs falling from his mouth. 'They beat the marmosets in a full-time penalty shootout yesterday – six goals to four. It was the roughest, toughest game in the history of the cup.'

'A taste of what's to come ...' Whisker said under his breath.

Frankie looked at both of them. 'Where's your confidence, lads? You'll never defeat an opposition unless you believe you can defeat 'em.'

'Okay,' Horace squeaked. 'We can do that. Can't we,

Whisker?'

'Sure,' Whisker said, sounding anything but confident. 'Think positive.'

'I'll tell you a secret,' Frankie said, putting down his fork. 'It's the key to my success. You'll find it all in my biography – *Frankie Belorio, the Champ Tells All,* which sells in all good bookshops – but here it is from the bilby's mouth.

'I was once a kid just like you. Yeah, I know it's hard to believe a big strong superstar like me was once a mere child, but I was. Anyway, do you think I was the fastest or the strongest kid when I was your age?'

'Err … no,' Whisker replied.

'Well, actually I was,' Frankie said, 'but that's beside the point. The point is, there were plenty of young bilbies who were almost as big and nearly as strong as me, but they never turned pro, and they never won the league's most valuable player four years runnin'. And why?'

'They suffered horrible, career ending injuries,' Horace guessed.

'Yes, that was partly to blame,' Frankie conceded. 'But the main reason was *this.*' He pointed to the middle of his broad muscular chest.

'Your oversized pectoral muscles,' Horace gasped.

'No,' Frankie replied. 'It's what's directly under here: my heart.'

'Zoologically speaking, your heart's actually a little to the left,' Horace pointed out. 'Just in case you didn't know.'

Whisker elbowed Horace in the ribs. 'Go on, Mr Belorio.'

Frankie tapped his chest and continued, 'Now, I'm not talkin' 'bout some touchy-feely love thing here, I'm talkin' about the real deal – a big meaty organ that pumps blood from my head to my toes. It's what keeps me going – literally. Think about this. When I miss a shot or get knocked flyin', and I'm lyin' face down in the turf, what keeps me goin'? My heart keeps me goin'. With every beat it says *Frankie, I'm still pumpin', I haven't given up. What about you?* So I dust off my paws and tell myself that as long as my heart keeps beatin', I'm gonna keep on fightin'. That's what makes a true champ, boys: you never give up … Oh, and a loose fittin' uniform – none of this new skin-tight rubbish. You'll never win a game if you're more restricted than a hippo in a corset …'

Frankie drifted off into a rambling diatribe on contemporary sports fashion, but Whisker's mind lingered on the champion's advice. As Delores brought out sizzling dishes of fried potato fritters and sweet chilli dumplings, Whisker repeated in his mind, *Never give up. Never give up.* It was a phrase he knew all too well, but one he'd somehow pushed to the back of his mind.

The dishes kept coming and the guests kept arriving. From their luxurious vantage point, the rats could see the rest of their companions marching up the gangplank two-by-two, carrying an assortment of boxes and brown paper shopping bags. The last guests to arrive were Ruby and the Captain. After seeing Horace's three sisters waving through the lounge windows, Ruby decided not to join the others and instead began loading the supplies into her new cart. Fred, having already eaten his weight in Ship-Shaped Chips, went to assist her.

When the loading was done, the two of them were joined by Rat Bait, eager to see if his small hired vessel would support the extra weight. Together, they disappeared down the hill with a stack of Frankie cut-outs protruding from the top of the cart. Frankie was too busy talking about Death Ball and sucking down sorbet to notice his seven painted faces staring back at him.

'Papa Niko told us you were working on a new set play for the winter season,' Horace said through a mouthful of mango gelato.

Frankie's eyes lit up. '*The Double Decoy – Centre Steal.* It's my greatest play yet.' He stopped and looked around suspiciously. 'Listen, if you can keep a secret from the reporters, I'll give you the inside scoop.'

Horace and Whisker nodded excitedly.

Frankie plucked a pencil out of Delores' apron on her way past and unfolded a white cloth napkin on the table.

'It goes like this …' he whispered, drawing a large circle in the centre of the napkin.

Talking at a million miles an hour while scribbling frantically with his pencil, Frankie brought the play to life before their eyes. Whisker could barely keep up.

'… and then the winger runs this way, but the opposition thinks the player in the centre has the ball, and half of them are already committed to the other winger, who is actually the centre, actin' as the keeper … and the whole thing ends with a sneaky goal!'

Frankie had to repeat himself several times before the two rats fully understood the play, and by that stage Papa Niko was peering over their shoulders, clapping his paws excitedly. Frankie was ready to launch into a detailed history of set plays from his last ten seasons when the restaurant band began to play.

'Come on,' Frankie said, dropping the napkin and leaping up from his chair. 'Grab a partner, it's time to dance!'

In moments Frankie was on the parquetry dance floor,

surrounded by adoring fans. Mama Kolina pulled Papa Niko up to dance, the Captain politely escorted Granny Rat over for a waltz and Athena dragged Pete into the action. To everyone's surprise, Pete was soon tapping his pencil leg and jiving away to songs of Betty Confetti and the Slew Foot Four.

'Who are you going to dance with, Whisker?' Horace asked cheekily as Hera and Aphrodite approached them in the lounge.

'M-me,' Whisker stammered, his tail coiling around the leg of the couch. 'Dance with? I, well … you see …' He shot a quick glance out the window, hoping to see the one rat he wanted to dance with, but the gangplank was deserted.

I doubt she'd dance with me, anyway, he thought, downcast. *She won't even talk to me.*

'Whisker?' Hera cried, pushing Aphrodite out of the way. 'WHISKER!'

'Yes – Hera,' Whisker sighed, turning from the window. 'What can I …'

'You said yes!' she exclaimed. 'Oh, that's fabulous. We'll make such a swell dancing duo. Come on, let's tango.'

Before Whisker could protest, Hera had grabbed him by the paw and was dragging him over to the dance floor, leaving Aphrodite fuming in the lounge behind them.

As the trumpets blared, *HONKA TONK TONK,* and the drums boomed, *DUM DUM DE DUM,* Whisker realised there were worse things in life than dancing with the queen of the gods.

It sure beats sitting in the corner being miserable, he thought. Finding the confidence, he slowly began to lighten up and enjoy himself.

Everywhere he turned he saw smiling, laughing faces. Joyous bodies swayed to the rhythm of the music. Heels tapped, hips shook, shoes shuffled and tails wiggled. Horace even pulled out his trademark dance move, the *Hookinator Handstand,* much to the delight of the crowd.

As Whisker spun in crazy circles with Hera, he noticed that even Delores and her fellow waitresses had swapped their menus for dancing shoes and were up grooving with the diners. The entire restaurant appeared to be on the dance floor – the entire restaurant except for two solitary figures.

Whisker saw them almost simultaneously. The first leant cross-armed against an entrance pillar, glaring angrily at him with her emerald green eye. The second was already halfway out a side door, his orange and white fur disappearing into the shadows, his black coat rippling behind him. He shot a suspicious glance over his shoulder with a pair of cunning orange eyes before slipping silently through the doorway.

Whisker froze mid-spin.

His paws slipped from Hera's grasp.

His heart skipped a beat.

He's here, he thought in astonishment. *Of all places ...*

And in a flash, Whisker was gone – darting past the dancers and vanishing through the doorway on the trail of a fox in a long black coat.

FIFTEEN

The Fox with No Name

Whisker found himself standing in the centre of an empty stone corridor. High, windowless walls rose above him, disappearing into the blackness in both directions. There was no sign of the fox.

Where did he go? he thought, scanning the passage for movement.

'HEY!' he shouted, his voice echoing off the stone walls. He waited for a reply, but all he could hear was the stomping of feet and the crashing of cymbals as the restaurant band continued to play.

Unsure which way he should turn, Whisker raised his nose and sniffed the air. A faint scent of musky cologne lingered in the passage. Sensing the smell was stronger to his right, he set off in that direction. Staying close to one wall, he used his whiskers to guide him along the corridor until he reached a wooden door.

He fumbled in the darkness until he located a cold metal handle and gave it a sharp twist. There was a soft *click* as the latch released and a thick, oak door swung outwards, filling the passage with blinding white light. Whisker shielded his eyes with the back of his paw and staggered forward.

When his eyes finally adjusted to the brightness, he realised he was standing on a first floor balcony, facing a sunlit courtyard. A grass-covered square was surrounded by walls on all sides and filled with fish-shaped topiary trees and an enormous stone fountain. Water squirted from the mouths of three giant fish in the centre of the fountain and splashed into a boat-shaped pool at its base. The balcony ran the entire perimeter of the courtyard and was accessed by a door at either end. A number of glass-paned windows hung open along each wall.

Over the soft gurgling sounds of the fountain, Whisker heard muffled voices coming from a window to his left. Hoping the voices would lead him to the fox, he pricked up his ears and listened carefully.

'… Business as usual then?' asked a thin, raspy voice.

'Aye,' replied a younger, quivering voice, 'but we're running short on workers and production's ramping up. You wouldn't happen to –?'

'No,' snapped the first voice. 'That was never part of the deal. If you can't meet the deadline then –'

'We'll meet the deadline,' interrupted a third voice, deep and confident. 'I can assure you that more workers are being recruited as we speak.'

'Good,' hissed the first voice. 'At least you have things under control.'

'Always,' said the deep voice. 'Now, if we're done talking, I'd like to get this game underway.'

Whisker heard the shuffle of chairs, the creak of a door and the tinkle of coins. Seizing his opportunity, he lowered himself onto his stomach and slithered closer. He reached a black marble statue of a mink, perched to the right of the window and, using the shiny statue as his cover, raised his head and peered inside.

Illuminated by a small candle chandelier, Whisker made out the dimly-lit interior of an elegant wall-papered room. A round table stood in its centre, covered by a layer of green felt. High stacks of Aladryan gold coins were piled across its surface, sparkling in the candle light. Seated comfortably at the table were two smartly dressed meerkats, a cloaked figure with his back to the window and the fox. The trader's penetrating amber eyes stared, unblinking, at the piles of coins around him.

Whisker felt a wave of dread run through his tail. In those eyes he glimpsed something cold, calculating and strangely familiar.

Have I seen him before? Whisker thought uneasily.

Trembling, he looked away, catching sight of a fifth animal lingering in the darkness at the back of the room. She was a young mink, similar in height and appearance to the waitresses in the restaurant. In her paws she held a small deck of playing cards.

'Gentlemen,' she said, stepping into the light, 'the rules of *Four-Suited Showdown* are as follows: each player must first nominate a different suit – *hearts, diamonds, clubs* or *spades.*'

♥ ♦ ♣ ♠

'Four cards are then dealt to each player, one at a time. After each card is received, players have the option to bet or withdraw from the round. At the end of the round, the player with the greatest number of cards of their nominated suit is the winner. If two players have the same number of suited cards, the highest card wins –' She paused. 'And now, gentlemen, please make your selections.'

The fox with no name

'*Diamonds*,' the fox said without hesitation, his deep voice stern and determined. 'My lucky suit.'

'I'll take *spades*,' a meerkat chimed in, his eyes fixed on the glittering piles of gold. 'The quickest way to riches is with a good ol' spade – and I don't mean by digging.'

'*Clubs*,' said the second meerkat, raising his paw.

The cloaked figure, left with no choice but to accept *hearts*, simply tapped a long, ape-like finger on the table, signalling for the game to begin.

As the young dealer stepped closer to the table, her foot caught on something resting against the fox's chair. Trying to regain her balance, she stumbled forward and a thin, black walking cane toppled towards the ground. With lightning quick reflexes, the fox threw out an orange paw and grabbed the cane in mid-air.

'Do watch yourself, my dear,' he said in a restrained voice. 'A new cane of this quality would be hard to replace on waitress's wages.' With a contemptuous smirk, he hoisted the cane into the candlelight and Whisker glimpsed an enormous pink stone set in its hilt.

A rare pink diamond, Whisker thought in amazement, *and it's huge ...*

As Whisker continued to stare at the glittering jewel, he noticed a small gap between the wooden handle of the cane and its lower shaft. The knock had clearly separated the two sections, revealing a thin shaft of steel at its core.

A sword blade, Whisker guessed in horror. *That's no cane, it's a sheathed sword.*

As the mink stammered her humble apologies to the fox, the fox slid the cane out of sight under his long coat, and the game was underway.

Whisker wasn't the gambling type and he'd certainly never sat at a high rollers' table before, but he knew enough about card games from Rat Bait and Ruby to understand the contest unfolding in front of him. From his unique vantage point, he could clearly see the cards in the hand of the mysterious cloaked figure and followed his every move with interest.

The stranger commenced the game with a pile of gold four times the size of the other players' piles and was not afraid to open each round with a sizeable bet. By the end of each round, however, when all four cards had been dealt, he would frequently concede defeat to another player without revealing his hand. Whisker knew this was a common strategy used by card players to keep their opponents guessing, but the disturbing thing about the stranger's actions was that every hand he discarded contained three or four hearts.

He's deliberately losing, Whisker said to himself as the cloaked figure threw an ace, king, jack and nine of hearts face-down on the table with a muttered excuse of, 'Yet another dismal hand.'

In no time, the enormous pile of gold was half its original size. The first meerkat, having meticulously arranged his winnings into ten-coin stacks, suddenly stood up from his chair and declared he'd had enough. As he fossicked through his oversized pockets, searching for his money bag, Whisker counted the number of stacks in front of him. There were ten. Locating his bag, the meerkat scooped up his winnings and hastily disappeared through the door.

It wasn't long before the second meerkat stood up and politely excused himself as well. Whisker had just enough time to count ten piles of ten coins before the meerkat swept the coins into a small suitcase.

One hundred gold coins, Whisker thought, puzzled. *The exact same number as the first meerkat. Surely that can't be a coincidence?*

While Whisker tried to fathom the strange series of

events unfolding in front of him, the fox and the cloaked figure continued their game of *hearts* versus *diamonds*. Whisker was so engrossed in his thoughts that he almost missed the fox pushing his entire pile of coins into the centre of the table in one enormous bet.

The fox stared at the cloaked figure with a perfect poker face. The stranger responded by moving his remaining coins into the betting pool. Whisker looked at his hand: three spades and a club. Without a single heart card he was destined to lose.

Growing even more perplexed, Whisker thought back to the conversation he'd overheard when he first arrived.

What if the coins weren't a bet at all, he asked himself. *What if they were a secret payoff? The card game would provide the perfect cover …*

As thoughts of mysterious dealings flittered through Whisker's mind, the fox slowly placed his cards face up on the table.

'Four diamonds,' he said in an expressionless tone. 'Ace high. A rather pertinent way to end the game, don't you think? Some would even call it symbolic.'

Without a word, the cloaked stranger dropped his cards face down on the table and strode from the room. The mink took one anxious look at the fox and hurried out the door.

Alone at the table with one hundred gold coins, the fox lazily reached down and removed the cane from his trench coat. Whisker watched with curiosity as he placed his paw on the handle of the cane and began to draw the hidden blade. There was a soft grating sound as the shaft slid from its sheath, its polished surface gleaming in the candlelight. The fox raised the sword above the coins and studied it closely.

'They're finally gone,' he murmured, as if talking to the blade. 'It's just you and me now. There's no point hiding in the shadows … is there?'

Without warning, he threw his wooden sheath aside and leapt towards the windowsill. Taken by surprise, Whisker felt the fox's strong paw grip the collar of his shirt as he was hoisted through the open window. The next moment he was lying on his back in a pile of gold coins with the fox glaring down at him and a sword pointed at his throat.

'Isn't this a fine catch,' the fox sneered, locking eyes with Whisker.

'I-I-I can explain everything,' Whisker stammered in pure terror.

'I suggest you do,' the fox hissed. 'And make it fast.'

'A question,' Whisker gulped. 'I-I only wanted to ask you a question.'

The fox continued to study him coldly. 'Ask away,' he said mockingly. 'You have nothing to be afraid of.'

With a sword pointed at his throat, Whisker knew he had everything to be afraid of.

'M-my parents,' he whispered. 'I want to know what happened to my parents – a-and my little sister, Anna. Where is she?'

'Sister, 'ey?' the fox said impartially. 'What makes you think I know anything about her?'

'Y-you sold the boat she was sailing in,' Whisker spluttered, '– to Rat Bait – on Drumstick Island.'

'Hmm,' the fox considered, without lowering his sword, '*Rat Bait,* did you say? Oh yes, I remember him now. Wasn't he that has-been pirate you befriended in the Captain's Inn?'

'The Captain's Inn?' Whisker gasped. 'How did you –?'

'I make it my business to know,' the fox snapped. 'It's not every day an apprentice traipses through the back door of the famous Captain's Inn pretending to be a captain.'

Whisker froze.

'That's right,' the fox leered. 'I know all about your little *charade.*'

'Ch-charade,' Whisker gabbled. 'I-I …'

'Come now,' the fox bristled, staring menacingly into Whisker's eyes. 'There's no point denying it. I can spot a lie a mile away.'

As the memory of that distant night flooded back into Whisker's mind, he suddenly realised where he'd seen the fox before.

'Y-you were there,' he gasped, '– in the Inn. I saw you leave when Captain Sabre arrived.'

The fox pressed his razor-sharp blade against Whisker's cheek and hissed, 'Captain or not, I make a concerted effort *not* to associate with pirates.'

Whisker flattened himself against the coins and tried to squirm backwards.

'C-can't we talk about this?' he pleaded. 'All I want is an answer. I'm begging you.'

'Answers are expensive commodities,' the fox said, twisting the blade like a corkscrew.

Whisker felt a sharp pain in his cheek as the tip of the sword pierced his skin.

'I can pay you,' Whisker cried fumbling for the bag on his belt. 'I've got gold.'

'Gold I have,' the fox said, without blinking. 'Take a look around.'

Whisker knew it was pointless. He felt a hundred

golden coins digging into his back and wished his two measly coins were diamonds.

'S-s-surely there's something you want,' he pleaded in desperation.

For the first time during their turbulent encounter, the fox's expression lightened.

'Perhaps there is one thing I could use,' he said wistfully, drawing back his sword. '... Something a little harder to obtain.'

'Name it,' Whisker said, with a sudden rush of hope. 'Whatever it is, I'll find it for you. I promise.'

The fox studied him closely. A sly grin crept across his face. 'It's a little *trinket* of sorts,' he said, his tongue lingering over every word. 'I doubt a pirate of your calibre will have any trouble locating it.'

With a horrible realisation, Whisker felt his tail drop limply over the side of the table.

'You can't be serious!' he gasped.

'Oh I'm deadly serious,' the fox said, narrowing his gaze. 'You're going to bring me the Trophy of Champions.'

SIXTEEN

The Weight of the World

Anxious and alone, Whisker crept down the dark passageway towards the restaurant. A fateful silence hung in the cool air. His back ached. His cheek stung. His tail dragged lifelessly behind him.

The fox's last words still rang in his ears:

… Bring me the Trophy of Champions, nothing less, and you shall have your answer. Tell a soul and the deal is off. You know where to find me.

The fox had revealed nothing during their conversation – not a single clue that Whisker's family were even still alive. Yet Whisker knew he had no other choice. Winning the cup was no longer just a dream, it was now a necessity.

With every step he took, he felt the enormity of the burden weighing him down. Part of him longed to ignore the fox's warning and share his secret with his friends, but deep down inside he knew he could never take that risk. The fox had an uncanny knack of finding things out and Pie Rats loved to talk.

They'll understand in time, Whisker said to himself. *Besides, it's safer if they don't know.* He knew that even if his loose-lipped companions managed to keep their mouths shut, he still had to face the fox alone. Whisker doubted he could stare into those piercing orange eyes and lie convincingly when asked, 'Who else knows?'

A horrible feeling in the pit of his stomach told him that if his parents and sister were alive, they were at the mercy of the fox. One false move and his actions could seal their fate. *This is the way it has to be,* he said to himself. *No one else can know.*

He saw a thin sliver of light on the passage floor and realised he'd reached the restaurant door. Taking a deep breath, he paused to compose himself. It wasn't just his run-in with the fox that plagued his mind. It was the entire series of events he had witnessed in the high rollers' room. Unanswered questions filled his head. Suited cards flashed before his eyes – diamonds, hearts, clubs and spades ...

Curiosity drowned the rat, he told himself. *You have enough to worry about. Let it go.*

Putting on his best poker face, he opened the door and stepped inside. The restaurant was deserted. Not a single musician, dancer or hungry diner was in sight. The tables had been cleared. The dance floor had been swept.

Unnerved by the emptiness, Whisker tiptoed across the soft carpet, barely daring to breathe. He'd almost reached the front door when a soft voice broke the silence.

'Missed the last dance, did you?'

He turned to see Ruby stepping out from behind a pillar, her arms crossed and her chin raised high. He half expected her to start yelling at him but all she did was stare at him with a sad green eye.

'Oh, h-hi, Ruby,' he stammered.

'Been anywhere special?' she asked coldly.

'Th-the bathroom,' he lied. 'Something in the food

didn't agree with me – a wild mushroom, perhaps? B-but I'm fine now, thanks for asking.'

'You were gone for over an hour,' she said, unmoved.

'Yes, well, I, err … got lost on the way back,' he gabbled, 'and I … ended up in a courtyard – and there were these big, fancy trees pruned into the shape of fish and a colossal stone fountain. And I was so thirsty, I –'

'Is this how it's going to be, Whisker?' she cut in.

'How's *what* going to be?' he spluttered.

'This!' Ruby hissed, stamping her foot. 'You lying to my face because you're too gutless to tell me you've got the hots for some air-headed goddesses. There, I said it!'

'N-n-no,' Whisker protested, waving his paws in front of him. 'It's not like that, honestly.'

'Well what's it like?' she shot back. 'One minute you're dancing with Hera like she's the only girl in the world and the next minute you're both sneaking off to some secret courtyard together.'

'Hera?' he gasped. 'Me? That's ridiculous. We were just dancing, I swear. She doesn't even know there's a courtyard.'

'So how do you explain the red lipstick?' Ruby probed.

'*Lipstick?*' Whisker cried in bewilderment. 'W-what lipstick?'

Ruby pointed to Whisker's right cheek. He touched the tender spot with his finger and suddenly realised what she was looking at.

'You've got it all wrong, Ruby,' he said, holding up his finger. 'Look, it's not lipstick, it's blood. I cut myself in the … in the courtyard.'

'On a fish-shaped tree no doubt?' Ruby scoffed. 'Don't even try it. You're a worse liar than Horace.' She screwed up her face into a disgusted frown. 'I thought you were special, Whisker. I thought *we* were special … but I guess I was wrong. You're nothing more than a dirty – lying – scumbag.' She prodded him in the chest. 'And as far as scumbags go, the liars are the worst!'

With one last filthy glare, she spun on her heel and stormed out of the restaurant.

The voyage back to Dagger Island was the most unpleasant journey of Whisker's life. Hera refused to talk to him for deserting her on the dance floor (he soon discovered she'd spent the final ten songs hauled up in the powder room to avoid the embarrassment of dancing alone); Aphrodite refused to look at him for dancing with Hera in the first place; and Ruby refused to look at him, talk to him or go within spitting distance of him for more reasons than he cared to count.

Horace (who was still talking to him) lightened the mood somewhat when he pulled out a familiar white napkin and handed it to Whisker.

To my biggest
fan Whisker,
NEVER GIVE UP!!

Frankie
Belorio

'Frankie's autograph, as promised,' Horace said, pointing to a scribbled message on the back. 'Sorry about the tomato sauce stains. It was all I could rustle up at short notice.'

'Thanks,' Whisker said politely, folding the napkin into his brown bag. 'I'll treasure it always.'

'So what really happened to you in there?' Horace whispered. 'You can trust me to keep a secret.'

'L-like I said,' Whisker replied, his ears turning red, 'I went to the bathroom with a stomach ache and got lost, that's all.'

'And it took you ten songs and an encore to get back?' Horace asked suspiciously.

'I-I don't know,' Whisker said, defensively. 'I found a courtyard and got a drink, didn't I? – Look, I've already told you all of this. What more do you want to know?'

'Forget it,' Horace muttered. 'Keep your lousy toilet adventures to yourself.' He waved his hook dismissively through the air and wandered off to talk to Fred.

Whisker didn't know where to turn. His entire world was crumbling down around him and all he could do was make things worse. The futility of the situation reminded him of Eaton, the little mouse who spied for the Cat Fish after Sabre threatened to harm his sister, Emmie. Eaton had grown more and more anxious during his time on the *Apple Pie* as he wrestled with his dark secret. Trapped by his own desperate lie, Whisker was beginning to understand how the poor boy felt.

Longing to escape from the crew – and from himself, Whisker slumped over the starboard bulwark of the ship and stared out at the darkening sea. His despondent thoughts slowly turned to the Pirate Cup.

There were four events left to win: the Treasure Hunt,

the Sea Race, the Death Ball final and the bonus Stealth Raid. The Pie Rats had to beat the Cat Fish in the Death Ball final and at least two other events to be certain of the championship. Whisker was quietly confident their Trojan Pasty Stealth Raid would snare them the bonus point and he clung to the hope he could still win his pet event, the Treasure Hunt. He knew the forest better than anyone and, as long as he survived the ambushes, his superior climbing ability would give him the upper edge. The Sea Race would be hard to win against the cats' three-masted ship, the *Silver Sardine*, but the Pie Rats' secret kite sail, the Eagle, at least gave them some chance.

He pushed any thoughts of failure to the back of his mind.

You can't win unless you believe you can win, he told himself. *Now is the time for belief.*

Quietly pondering his course of action, Whisker stared across the empty ocean. It was a cloudy evening with a large waxing moon and a line of rain clouds building on the horizon. Whisker noticed a flaming orange glow coming from the north in the direction of Dagger Island.

The lookout tower, he thought, puzzled. *But the flames aren't purple, they're …*

Fearing the worst, he extended his spyglass for a closer look – and froze in horror.

'What is it?' Horace demanded, rushing over.

Whisker was speechless.

Horace snatched the spyglass from Whisker's paws and held it to his eye.

'Shiver me cinders!' he cried.

Dead ahead, the top of the tower was ablaze with scorching orange flames. Nearby, a blazing inferno of fifty-foot flames rose in a circle from the forest floor.

Whisker watched in horror, unable to move, as the entire Death Ball arena went up in flames.

Riding a strengthening eastern breeze, the Pie Rats sailed into the marina on Dagger Island to find the northern and southern piers in total chaos. Scared, singed and panicked spectators crammed into boats and ferries, fleeing for their lives. Rowboats, rafts and canoes, overflowing with passengers, splashed past the Pie Rats in a frantic bid to escape.

'Sail for yer lives!' shouted an old badger in a dingy. 'The Blue Claw are upon us!'

'Oh my precious paws,' Pete gasped, steering the hired vessel alongside the southern pier. 'This gets worse by the minute.'

The Captain drew his sword and leapt onto the pier. 'Crew at arms,' he bellowed. 'The Hermit needs our help.'

While Mama Kolina gathered her terrified daughters around her, the rest of the companions drew their weapons and sprinted down the gangplank. Whisker glanced over his shoulder as he scampered over the decking and saw the *Apple Pie* and the *Golden Anchor* moored on the northern pier. Anchored a short distance from shore was the *Velvet Wave*. A flickering purple glow radiated from the trophy room, illuminating an empty crow's-nest and three deserted decks. Unguarded on its lavish purple plinth stood the Trophy of Champions.

Whisker's heart pounded in his chest. In the midst of the chaos, he suddenly had the answer to all his problems – he didn't have to win the trophy, he simply had to steal it.

As he neared the end of the pier, a plan of attack materialised in his head: *swim to the Velvet Wave; steal the trophy; sail the Golden Anchor back to Two Shillings Cove … leaving the Hermit and the Pie Rats to fight the Blue Claw alone –*

Whisker cut himself short.

What kind of lying, stealing, deserting scoundrel are you? he asked himself, horrified that he had even considered the idea.

As the flaming belltower toppled out of sight behind a line of trees, Whisker turned his back on the trophy and scrambled up the path to the athlete's village, determined to do one thing right.

Reaching the campsite, he was met by a scene of total devastation. The ticket booth had been smashed to smithereens. Sticky liquid oozed from shattered barrels onto the floor of the Champions Tavern. Stalls had been ransacked, tents lay flattened and claw marks covered every tree trunk in sight. The village had escaped a torching, but no one was sticking around for the clean-up.

Frenzied spectators darted past Whisker as he made his way through the disaster zone.

'Have you seen the Hermit?' he shouted, grabbing the sleeve of a passing wombat.

'Who?' puffed the plump marsupial. 'I ain't heard of no *Hermit*.' He pulled away and continued his escape.

'If it's a pirate yer looking for then 'e's as good as sausage meat,' said a second wombat, lumbering past. 'Them crustaceans took care of every pirate they could get their filthy claws on.' She snorted loudly in disgust. 'They're long gone now, but I wouldn't hang around if I was you. The Blue Claw'll be back with reinforcements, mark my words …'

Ignoring the wombat's warning, Whisker took off in the direction of the supply tent. He reached the demolished structure to see Ruby and the Captain staring at a torn piece of canvas with the words *Pirates never prosper* written in blood-red letters. There was no sign of the Hermit.

'Tell me it's not ...' Whisker gasped.

The Captain reached down and touched the sticky, red substance with his fingers then raised his paw to his lips.

'Tomato sauce,' he said, sticking out his tongue, 'The crabs must have found Horace's sauce shooters.'

Whisker felt a wave of relief pass through him.

'But where's Grandfather?' Ruby asked, looking around anxiously. 'And Smudge? You don't think they've been captured, do you?'

Before the Captain could reply, there was a tiny buzz of wings and Smudge crawled out from under the canvas, dragging a small metal object behind him.

'Smudge!' Ruby cried, her voice filled with panic. 'Have you seen the Hermit?'

Smudge gestured over his shoulder to the collapsed tent.

'He's in there?' Ruby exclaimed.

Wasting no time, the Captain began scrambling through the debris shouting, 'Father, can you hear me?'

THWUMP, THWUMP, THWUMP.

A loud tapping sound echoed from a lump in the centre of the tent. The Captain drew his sword and sliced a hole in the crumpled canvas roof, uncovering Pete's impenetrable iron chest and a pile of shredded books.

THWUMP, THWUMP, THWUMP.

The tapping sound came directly from the chest. Ruby threw the books aside, then grabbed the lid with both paws and tried to prise it open.

'It – won't – budge,' she groaned.

'You'll never get it open that way,' Whisker said, pointing to the key hole. 'It's got a self-locking mechanism. As soon as it closes, the lock activates. You'll need the key.'

'Well, we don't have the key,' Ruby snapped.

'But fortunately Smudge does,' the Captain said, picking up the tiny brass object from the ground.

He handed the key to Ruby. She hastily inserted it into the lock and gave it a twist. With a loud *KERTHUNK*, the lid sprang open and the Hermit leapt out like a jack-in-a-box, clutching the Book of Knowledge in his arms.

'Hermit – is – safe, yes, yes,' he said, gasping for air.

'Thank Ratbeard for that,' the Captain rejoiced.

'Hermit hid in chest when crabs arrived,' the Hermit panted. 'Claws no match for sturdy lock, no, no!'

The rest of the crew bounded up behind them, overjoyed to see Smudge and the Hermit alive. Granny Rat leapt off Fred's shoulders and threw her wrinkly arms around her husband. Caught up in the moment, Whisker wished he had someone to hug.

'Here comes Gustave,' Horace coughed through a thick cloud of smoke. 'Maybe he can tell us what's going on.'

Gustave hopped towards them, looking more like a dishevelled vagabond than a rich Baron. The ends of his ears were singed black, his purple coat was covered in burnt patches and his white fur was now a dirty grey colour. Out of breath, it took him some time before he finally spoke.

'Blue – Claw – attack,' he puffed. 'Four Claws-Of-War on ze eastern side of ze island.'

'A tip off?' Pete said.

Gustave shook his ash-covered head. 'Ze Sea Dogs

172

vere practicing on ze firing range at sunset and must have caught ze attention of a passing patrol ship. Several platoons of crabs came ashore and captured Brawl's crew before ambushing Penelope and her girls in ze waterhole.'

'What about the others?' Horace asked.

'Ze penguins vere out fishing and ze marmosets and Cat Fish escaped up trees,' Gustave explained. 'Unfortunately, half ze spectators vere also arrested.' He pointed to a column of smoke where the bell tower once stood. 'Ze Blue Claw torched ze tower and Death Ball arena before ransacking ze athlete's village. Luckily zey did not make it as far as ze marina.'

'Can we do anything to help?' the Captain asked, surveying the flattened remains of the camp.

'My sons have ze fire under control,' Gustave replied. 'I suggest you salvage your belongings and make your vay to ze marina.'

'But what about the trophy?' Whisker exclaimed. 'You can't just cancel the competition.'

'Cancelling ze cup would be a symbol of defeat,' Gustave replied bluntly, 'and *defeat* is not a vord I use. Ve vill simply have to go to Plan B.'

'*Plan B?*' Horace repeated.

'Yes,' Gustave said. 'Every Pirate Cup has a Plan B. It is not ze first time an incident like zis has occurred.' He pulled out several sealed envelopes from a coat pocket and handed one to the Captain.

'Zis envelope contains a secret map of ze backup Pirate Cup location,' Gustave explained. 'It is not as lavish as ze current site but it vill be sufficient for ze remaining events – vhich, I might add, vill be condensed into two final days of competition.'

Whisker glanced at the writing on the front of the envelope:

'Now if you vill excuse me,' Gustave said, stuffing the remainder of the envelopes into his pocket, 'I have much to do.' With a polite bow, he turned to leave, colliding with Rat Bait in a puff of ash. Rat Bait tipped his hat in apology and Gustave hopped off into the smoke.

'Something tells me the Blue Claw didn't stumble upon this island by accident,' the Captain said quietly, as he opened Gustave's envelope.

The crew huddled around him as he slowly unfolded the secret map.

'Ratbeard save us,' Pete gasped, pointing to the location. 'Surely this is a joke.'

'What?' Fred grunted. 'It looks like a lovely place to me.'

'That's because you can't read!' Pete snapped. 'Baron *Reckless* has chosen the least secretive location on the entire Isle of Aladrya: the hill at the top of Two Shillings Cove.'

SEVENTEEN

Plan B

It was raining steadily when the Pie Rats finished loading their sauce-splattered belongings onto the *Apple Pie*. Their entire arsenal of finned pies and bulrush-arrows had been destroyed and only a few tents and a handful of spare uniforms were salvageable from the wreckage.

Ruby was relieved to find her silver bow half-submerged in a patch of mud near the tavern. She wiped it clean on a patch of grass and examined it closely. Apart from a few claw marks on its upper edge, the weapon appeared undamaged.

'I've got real arrows on the *Apple Pie*,' she declared loudly, throwing the bow over her shoulder. 'The next nasty pest that comes into range is history!'

The filthy look she shot Whisker told him that she had not forgotten his dance floor disappearance.

To avoid yet another uncomfortable journey, Whisker chose to sail with Rat Bait and Smudge aboard the *Golden Anchor*.

The one-masted vessel scouted ahead, scanning the ocean for Claws-Of-War and other unwelcome ships. Whisker was glad to be aboard his family's boat again, and he was equally happy to have a scoundrel and a mute fly as his travelling companions.

Smudge was perfectly content keeping lookout, and Rat Bait was more interested in discussing Plan B than prying into Whisker's affairs.

'Did ye get a look at Gustave's map, young Whisker?' Rat Bait asked, raising one of Athena's bright pink umbrellas above his head.

'Only briefly,' Whisker replied, brushing his soggy fringe out of his eyes.

'Well yer'd best take another look,' Rat Bait said, removing a familiar envelope from his pocket.

'Hey!' Whisker cried. 'I thought the Captain had the map.'

'He does,' Rat Bait shrugged, removing the contents. 'I be procurin' a second map from Gustave when he bumped into me.'

'You pickpocketed Baron Gustave?' Whisker gasped.

Rat Bait shrugged again. 'That be one way o' lookin' at it. I figured that with Capt'n Brawl and Lady Pond Scum in the clink, there be plenty o' spare maps to go 'round.'

He handed his umbrella to Whisker and began unfolding the map. Whisker immediately recognised the Fish 'n Ships Inn in the lower left corner of the map. A large farm was visible above it, accessed from the Hawk River via a steep flight of stairs.

'The remainin' pirate crews have been instructed to dock their ships on the small wharf just below the farm,' Rat Bait explained. 'The bulrushes will provide plenty o' cover to the south an' there's li'l danger o' boats passin' by, with the rocks upstream t'wards Oakbridge. Sailin' through the cove is the tricky bit, but we should escape attention at this hour o' the night.' He ran his finger to the lower right corner of the map. 'Gustave intends to moor the *Velvet Wave* on a fishin' jetty further down the river. He's a regular guest at the Fish 'n Ships Inn, an' I doubt his ship'll raise any suspicions.'

'How do you know all of this?' Whisker asked suspiciously.

'I be listenin' in to a conversation or two through a patch o' smoke,' Rat Bait said with a grin. 'It's all in me job description. Anyway, with twelve hungry sons to feed, not to mention the Blue Claw ambush, Gustave's supplies are runnin' low an' he's plannin' a dock delivery for tomorrow evenin'.'

'You don't suppose he'd like a couple of Trojan Pasties added to his order?' Whisker murmured.

'Aye,' Rat Bait replied. 'If ye can get the pasties baked in time.'

'Oh,' Whisker said, sensing a snag in his already flawed plan. 'That could be a problem. Mama Kolina's stove was destroyed in the raid, and I doubt the galley oven is big enough for a Trojan-sized anything.'

'Ye could always try the forge,' Rat Bait said, running his finger across the map to a building in the middle of the apple grove. 'If me memory serves me correctly, there's a large pottery kiln in the back corner.'

'You sound like you've been there before,' Whisker said.

'Aye, that I have,' Rat Bait chuckled. 'Many years ago, mind ye. A secluded farm be the perfect hideout for a mischievous rat. There be plen'y o' food plus a well for fresh water – not to mention how close it be to the Fish 'n Ships Inn.'

So close, Whisker thought, staring at the map. *And the fox is right there waiting for me.*

As he studied the detailed layout of the farm, he felt the

rising realisation that his chances of winning the trophy were further away than ever. His beloved and familiar eucalypt forest was gone, and in its place stood a pumpkin patch, an apple grove and a rose maze – hardly the wild terrain on which he'd practiced.

Whisker continued to study the map as the *Golden Anchor* sailed into the dark cove and then made its way towards the wide river mouth. The driving rain provided the perfect cover for the fleet of pirate ships, and Whisker could barely see the lights of the town scattered up the hillside.

'What can you tell me about the maze?' he whispered to Rat Bait as they passed the deserted fishing jetty. 'It seems like an odd thing to have on a farm.'

'The Maze o' Roses,' Rat Bait said dreamily. 'The bushes once produced the finest white roses in the whole of Aladrya. For many years it was known as the *Lover's Labyrinth*.'

'I thought red roses were the symbol of love, not white roses,' Whisker said, searching his memory. 'My mother used to sell them on her fruit and vegetable stall.'

'Aye,' Rat Bait replied. 'There be a single scarlet-red rose bush in the centre o' the maze. Lovers would come from miles around every summer to take part in a special race. The first couple out o' the maze with a red rose in their grasp would be crowned the *Soul Mates of Summer …*' He sighed longingly.

Whisker studied the old rogue's face. 'You won the race?'

Rat Bait nodded listlessly.

'But what happened to your –?' Whisker began.

'Summer ended,' Rat Bait replied gruffly. 'That's all

ye need to know.' He hurriedly stuffed the map into his pocket and pointed to the approaching cargo wharf. 'Steer her in, Son.'

Pushing Rat Bait's story from his mind, Whisker coiled his tail around the rudder and the small boat turned to its port side. Beyond the wharf, Whisker could just make out a rough set of stairs, carved into the cliff face. Water trickled down the steps to a thick patch of bulrushes. The tall reeds partly obscured several other pirate vessels already docked. Even through the pouring rain, Whisker could easily recognise the metallic hull of the Cat Fish's armoured ship, *the Silver Sardine*.

Silver versus gold, Whisker shivered, running his paw over the slippery rail of the *Golden Anchor*. *This time there's much more at stake than treasure …*

The Silver Sardine

It was nearly dawn when the soggy Pie Rats assembled on a steep bank of earth overlooking the new sporting arena. Horace's family had taken refuge in the old forge with Fred and the Hermit, and were busy baking Trojan Pasties and beautifying Frankie cut-outs, while the rest of the rats surveyed the Death Ball grand final site. In its current state, the 'dry' dam looked more like a swamp than a professional playing field. Crater-like puddles of rainwater dotted the grassy ground, shimmering in the pale moonlight.

'At least it's stopped raining,' Horace said, swishing the end of his hook through a muddy puddle. 'Head-high grass and a killer opposition is enough to contend with.'

'Phooey to that,' Pete grumbled, glancing up at the clearing sky. 'A flooded oval would have been perfect. Cats hate water nearly as much as we hate cats.'

'What about the crowd support?' the Captain asked, studying the sloping bank of the dam. 'Can we count on any out-of-bounds balls heading our way?'

Rat Bait shook his head. 'The numbers be stacked against us. The cats be the competition favourites and the safe bet for any gamblin' types.' He stroked his chin thoughtfully, 'What we need is a good ol' fashioned rent-a-crowd to boost our numbers.'

'At this late notice?' Pete huffed. 'Forget it.'

Whisker, who until this point had remained a silent bystander on the outskirts of the gathering, decided to voice his opinion.

'How far is it to the town of Oakbridge?' he called out.

'A few hours' walk by road,' Rat Bait said. 'Give or take an hour or two – it's all uphill.'

'And what about by air?' Whisker continued.

Smudge raised one arm upwards while extending a

second arm to his side like the hands of a clock.

'You can be there by seven o'clock,' Whisker interpreted.

Smudge nodded.

'What's in Oakbridge?' Granny Rat asked suspiciously.

'Let me guess,' Pete muttered. 'Trembling Tribble, our timid teacher friend.'

'Not just Mr Tribble,' Whisker said, 'but Eaton and Emmie and an entire primary school of enthusiastic children. The perfect rent-a-crowd.'

There was a soft muttering of voices from the crew.

'It does have potential,' the Captain said, considering the idea. 'The school term has just resumed and we could pass it off as a farm excursion ...'

'Make it happen,' Granny Rat snapped. 'There's plenty of time to mobilise the little nippers. The game won't commence until after lunch.'

'Says who?' Horace exclaimed. 'Gustave hasn't announced today's schedule yet.'

'Says *me*, you insolent iguana!' Granny Rat snapped. 'I've been right with my predictions thus far, haven't I? The Sea Race is *always* held on the last day of competition, which means the other two events will be jammed into today's program – starting with the least gruesome event, the Treasure Hunt.'

'Alright, Coach,' Horace grizzled. 'But we still don't have an on-field strategy to defeat the cats. They're stronger, nastier and will tear us to shreds the moment we touch the ball.'

'They'll have to catch you first,' Granny Rat retorted, waving a wrinkly finger over the field. 'Look at those clumps of grass – you've got more cover than a chameleon in a bramble bush.'

'Yeah, but chameleons can change colour,' Horace pointed out, 'and our bright red uniforms are hardly standard issue camouflage apparel.'

'Then find an alternate uniform,' Granny Rat snapped, quickly losing patience. 'I'm sure there's a loophole in the rules that you can exploit.' She turned to Pete. 'Well? You're the know-it-all.'

Pete screwed up his nose.

'There is *one* clothing-related rule I recall reading,' he said dryly. '*Rule 37a: Teams are entitled to wear a contrasting uniform in the instance their opponents are dressed in similar colours.*'

'I think that qualifies us,' the Captain said, pointing to his soggy red shirt. 'The orange jerseys of the Cat Fish are arguably similar to our red and gold uniforms.'

'So where do you propose we get these alternate uniforms?' Ruby asked, frowning.

'No idea,' Pete sniffled. 'Why don't you ask Whisker? He runs the costume department.'

Whisker thought for a moment and then gestured towards the small campsite on the top of the ridge.

'Perhaps Mama Kolina could rustle up a few outfits from our tattered tents,' he suggested. 'They're the perfect colours – khaki green with a few dirty-brown sauce stains.'

'Tent tracksuits it is,' Granny Rat said, without waiting for a debate. 'Rat Bait, get every scrap of canvas you can find and report to Mama Kolina pronto. Smudge, I want you back here with our rent-a-school-crowd by midday sharp, understood?'

Smudge and Rat Bait both saluted and hurried off into

the misty darkness.

'First I lose my sleeping bag and now I've lost my tent,' Horace mumbled, giving Whisker an accusing look. 'How am I supposed to get any sleep?'

'Sleep is the last of your priorities,' Granny Rat said gruffly. 'You've got a treasure hunt ambush to organise. I want you and Pete to find an appropriate spot on the farm and set up your cannons. When the hunters run past, blast them off their feet with whatever half-baked projectiles you can get your paws on.' She gave Horace a hard stare. 'And this time, you'd better *hit* your targets.'

'Aye, Coach,' Horace and Pete droned in unison.

'But what about me, Gran?' Ruby burst out. 'I've been practicing my archery for weeks. Surely *I* should be a part of the ambush team.'

'I'm sorry, sweetheart,' Granny said firmly, 'but I can't waste your speed behind a bow. You'll be running with Wafer as our second hunter.'

'With him!' Ruby exploded, yanking a pawful of grass from the dam and throwing it in Whisker's direction. 'No way! I need a teammate I can trust.'

Whisker felt like he'd just been hit by a wave of arrowheads.

'This is not negotiable,' Granny Rat said, turning her back on Ruby. 'As for you, Wafer, I expect you to start acting like a member of this team and not a two-faced toad – no hiding under jetties and no skulking off without telling anyone. Got it? You have until Gustave's announcement to be ready.'

She took the Captain by the arm and hobbled off towards the camp, leaving Ruby fuming with rage and Whisker trying to control the violent spasms in his tail.

EIGHTEEN

Riddles and Roses

TONK, TONK, CLANG.

The small cowbell broke the stillness of the sleepy farm. Rain-covered clover glistened in the dawn light. Misty patches of cloud rolled down the side of the steep hill like cottonwool tumbleweeds, thinning as the autumn sun warmed the crisp air. It was a splendid day for a treasure hunt.

Two members of each of the remaining four pirate teams gathered in the greenhouse at the top of the farm in anticipation of the event. Word had spread that Whisker was the player to beat, and the other teams made it perfectly clear that 'the dirty rat was going down.'

Cleopatra and Prowler stood snarling and hissing from the shadows of a leafy banana tree. Prince Marcabio and Princess Mayenya plotted his demise from behind a tomato trellis, and the two penguins gave him dirty looks and directed a barrage of rude flipper gestures in his direction. Even Ruby acted like he was a hated opponent.

'Got someone special to impress?' she asked snidely as he waited in earnest for Gustave to arrive. 'You weren't taking the competition this seriously two days ago.'

'I-I-I …' Whisker spluttered. 'It's …'

'Forget it,' Ruby snapped, 'I don't want to hear another one of your lame excuses.' She lowered her voice as Gustave entered through a concealed doorway. 'But know this, apprentice: I'm running for the team, not for you.'

'Don't worry,' Whisker sighed. 'I know exactly where you stand ...'

Baron Gustave's announcement turned out to be more of an *on-your-marks-get-set-go* than a rundown of the morning's events. From the outset, it was immediately clear that the Treasure Hunt was going to be much more than a simple duck-and-dodge obstacle course.

'Zere are clues hidden all over zis farm,' Gustave explained. 'Each clue vill lead you to your next location. Your first clue is concealed in an object zat represents your team. You vill find it somewhere in zis greenhouse. Votch out for ambushes – and happy hunting.'

The competitors took one look at each other and leapt into action. The low sun filtered through the hazy glass panes of the greenhouse, illuminating an overgrown jungle of tropical plants and flowering shrubs. Creepers criss-crossed the metal framework high overhead to form a huge, green arbour. Tall weeds and patches of moss covered the slippery paths. The air was heavy and damp.

Whisker felt like he was back in the rainforest on the Island of Kings. But this time he wasn't hunting for a key, he was hunting for a clue.

'We need to find a pie,' he whispered to Ruby as they barged through the thick vegetation. 'It represents our team perfectly. You search the northern wall and I'll take the south. Hoot like an owl if you see anything.'

'Who elected you captain?' Ruby snapped, stepping in Whisker's way. 'I'll go south and you can head north.' She turned her back on him and disappeared into the dense foliage.

Left with no other option, Whisker took off through the tropical plants along the northern wall. He spotted a porcelain banana hanging from a paw paw tree and glimpsed a sardine tin in a bed of orchids before he reached the end of the wall. With no pies in sight, he began working his way along the eastern side of the greenhouse.

High above him, a glimmer of sunlight caught his eye.

He tipped his head back for a closer look. A long, rectangular shape was suspended from the very top of the glass roof. It wasn't a pie, but it was undoubtedly the object he was searching for: a spring-loaded rat trap. The trap was baited with a folded piece of paper, ready to spring shut the moment he touched it. It sent a shiver down his tail.

Just my luck, Whisker thought as he grabbed hold of the closest vine. *Even Gustave wants me dead.*

With a *HOOT, HOOT,* he began scaling the side of the greenhouse, using creepers and branches to aid his ascent. Hanging on for dear life, he reached the top of the wall and began climbing upside-down across the snaking vines of the roof. As he approached the rat trap, he realised the vines in front of him stopped short several metres from the suspended object. With nothing but glass to hold, he knew he would have to climb back down and approach from a different wall.

In frustration, he looked below to see two penguins waddling out a small rear door carrying an ice-cream cone and a scrunched up ball of paper.

No time for climbing, Whisker told himself, grabbing hold of a loose vine. *I'll have to do this jungle style.*

As Ruby appeared beneath him, Whisker drew his

sword and slashed at a section of the vine, separating it from its lower stem. Holding onto the vine with his free paw, he launched himself off the roof with a hard kick. His body swung downwards in an arc, gathering speed, and then rose upwards towards the rat trap. Angling his scissor sword forward like a lance, he skewered the note, flicking it free before the trap slammed shut with a mighty *SNAP!*

The impact threw Whisker backwards. Losing his grip, he plummeted down, crashing through leaves and branches and landing with a cushioned *thud* in a moist garden bed. The note fluttered down after him.

Ruby plucked it gracefully out of the air.

'What does it say?' Whisker groaned, pulling himself out of the soil.

Ruby unfolded the note and read in a whisper:

lost rabbits love scarlet roses

Her brow contorted into a frown. 'What in Ratbeard's name is that mumbo jumbo supposed to mean?'

Whisker's mind flashed back to his conversation with Rat Bait on the *Golden Anchor. The Lover's Labyrinth*, he recalled. *Where scarlet roses grow …*

He turned to Ruby, trying to contain his excitement.

'The Rose Maze,' he whispered. 'It has to be our next destination. Come on. There's a back entrance this way.'

Whisker and Ruby burst into the sunlight at the rear of the greenhouse to the sound of breaking ceramics.

The porcelain banana, Whisker thought.

As they rounded the deserted campsite and made their way down the rocky slope, the two rats heard a mighty *SMASH tinkle, tinkle* and turned to see Prowler leaping though a large hole in a shattered pane of glass clutching a sardine tin in his paws. Cleopatra and the marmosets bounded after him.

'Here they come!' Whisker exclaimed.

'Are you sure we're heading in the right direction?' Ruby panted, pointing ahead to the maze. 'The roses are white, not scarlet.'

'I'm positive, Whisker puffed. 'There's a bush of scarlet-red roses in the centre of the maze.'

'Do you know how to reach it?' Ruby asked.

'Err … not exactly,' Whisker replied, pulling Gustave's map out of his drawstring bag.

He quickly scanned the drawing of the maze as he ran, hoping to locate a hidden word or symbol. He saw nothing.

'What about the note?' he said, turning to Ruby. Take another look.'

Ruby held the note up in front of her. Her emerald-green eye lit up with realisation.

'Look!' she cried, almost tripping over a tuft of grass. 'The first letter of each word is written in italics: *L R L S R*. Does that mean anything to you?'

'No,' Whisker said, staring up at the thorny wall of roses ahead of him, 'but we need to pick a direction – and fast. It's either right or it's …'

'*LEFT!*' Ruby shouted. 'It has to be left. The letters must stand for directions: *left, right, left, straight, right.*' She grabbed Whisker's paw and pulled him into the dense maze. 'Hurry!'

As Whisker darted through the maze, clutching Ruby's paw tightly, his mind flashed to a different race – a race once won by a scandalous rogue and his young sweetheart.

'*Right,*' Ruby snapped, roughly dragging Whisker around the next corner. 'Keep up or I'll leave you behind.'

'So much for a lover's labyrinth,' Whisker muttered, copping a thorny branch in his face.

The thick, tangled walls of rose-bushes grew taller and denser as the rats turned *left* and then followed the passage *straight*. The sunlight transformed the uppermost roses into majestic golden blooms. On ground level, deathly-pale rosebuds and icy-blue shadows filled the maze.

The rats reached the final turn *right*, almost colliding with two penguins hurrying in the opposite direction. One of the penguins held a single red rose in his flipper. Tiny white words were scrawled over its outer petals. He quickly stuffed the rose out of sight before Whisker could decipher its message.

The penguins disappeared around a bend and the rats sprinted down a long, straight passage. Reaching the far end, they saw a small alcove to one side containing a solitary bush with blood-red roses.

'Find a rose with writing,' Ruby instructed.

As Ruby scoured the top of the bush, Whisker dropped to his knees and began searching the lower flowers. He had barely examined a dozen roses when he heard a scuffing sound behind him and spun around expecting to see one of the other teams. All he saw was a flash of blue-grey fur through a small hole at the bottom of the rose wall. Looking closer, he realised the hole led to an outer passage and was only visible from ground level.

'I think I've just found a shortcut out of here,' Whisker whispered.

'Good,' Ruby hissed back, 'because I've just found our clue.' Using the end of her fingernail as a knife, she severed the rose from its stem and threw it to Whisker. 'Decipher this, detective.'

A windowless tower,
tall and round.
Not rising up but
falling down.

Whisker took one look at the message and stuck the rose between his teeth like a tango dancer. Following Ruby's lead, he threw himself headfirst into the hole, wiggling under branches and thorns. It wasn't long before he emerged from the opposite side of the wall with a shirt-full of thorn holes for his troubles.

'Well?' Ruby asked as he scrambled to his feet, 'Have you figured out the message yet?'

Whisker removed the rose from his mouth and grabbed Ruby's arm.

'I'll tell you on the way,' he cried, taking off down the passage. 'Right now we have two penguins to beat.'

Paw-in-paw, Ruby and Whisker overtook the penguins a few metres from the entrance. There was no triumphant cheer or round of applause as they burst from the *Lover's Labyrinth,* but Whisker was silently celebrating. They were winning the race and they were winning together.

The rats sprinted a short distance up the ridge, leaving the penguins waddling in their wake. Without warning, Whisker suddenly changed direction and pulled Ruby into the Apple Grove.

'This way,' he said, weaving past a thick trunk.

'Hey!' Ruby protested. 'There's no tower in here. The closest thing is the forge chimney, but that's hardly *falling down.*'

'You're right,' Whisker agreed, dodging a pile of Granny Smith apples. 'We're not headed for a tower. We're headed for a well. It fits the description perfectly: *A windowless tower, tall and round. Not rising up but falling down.* A well isn't literally falling down but it is falling into the earth.'

'I hope you're right,' Ruby said, glancing over her shoulder. 'The marmosets have just left the maze and they're not headed in our direction.'

Beginning to doubt himself, Whisker took another look at the map. Scanning its inked surface, it only took him a moment to spot a fallen tree crossing the creek.

'Round, tall and windowless,' he thought aloud. 'It ticks all the boxes – except the *falling down* bit. The tree has already *fallen* down.'

'Fingers crossed,' Ruby muttered. 'One of our teams is right. The other is out of the competition.'

Hoping desperately they had the right 'tower' Whisker continued his scramble through the grove in the direction of the well. He was soon surrounded on all sides by gnarled trees and thousands upon thousands of apples. The ripe fruit dangled from branches and lay in rotting heaps at the bases of trunks – every colour under the sun: red, green, pink, golden and brown.

We should be baking Trojan Apple Strudel, he thought, as the forge came into view.

Through the gaps in the trees he could see thick, grey smoke drifting upwards from the top of the chimney. The heavenly songs of Mama Kolina and her daughters filled the forest. Ruby pulled a sour face.

'The well's just ahead,' she said, pointing past the forge. 'Unless you'd prefer to visit the house of the *three little pageant queens* for breakfast …'

Whisker shook his head and kept on running, annoyed that it wasn't Fred's out-of-tune singing they had heard.

The stone well lay in the centre of a small clearing at the eastern end of the Apple Grove. Sunlight streamed through a hole it its brick-tiled roof to reveal four ropes descending into the watery darkness.

One rope for each team, Whisker thought in relief. *We must be in the right location.* He rushed over to the well and took hold of the closest rope.

In moments, a wet coil of rope lay on the ground and a water-filled bucket was making its way to the surface.

Ruby reached her paw inside the bucket and removed a round river stone. She brushed the water off its smooth surface to reveal several lines of chiselled text:

'It's a reference to water,' Whisker said, peering over her shoulder. 'Somewhere we can relax and paddle our toes – the creek perhaps? The stone is a dead giveaway –'

'Not necessarily,' Ruby cut in. 'Look at the fourth and fifth lines: the *bull* who *rushes* … The words *bull* and *rushes* are in italics – like the last clue – which means they must have a double meaning. I haven't seen any rushing bulls on this farm but I have seen *bulrushes*. I picked some when we docked last night.'

'The wharf,' Whisker acknowledged. 'There are bulrushes everywhere and it's the perfect place to *paddle our toes.*'

'We'd better *rush* on down then,' Ruby said, cracking a rare joke. 'The river stairs aren't far from here.'

Handing the stone to Whisker for safekeeping, Ruby hurried through the trees in the direction of the Hawk River. Whisker slipped the stone into his bag and darted after her.

NINETEEN

Slow and Steady

As the trees thinned and the edge of the cliffs became visible, Whisker was suddenly aware of a pungent burning smell in the air. Wondering if the scent was coming from the forge, he looked to the air for any signs of smoke.

The morning sky was clear, but the falling autumn leaves told him the wind was blowing in the opposite direction. Taking no chances, he pulled Ruby behind a tree and raised a finger to his lips.

'Can you smell that?' he whispered.

Ruby inhaled deeply and then contorted her face into a repulsed frown.

'Flaming fur-balls,' she hissed. 'I'd bet my scissor swords on it.' She peered around the side of the tree for a closer look. 'There's a burnt patch on the ground near the top of the stairs. The cannons must be stationed further along the cliff, ready for an ambush.'

'Can we sneak past them?' Whisker asked.

'Not likely,' Ruby said. 'Our safest option is to wait until they fire at another team and make a dash for the stairs while they're reloading.'

'We both know that isn't going to happen,' Whisker

murmured. 'We'd lose too much time.'

'Alright,' Ruby said. 'We'll have to create our own distraction. What's in that magic sack of yours?'

Whisker loosened the drawstring of his small bag and peered inside. 'I've got the Hermit's compass, a white napkin, two gold coins, an extendable spyglass, a map of the farm and the river stone.'

'I'll take the stone,' Ruby demanded. 'Please.'

Whisker slid his paw into the bag and removed the discus-shaped rock.

'Perfect,' Ruby said, eyeing it closely. 'Here's hoping the trigger-happy Cat Fish shoot first and think later.'

Stepping wide of the tree, she raised the stone behind her back and hurled it towards an apple tree dangling over the cliff. The smooth object whizzed through the air, colliding with an outstretched branch.

Leaves shook. Apples fell. Cannons exploded. The next moment, two flaming fur-balls raced past the rats and exploded in a shower of sparks at the base of the tree.

'NOW!' Ruby shouted. 'RUN!'

Whisker took off like a paper plane in a windstorm. With powerful strides, he sprinted from the grove, leapt over a tree root and bounded across the cliff top towards the stone stairs. As he reached the top step, with Ruby close behind, he heard a third *KABOOM!*

'DOWN!' Ruby cried, grabbing Whisker by the tail.

Losing his balance, Whisker toppled forward, collecting Ruby on his way as a flaming projectile crashed into the upper steps. The two rats rolled in a ball of flailing arms and legs, coming to a halt halfway down the stairs.

Bruised and battered, they slowly untangled themselves and staggered down the remaining steps. Sheltered from further shots by the surrounding cliffs, they began hunting for their next clue.

They focused their attention on the southern side of the wharf, where the bulrushes grew thicker, searching between wooden wharf-boards, behind mooring bollards and under the wharf, with no success. Growing impatient, Ruby expanded her search to include the rest of the wharf and the tips of the closest bulrushes.

Still no success.

'We must be missing something,' Ruby said, slashing the reeds with her scissor swords. 'What else did the rock say?'

'I don't know,' Whisker muttered. 'You threw it in a tree, remember?'

Ruby rolled her eye. 'Search the entire wharf again. And make it snappy. We've lost enough time as it is.'

Whisker knew a second search would reveal nothing. He'd been ultra-thorough the first time around – and so had Ruby. Hoping for a flash of inspiration, he tried to recall the words of the clue: *Sitting, watching, paddling toes. The bull who rushes never knows.*

He looked across at Ruby, frantically searching under a mooring rope and, suddenly, he knew exactly what to do. Taking a calming breath, he sat down on the edge of the wharf, dangled his legs over the side and slipped his toes into the cool water. Then he waited.

'Whisker,' Ruby hissed, storming towards him like an angry bull. 'What on earth are you doing?'

'I'm following the advice of our friendly river stone,' he said calmly. 'Come and join me. The water's lovely.'

Ruby considered his offer for a moment and then, without bothering to remove her boots, plonked herself down next to him.

'Humph,' she muttered. 'Sitting around never won anyone a race ...'

Before Ruby had finished speaking, a stream of bubbles appeared on the surface of the water. Both rats watched with open mouths as a dark shape appeared beneath them, rising from the depths of the river.

'What is it?' Ruby whispered, as the round shape drew closer.

'Not what but *who*,' Whisker responded. 'Look. You can see the patterned shell.'

As the rats continued to watch, the small head of a green turtle pierced the surface of the water. Whisker recognised the turtle immediately as the third judge from the diving competition. The turtle gazed up at them with sleepy eyes and yawned, 'Nice morning for a paddle, don't you think?'

'Um ... sure,' Whisker responded.

'I like to start each day with a nice little dip in the water,' the turtle went on. 'It soothes my joints and reminds me of a time when I was a sprightly eighty-year-old ...'

'Sorry to interrupt, Mr Turtle,' Ruby broke in, 'but we were kind of hoping you could give us our next clue – today.'

The turtle sighed. 'Young folk – always in a hurry. No one stops for a friendly conversation anymore.' He yawned again. 'Very well. Listen carefully: *Red and yellow mixed as one, but some don't ripen in the sun.*' And with a polite 'Cheerio,' he closed his eyes and sank beneath the surface.

Whisker turned to Ruby, excitedly. 'It's an art riddle. Red and yellow mixed together make what colour?'

'Orange,' Ruby replied. 'That's easy.'

'And what turns orange when it ripens?' Whisker asked.

'Pumpkins – another easy one,' Ruby answered. 'There's an entire patch of them on the other side of the creek. I'm guessing if we find an unripe pumpkin, we'll have our next cl-'

'Thank you very much,' purred a sweet voice behind Ruby, 'You've just saved me from getting my toes wet.'

Whisker spun around to see Cleopatra standing halfway along the wharf, grinning from ear to ear. Prowler was visible in the distance, racing silently up the stairs.

'Catch us if you can,' Cleopatra hissed, dashing after him.'

'ARGH!' Ruby yelled, leaping to her feet. 'I hate those cats!' She took several strides down the wharf, but skidded to a halt as the cannons roared to life from the cliff top.

Whisker looked up in horror to see two flaming penguins leap off the top of the cliff and dive into the river in a hiss of steam. They rose to the surface, shaking their singed flippers at the escaping cats.

'Come on!' Whisker cried, pulling Ruby backwards down the wharf. 'We'll never get past those cannons.'

'But there's no other way up,' Ruby protested.

'You're forgetting the ships,' Whisker said, leaping onto the gangplank of the *Silver Sardine.*

'Are you out of your mind?' Ruby gasped. 'I'm not boarding that floating funeral parlour.'

'The cats are up there, not down here,' Whisker said, pointing across the ship. 'Look. The bowsprit is almost touching the southern cliff face. It's a simple climb up the rocks and a short run to the pumpkin patch. We can avoid the cannons and bypass the entire Apple Grove.'

Gritting her teeth, Ruby followed Whisker up the gangplank onto the *Silver Sardine*. Flattened sardine tins lined the hull and bulwark of the vessel, reflecting sunlight in all directions. Shielding their eyes from the dazzling light, the rats staggered along the gently-swaying deck until they reached the sword-like bowsprit extending from the bow of the ship.

Clutching the edge of the jib sail, they shimmied their way along the razor-sharp blade and then leapt onto a small ledge partway up the cliff.

The nimble climbers took a diagonal route up the rocks, arriving at the top of the cliff, to the south of the Rose Maze. From their elevated vantage point, they could see the mouth of the rushing creek and the fishing jetty to the south-east. As predicted, the *Velvet Wave* was moored on the small jetty, its flaming trophy guarded by a line of white rabbits.

Whisker caught sight of two furry bodies being swept down the centre of the gushing creek. They splashed their arms hysterically as they tried to stay afloat. One of the rabbits threw them a rope before they were sucked into the Hawk River.

'It appears the marmosets took more than one wrong turn,' Ruby muttered.

Drawing their eyes from the dramatic rescue, the rats raced down the hill towards an ancient stone bridge.

They crossed the lichen-covered stones of the bridge to see the field of pumpkins stretching out in front of them. The glorious, golden vegetables dotted the leafy ground like miniature suns. There was no sign of the cats, but Whisker knew they could arrive at any moment.

He hurried over to the pumpkin patch and began

searching the crop. Every leaf he turned concealed another succulent orange vegetable. It was a bumper harvest, a farmer's dream. Every pumpkin was ripe and ready for the market. But Whisker wasn't there to make pumpkin pie, he was there to find the one pumpkin that not even Fred would throw in the cooking pot: a hard, green undersized reject.

The longer he looked, the more desperate his searching became. Over the loud gurgle of the creek he could hear the frustrated mutterings of Ruby as she, too, struggled to locate any pumpkins of 'value.'

Then he saw it: a small, round shape lying on its lonesome under a thick layer of leaves. Barely bigger than his fist, it was a pottery pumpkin, glazed lime green.

'Ruby,' he hissed. 'Over here. I think I've found it.'

Ruby reached him in moments.

'That's got to be it,' she said, running her paw over the smooth surface. 'I can't see anything written on it, but it definitely *won't ripen in the sun.*'

Together, the two rats turned the clay object over, searching for a clue on its base. They heard a soft *tinkle, tinkle* from inside.

'Maybe that's our clue,' Whisker said.

Ruby wasted no time in drawing one of her scissor swords and, with a powerful blow, smashed a hole in the side of the pumpkin. Whisker reached his fingers through the opening and pulled out five clay seeds. One side of each seed was blank. The other side contained a single word.

'I'm guessing we need to arrange them into the correct order,' Whisker thought aloud, laying the seeds on a leaf.

awaits   the   circle   victory   in

'How about this,' Ruby said, shuffling the seeds around.

Whisker shook his head.

Ruby let out a small 'humph' and then hurriedly reordered the words.

'That's it!' Whisker exclaimed, trying to keep his voice down. 'The finish line must be the dry dam – it's a perfect *circle.*'

'So what are we waiting for?' Ruby said, brushing the seeds aside with her paw. 'The dam's only a short sprint from the fallen tree.'

Side by side, the rats took off in the direction of the second river crossing. The vibrant colours of the field flashed past them in a blur as they leapt over leaves and hurdled pumpkins.

Whisker burst through an enormous line of leaves and skidded to an abrupt halt. Directly in front of him, lying deathly-still on the ground, was the unmistakable blue-grey body of Prowler.

Whisker half expected the cat to spring up and bite off one of his ears, but all Prowler did was gaze in his general direction with stone-cold eyes.

As Whisker stared warily at the silent cat, he noticed a dozen small, feathery objects protruding from Prowler's fur.

Before Whisker could figure out what they were, he heard several *vrooshing* sounds over his shoulder.

Ruby gasped in panic, pulling Whisker behind a

pumpkin as a red, feathery shape whizzed past them. As he hit the ground, Whisker felt a needle-like pain in the tip of his tail. He looked up to see a red dart sticking out of his skin. A numb feeling began spreading through his tail.

'Tranquiliser darts!' Ruby hissed, yanking the object free. 'They must be the marmosets' handiwork. Can you move?'

'I think so,' Whisker squeaked, wiggling his fingers and toes. He tried to lift his tail but it remained motionless on the ground.

'You're lucky you only copped one dart,' Ruby whispered. 'Prowler won't be going anywhere in a hurry.'

Whisker took another look at the frozen feline. Prowler was still staring at them, unable to move a muscle. The remains of a second pottery pumpkin lay strewn over the ground beside him. There was no sign of any seeds.

'Where's Cleopatra?' Whisker asked in alarm.

'No idea,' Ruby answered, 'but if she's good at word games we're in big trouble. Come on!'

Leaving Prowler where he lay, Ruby began crawling through the leaves. Whisker followed silently after her, keeping his body close to the ground.

There were further *vrooshing* sounds and a stream of darts raced through the air, striking the tops of pumpkins to either side of them.

Head down, Whisker scrambled forward, his tail dragging paralysed behind him.

'This way,' Ruby whispered from up ahead. 'I can see the creek.'

A few steps later, Whisker was peering through the pumpkin leaves at a shady riverbank. A fallen, moss-covered tree lay to his right. To his left sat a green-eyed Abyssinian cat, grinning at a pawful of porcelain seeds.

TWENTY

The Other Side

Whisker didn't wait to see what Cleopatra had discovered. He stuffed the limp end of his tail into his pocket, scrambled out of the pumpkin patch and leapt onto the trunk.

Ruby was right behind him.

Startled by the sudden movement, Cleopatra's green eyes flashed in the rat's direction.

'Pesky Pie Rats,' she snarled, scattering the seeds. 'I'll be dammed if you reach that dam before me.' Hissing and spitting, she bounded after them.

Ruby ran a perfectly straight line and quickly overtook Whisker, struggling to maintain his balance without the use of his tail. He swayed awkwardly from side to side, almost toppling into the water. As wayward as his path was, it proved to be his saving grace.

Reaching the centre of the trunk, he saw three horrifying things at once: Ruby lurching backwards through the air yelling *'AMBUUUSH,'* a water-filled bucket swinging straight past him, and two penguins clutching a long rope from the top of a tree.

Steadying himself, Whisker made a desperate snatch for Ruby's arm, but his fingers clutched at thin air. He watched helplessly as she plummeted into the creek with a loud *SPLASH* and disappeared beneath the frothing rapids. A moment later, her head burst from the surface.

'RUN, YOU FOOL!' she spluttered, as the current swept her away. 'I can swim …'

Before Whisker could move, he heard a startled *hiss* behind him and spun around to see Cleopatra throwing herself onto the trunk. Above her, the flying water bucket hurtled back on its return journey.

With no time to leap clear, Whisker braced himself for the impact. The bucket hit with seismic force, knocking the breath out of his lungs and saturating him with icy cold water. Gasping for air, he threw his arms around the bucket and held on for dear life. There was more than one way of reaching the other side – and he was riding it.

The *bucket express* carried Whisker's shell-shocked body all the way to the willow trees on the far bank. As it began to slow down, Whisker leapt free, commando-rolling into a patch of clover and springing to his feet.

It was now an uphill dash to the finish line.

Whisker had a head start, but he was winded, woozy and sopping wet. Cleopatra, on the other hand, had speed. Oodles and oodles of speed. By the time Whisker had cleared the thicket of trees, the Egyptian speedster was already bounding off the trunk.

He increased his pace, his legs pumping, his heart pounding in his chest. The words of Frankie Belorio flashed through his mind: *Keep on running. Keep on fighting.*

Cleopatra's footsteps thundered behind him. With grit and determination, he clambered higher up the hill. Ahead of him, the southern edge of the dam came into view.

Frenzied spectators threw their paws in the air, cheering the runners home.

Fifty metres to go, he told himself.

Cleopatra was closing fast, tearing up the hill like a hungry cheetah.

Whisker's muscles burned. His lungs heaved. His tail did nothing. Losing the strength in his legs, he began to falter.

Forty metres. Keep it together.

The crowd was suddenly all around him, shouting and screaming. He could feel Cleopatra's breath on the back of his neck. He could hear her snarling victoriously.

Thirty metres, he panted, willing himself on. *You can still win it.*

The purple ribbon of the finish line drew closer. Cleopatra was right beside him. Shoulder to shoulder, they tussled for the lead.

Twenty metres.

Reaching the edge of the dam, Cleopatra made her move. She broke away from Whisker with explosive acceleration and hurtled up the steep bank like a mountain goat on a sugar rush. Before he knew it, she was a full body length ahead of him. Then she was two bodies clear.

With only ten metres to go, Whisker knew he would never catch her.

It can't end like this, he told himself. *Come on …*

With a mighty *KABOOM! KABOOM!* two cannons roared to life from the centre of the dam. Caught unawares, Cleopatra was blasted off her feet by a wave of sticky, green goo. Startled onlookers screamed in panic as mangled chunks of Granny Smith apples sprayed everywhere.

Avoiding the brunt of the attack, Whisker brushed an

apple seed from his chin and kept on running.

Five metres to go. You've still got a chance.

Ahead of him, Cleopatra began dragging herself out of the putrid muck, clawing her way to the finish line. Fuelled by adrenalin, Whisker lowered his head and powered on.

Four metres.

Cleopatra stumbled forward, green-eyed and terrifying, her brown fur glistening with apple juice.

Three metres.

He was almost there.

Two metres.

Neck and neck, they approached the line, the ribbon close enough to touch.

One metre.

It was now or never.

With every last ounce of his strength, Whisker hurled his body forward. He heard the roar of the crowd. He felt the ribbon brush the tip of his nose.

Victory.

As he crashed to the ground in a tangle of purple material, he knew he had done it.

This one's for you, Mum, he said to himself as he lay in a heap, panting for breath. *Red roses and rotten apples. If only you could see ...*

To either side of him, Horace and Pete thumped their cannons in celebration. Granny Rat and the Captain cheered and paw-pumped the air.

'Caw, caw,' Chatterbeak screeched. 'What an explosive finish. Watch your backs, Cat Fish. The Pie Rats are coming for the trophy.'

'Awesome treasure hunting, Whisker!' Horace cried, rushing over.

'Awesome shooting, yourself,' Whisker said, untangling himself from the ribbon.

'Aw, shucks,' Horace replied, brushing the praise aside with his hook. 'I can't take all the credit. It was Pete's idea to plant the cannons on the finish line.'

'Thank Ratbeard the Cat Fish supporters stayed out of our way,' Pete added dryly. 'The fools all presumed our cannons were for the victory celebrations.'

'The celebrations vill have to vait, I'm afraid,' Gustave said, stepping out of the crowd. He gestured behind him to where a throng of rowdy Cat Fish supporters were leading a chant of, 'Death Ball! Death Ball! When do we want it? Now!'

'In an endeavour to avoid a riot,' Gustave continued, 'I have rescheduled ze Death Ball final for zis morning.'

Whisker felt his jubilation turn to despair. The Pie Rats' rent-a-crowd was nowhere in sight and, without their camouflaged uniforms, the entire team stood out like bright-red strawberries in a spinach patch.

'We begin in thirty minutes,' Gustave said firmly. 'Gather your vits and prepare to do battle.'

Fuming with rage at her inaccurate game-time prediction, Granny Rat called an emergency meeting in the grassy centre of the dam. Ruby arrived, sopping wet and shivering, and joined the five rats in a tight huddle.

'We've got good news and bad news,' Horace said, bringing her up to speed.

'Let me guess,' Ruby said, glaring at Whisker. 'We lost the Treasure Hunt, right?'

'Err, no, that's the good news,' Horace replied, 'The bad

news is that Gustave has scheduled the Death Ball final for nine forty-five this morning.'

Ruby shrugged. 'It's a good thing your mother has finished our uniforms, Horace.' She pointed a wet thumb over her shoulder. 'I saw her with Rat Bait and the Hermit a few minutes ago. They were lugging an entire cartful of clothing through the apple grove. I didn't spot Fred, but he may have been blending in with his surrounds.'

'That definitely halves the bad news,' Granny Rat said. 'What about our opposition?'

'Prowler won't be much good until at least the second half,' Whisker said, holding up his tranquilised tail. 'Those darts were quite a knockout.'

The Captain managed a small laugh and, for the first time since the Fish 'n Ships Inn, Whisker felt like he was part of the crew again. Ruby was still giving him the cold shoulder, but the others appeared to have softened after his winning performance in the Treasure Hunt. Whisker knew they would think otherwise if they discovered what he was secretly planning to do with the trophy.

Pushing the guilt to the back of his mind, he watched as Mama Kolina, Rat Bait and Fred appeared on the bank of the dam with their cart. Dressed in a flowing piece of canvas with a hole for his head, Fred looked more like a camouflaged potato sack than a Death Ball finalist.

'Frankie always said that *loose fitting uniforms were best*,' Horace murmured in bemusement.

Although Whisker's uniform was slightly more streamlined than Fred's 'sack', his long-sleeved top and three-quarter pants prompted a string of snide pyjama remarks from the assembled spectators.

The Cat Fish were clearly unimpressed with the Pie

Rats' last-minute uniform swap, but Sabre's animated protests to Gustave were in vain.

'It's in ze rules,' Gustave said firmly, pointing to a scroll in Chatterbeak's claws. 'Now if you vill excuse me, Captain Sabre, I have an important timepiece to attend to.'

Sabre grabbed the scroll from Chatterbeak and thrust it towards an old ginger cat wearing a top hat.

'Find me a solution, Tom,' he hissed. 'Now!'

While Sabre glared menacingly at Whisker and the rest of his camouflaged opponents, Gustave made his way towards a large grandfather clock on the southern bank of the dam.

'Next time I vill remember to bring ze spare hourglasses,' he grumbled to two rabbits as they moved the clock into position.

Whisker looked up at the clock's enormous face. The time read nine thirty-six.

Only nine minutes to the opening bounce, he thought, *and over two hours till Smudge is due back with our rent-a-crowd.*

He scanned the perimeter of the dam. An army of Cat Fish supporters dressed in orange and silver scarves stood shoulder to shoulder in an unbroken circle. Papa Niko and his daughters tussled for a front row position, but were soon forced to the very back of the crowd.

'Listen up!' Granny Rat snapped, gathering the crew in a huddle near the reserve bench. 'I want you to play for possession, not for position – the Cat Fish can't score if they don't have the ball. If they're as callous as they've been in the past two games, you should get at least one penalty shot at goal.'

She pointed to a nearby leader board and addressed the team with determined focus.

PLACE	TEAM	POINTS	DEATH BALL VICTORIES
1ST	CAT FISH	2	2
2ND	PIE RATS	1	2
3RD	MARMOSETS	1	1
4TH	PENGUINS	1	0

'It all boils down to this,' she said, 'if we win this match, we'll go from dead last to first place in one day. If we lose, the Cat Fish will take an unassailable lead. Even if we win the Sea Race and the Stealth Raid, the cats will have an extra Death Ball victory, guaranteeing them the championship.'

'It's all or nothing then,' Horace said, clicking his racket attachment into place. 'Right here, right now.'

Granny Rat shot him a wary look. 'This isn't a ten-second sprint, pipsqueak. It's a sixty-minute marathon.' She waved a wrinkly finger in the direction of the grandfather clock. 'You've got until the eleventh stroke of the hour to snatch victory. Make every second count.'

Whisker watched the rest of his crew take their positions on the field before he ventured through the thick grass to his spot on the wing. It didn't help his confidence that his old rival, Cleopatra, stood waiting for him, her fur still gleaming with apple juice. She arched her back and extended her claws as he approached.

'Isn't this a pleasant surprise,' she purred. 'Together again without a single apple-filled cannon in sight. What's going to save you this time, little rodent?'

'Who says I need saving?' he blurted out.

212

Cleopatra glared at him. 'You'd be wise to remember the food chain, apple boy. Big cats eat little rats.'

With a small gulp, Whisker realised he'd probably said enough. He tightened the drawstring of his baggy pants and waited for the action.

When the hands of the grandfather clock reached nine forty-five, the referee blew his whistle. With a delighted roar from the crowd, the game was underway.

Chatterbeak squawked frantically as he tried to follow the events on the field. 'Caw, caw, the cats take first possession and make a break though the centre circle … Master Meow passes the ball to Sabre … Sabre steps around a puddle. Out of nowhere he's tackled by a green potato sack and the ball bounces free … It flies through the air … It lands in a clump of grass … Wait a minute folks, the grass is moving. Possessed parsley! I think it's a Pie Rat. Yes, here comes Horace … or is it Whisker … Ruby, maybe …?' He waved his wings in agitation. 'Caw, caw, I have no idea. It's all a green blur in there …'

With the ball tucked firmly under his arm, Whisker wove through the grass in the middle of the field, struggling to see where he was going. He could hear Cleopatra hissing behind him and knew he must maintain his pace.

Head down, he told himself, splashing through a puddle. *Don't let her catch you.*

He saw the Captain darting out from behind a thistle and had just enough time to get a clean pass away before Cleopatra crashed through the grass, swiping wildly at him with her paw. He leapt clear, rolling to one side as her razor sharp claws sliced the stem of a large weed in two.

Scrambling after the Captain, Whisker knew that Death Ball had suddenly become a whole lot more deadly.

TWENTY-ONE

A Mischief of Rats

Thwarted by their canvas-clad opponents, the frustration of the Cat Fish grew as the grand final wore on. Unable to identify who was carrying the ball, the cats resorted to tripping and tackling any rat they came in contact with.

Whisker found himself illegally upended on at least three occasions. The referee, unable to see what was unfolding in the long grass, allowed the brutal game to continue without awarding a single penalty.

It wasn't a pretty sight, but with play restricted to the centre field 'swamp,' the Pie Rats managed to hold the Cat Fish to a scoreless first half.

Whisker had barely plonked his bruised backside on the bench for the fifteen-minute break when a throng of Cat Fish supporters leapt onto the field with an assortment of sickles, machetes and rusty harvesting equipment.

'Half-time entertainment?' Horace wondered, looking up from a broken string on his racket attachment.

'If only,' Pete sniffled, pointing a bony finger at the ginger cat. 'It seems our beloved opponents have found their own loophole in the rules.'

Pete was right. The ginger cat stood on the top of the

dam bank reading from Gustave's scroll, *'Playing surfaces must be maintained to a standard befitting an international tournament at all times …'*

In unison, the army of orange and silver spectators raised their tools and began slashing the tall grass and weeds of the dam.

'Oh, that's just swell,' Horace muttered. 'The gardening brigade is about to destroy the one thing that's keeping us in this contest: our cover.'

Ruby threw her water flask on the ground in disgust. Pete scratched something unpleasant in the dirt.

The sombre mood seemed to spread down the entire bench. As more grass disappeared in the centre of the dam, the Pie Rats' heads slumped further into their laps. Whisker could see it written all over their faces. They had accepted defeat long before they had even lost.

Who can blame them, he thought. *They're bruised, battered and utterly exhausted. For them this is simply another contest they're destined to lose.*

For Whisker, however, the next thirty minutes meant much more than a game of ball. It was his one chance of finding his family. Realising what he had to do, he slowly stood up from the bench and turned to face the crew.

He had never given a half-time speech, and he didn't know the first thing about Death Ball tactics, but what he was about to say had nothing to do with strategy. It had everything to do with spirit.

The weary line of rats peered up at him as he began his desperate plea.

'I-I know I am not your captain,' he said, nervously, 'nor am I your coach, but if I have learnt one thing during my time on the *Apple Pie*, it is that even the most insignificant

215

rats can have a voice. The task we face today is near impossible, to say the least. Our opposition is stronger, faster and vastly more experienced.'

He surveyed the sorry line of rats and then shrugged. 'But hey, what's new?'

There were several downcast nods.

'Umm, Whisker,' Horace said, 'I don't mean to be critical, but your doom and gloom pep talk is hardly raising anyone's spirits.'

'Bear with me,' Whisker said, searching his mind for a more positive approach to take. He recalled a passage he had read in his great-grandfather's book comparing rats with other species. For once, rats had come out on top.

Trying to remember the exact words, he looked directly at Ruby and whispered, 'We do not possess the rich colours of a peacock nor the glorious wings of a butterfly, but we can still be beautiful.'

Ruby stared back at him, her cheeks flushing pink. Trying to stay focused, Whisker turned to the Captain and said with passion, 'We are not a *pride* of lions, but we still have pride.'

The Captain raised an eyebrow in recognition.

Recalling another fact, Whisker addressed Pete. 'We are not a *school* of fish, but we love to learn.'

'That's true for some of us,' Pete murmured half-heartedly.

Growing in confidence, Whisker stepped towards Fred. 'We are not a *tower* of giraffes, but we can still be mighty.'

Fred straightened his hunched shoulders and gave Whisker a beaming smile.

Finally, with the rest of the crew hanging on to every word, Whisker turned to Horace.

'My friend,' he said with fire in his eyes, 'we are not a

pack of dogs nor a *barrel* of monkeys and we are definitely not a *litter* of cats. We are a *mischief* of rats and mischief is what we do best. So hold your head high, for on that field, mischief awaits!'

Horace leapt to his feet and saluted Whisker with his racket attachment, 'Now that's more like it! You can sign me up for a double dose of mischief.'

'I'm in, too, Whisker,' Fred said with a stirring round of applause.

'I hate peacocks and I loathe butterflies,' Ruby added, punching her paws together, 'so book me a spot on the victory podium.'

The Captain adjusted his eye patch and rose from his seat. 'As a wise rat once said, *it's better to go down fighting than sitting on a bench.*'

'For the record, I was referring to a game of chess when I said that,' Pete sniffled. He squirmed awkwardly for a moment before adding, 'But if you're desperate for a substitute, you know where to find me.'

Invigorated and energised, the Pie Rats made their way onto the now barren dam. A few flattened stalks of grass lay in shallow puddles in the centre of the playing arena, but most of the vegetation had been removed by the fanatical Cat Fish supporters.

Lying on the cats' reserve bench, Prowler began to move his arms and legs as the effects of the tranquiliser darts wore off. Whisker looked over his shoulder to see his own tail twitching haphazardly behind him.

As the clock ticked over to ten thirty, the referee blew his whistle and the final half of Death Ball was underway.

Whisker was amazed at what spirit could do. Although the soft squeaks of half-a-dozen Pie Rat supporters were drowned out by the roar of three hundred hostile Cat Fish fans, the rats played like every opposing cheer and chant was intended for *them*.

Granny Rat's game plan was simple: *make as much mischief as you can without conceding a goal*.

Ball in arms, the rats darted and wove between the cats' legs, jabbing them in the belly for good measure. Whenever the cats won possession, the rats would cling to their hind legs and yank their tails, causing the ball to bounce free time and time again. The size and strength of the Cat Fish proved no match for the nimble acrobatics of their smaller opponents, and they had no choice but to hurl the ball into the crowd as soon as they touched it.

Much to the dismay of the Pie Rats, the crowd began bounce-passing the ball from spectator to spectator in an attempt to move it closer to the cats' goal. In response, Granny Rat ordered her team into a defensive formation in the back half of the field. The Captain went to centre, Ruby and Horace moved to left and right fullback positions and Whisker joined Fred in the goal box as a shadow keeper.

The restructure proved invaluable. As the game wore on, the cats' master striker, Prowler, having fully recovered from the tranquiliser darts, subbed on for Siamese Sally and took a monumental shot at goal. Fred managed to get a finger-touch on the ball as it headed towards the lower right corner and Whisker's tail did the rest. Like an anaconda suffocating its prey, his tail coiled around the rubber ball, and with a deathly tight grip, jerked it to a halt.

The crowd booed. Prowler hissed. Whisker said a silent *thank you* to his tail and flicked the ball over the heads of the attackers. As it bounced towards a deserted wing on the far side of the field, Whisker noticed Granny Rat gesturing frantically and pointing to the cats' goal box.

'I think the old bat want us to mount an attack,' Horace whispered.

'But we can't risk leaving our defences open,' Whisker shot back. 'Not with the cats and the crowd breathing down our necks.'

'The crowd is no longer our concern,' the Captain shouted, sprinting after the ball. 'Take a look.'

Whisker's eyes flashed to the crowd. A sea of tiny bodies wearing maroon blazers were pushing past the Cat Fish supporters towards the front row. They squeezed between the legs of startled onlookers and scrambled over shoulders like an army of ants.

Eaton

Mr Tribble

Emmie

Everywhere Whisker looked he saw ecstatic students: hamsters, Guinea pigs, gerbils and dozens of mice. In the midst of the mayhem stood the most unlikely ringleader: Mr Tribble, the timid history teacher-turned holiday adventurer.

'Greetings, fellow Pie Rats,' Mr Tribble beamed, almost losing his spectacles. 'Better early than late, I say. My students are under strict orders to remember their best Oakbridge manners – and then to behave in the exact opposite way!'

By the time the bouncing ball had reached the sideline, Emmie and Eaton had clambered onto the heads of the two closest spectators and covered their eyes with their paws. Mr Tribble scooped up the ball from their feet and hurled it to the Captain.

The Captain charged past, catching the ball on the fly, and centred up for his shot at goal. Furious Fur stood alone in the goal box, but the rest of the cats were closing fast.

'Go, Uncle Black Rat!' Emmie squeaked from the sidelines.

'Let 'em have it!' Eaton added, heartily.

The Captain dropped the ball onto his foot and, with a mighty kick, sent the ball spinning towards the left corner of the goal. A moment later, Sabre crashed down on top of him with bone-crushing impact.

The Captain hit the ground head first and Furious Fur made a desperate lunge for the ball. Stretching out his shaggy paws, he clipped the side of the speeding object, deflecting it wide of the goal post.

The Cat Fish supporters let out a roar of delight. The Captain remained motionless on the ground.

A whistle rang out and the referee called for a halt in play. The entire Pie Rat crew rushed over to the Captain. Ruby reached him first and dropped to her knees by his side.

'He's got a pulse,' she said, touching his neck. 'Uncle, can you hear me?'

The Captain didn't stir.

'It appears he's suffered a nasty concussion,' the referee said, leaning over. 'I'm afraid he'll have to be stretchered off at once.'

'And what about our penalty?' Ruby said, glaring up at Sabre. 'My Uncle was tackled *after* he got the shot away.'

'I assure you, the tackle and the kick were simultaneous.' Sabre hissed indignantly. 'Ask the referee.'

The referee hesitated for a moment and Sabre gave him a deathly-cold stare.

'N-no,' the rabbit gulped, suddenly looking ill. 'There will be no penalty. The game will resume with a centre bounce when the injured player has left the field.'

'You can't be serious!' Ruby exploded. 'This is a –'

'I've made my decision,' the referee said, hopping away. 'There's no more to be said.'

'Arrrgh!' Ruby fumed, stepping after him.

'Come on, Ruby,' Whisker said, grabbing her arm. 'We haven't lost yet.'

'But we're about to,' Ruby hissed, pushing him away. 'Haven't you seen the time?'

Whisker glanced across at the clock – and gasped. The time read *ten fifty-five*. With all the action and excitement of the second half, he had totally lost track of the time. There was less than five minutes left to play and the scores were still locked at nil-all.

'The last thing we want is a penalty shootout,' Ruby said as Rat Bait and Papa Niko loaded the Captain's unconscious body onto a stretcher. 'The cats are the masters of set shots.

You saw their game against the marmosets. All six shots soared straight through the goal.'

'And we just lost our best striker,' Pete sniffled, hobbling onto the field. He pointed to his red pencil leg. 'A roundhouse kick is one thing, but I'm not much chop when the ball is lying stationary on the ground. Heavens, I'd be hard pressed attempting the run-up.'

Ruby raised two clenched fists in front of her. 'I hate to admit it but I'm much better with my paws.'

'I'll second that,' Horace said, holding up his racket attachment. 'When it comes to kicking, I've got two left feet – and I'm *right* footed.'

'I get it! I get it!' Whisker groaned in frustration. 'We're all useless at penalty shootouts.'

'You're not, Whisker,' Fred rumbled. 'I've seen you kick. You're almost as good as Frankie Belorio.'

'Hardly,' Whisker muttered. 'Frankie's got speed, accuracy and a killer strike – not to mention the best set plays in the world. And all I've got is-is …'

Of course! With a gasp of realisation, Whisker turned his back on his teammates and sprinted for the sideline.

'Hey!' Horace called after him. 'Where are you going?'

Whisker was in too much of a hurry to respond. He reached the reserve bench to see the hands of the grandfather clock ticking over to *ten fifty-seven.*

Just enough time, he thought, frantically opening his brown drawstring bag. He pulled out a single item, stuffed it into his pocket and darted back onto the field.

'Everythin' alright?' Rat Bait asked, passing Whisker with the stretcher.

'Fine,' Whisker called over his shoulder, 'although I could do with some more time.'

222

'Aye,' Rat Bait said knowingly, 'that can be arranged.' With a sly wink to Papa Niko, he slowed his walk to a snail's pace and said in a loud voice, 'It's safer for our patient if we take the long route 'round the puddles.'

Whisker reached his four teammates in the centre of the field and pulled out a crumpled, white napkin.

'Frankie's signature?' Horace said, puzzled.

'No,' Whisker said, reversing the napkin and spreading it on a muddy patch of ground. 'Something much better.'

Horace peered down at the collection of circles and squiggles covering the material. His eyes grew wide. 'Shiver me britches! It's Frankie's *Double Decoy – Centre Steal*.'

'Shush,' Pete hissed, glancing behind him to the watching Cat Fish crew. 'A decoy's not a decoy if you give the blasted thing away.'

Ruby turned to Whisker and frowned. 'If that kindergarten scribble can get us out of this mess, then I'm in. But you'd better get explaining – and fast.'

'Alright,' Whisker said. 'Listen up. Frankie's plan will only work with a few modifications …'

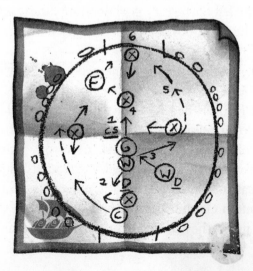

TWENTY-TWO

Eleven Strokes

A s the Captain's body was lowered onto the reserve bench, the grandfather clock ticked over to *ten fifty-nine*. With sixty seconds left to play, it was now or never for the Pie Rats.

In a positional change that had the Cat Fish baffled, Fred took Ruby's place in the centre circle, with Whisker crouching directly behind him. Horace stood a short way back, his entire right arm concealed under his canvas shirt. Ruby occupied Fred's usual position in the goal box, but was slowly creeping away from the posts. Pete waited up-field, to the left of the cats' goal, looking utterly terrified.

With the shrill of the whistle, the referee slammed the ball onto a dry patch of earth.

The crowd roared with excitement and Prowler made a mighty leap into the air. Facing him, Fred did the exact opposite. He hunched his huge, powerful shoulders and stooped down before the ball had even left the ground.

The rubber object exploded upwards, rising high above the competitors. As Prowler extended his paws for an easy catch, Whisker made his move. He sprang onto the mountainous shoulders of Fred and, in one perfectly executed move, the giant straightened his back, catapulting

Whisker upwards like an exploding cannon ball.

Whisker plucked the object from Prowler's fingertips and somersaulted over his head. He hit the ground running and dummied to Ruby, sprinting along the left wing.

Master Meow took the bait and bounded after her, his glass eye hampering his vision. Whisker wasted no time in throwing the ball back to Horace.

With his right arm still tucked out of sight, Horace caught the ball with his left paw and took off down the centre of the field. Ahead of him, Fred ran as a blocker and shoulder-charged Prowler before he knew what was happening. The dazed cat stumbled backwards, opening up a clear path for the two rats.

As they stampeded past Whisker, Horace stepped clumsily to one side, clipping Whisker's shoulder. With a startled 'YELP!' Whisker tripped forward, splashing into a shallow puddle and Horace's right arm sprang out from under his shirt.

Steadying his stumpy legs, Horace continued running, leaving Whisker flailing in the water.

'Get the pipsqueak!' Sabre bellowed, tearing after Horace. 'He's got the ball.'

Baring her fangs, Cleopatra darted off the right wing in pursuit of the rats.

With the attention focused on his teammates, Whisker scrambled out of the puddle, hooked his tail behind him and raced down the deserted right side of the field.

The Cat Fish supporters closest to Whisker tried desperately to grab Sabre's attention, but their voices were overpowered by a deafening chant of 'HORACE! HORACE!' from the Oakbridge students.

Spurred on by the sound of his own name, Horace

increased his strides to a pace that would match any rodent. Unluckily for Horace, his pursuers were cats.

From the safety of his own wing, Whisker saw Cleopatra and Sabre pounce in unison. Horace's tiny body was thrown forward, knocking Fred's legs from under him. Fred landed on Horace and the two of them crumpled to the ground. A moment later, Meow's hefty frame barged Ruby over the sideline and she disappeared into the frenzied crowd.

The loss of his teammates did nothing to slow Whisker's pace. Without faltering, he continued his wide, sweeping run in the direction of the cat's goal.

There was a howl of rage from the middle of the field as Sabre, wrestling the two rats for the ball, suddenly found himself clutching Horace's racket attachment. Covered by a mud-soaked napkin, its circular head had been disguised to look like a brown, rubber Death Ball.

Sabre's hazel eyes burned with rage. He threw the racket at the dazed rats and locked eyes with Whisker.

'After the apprentice,' he shouted, slashing his claws through the air. 'He's got the real ball!'

Whisker felt a shot of terror race through his ball-carrying tail. The double decoy had just been discovered and the entire Cat Fish death squad was now after him.

Cleopatra was on his trail in an instant. Furious Fur, his fur standing on end, bounded from the goal in an attempt to cut Whisker off. Behind him, Whisker heard the sound of hurried footsteps and knew that Prowler had recovered from his knock.

GONG –

The grandfather clock began to chime.

Eleven strokes, Whisker gasped.

GONG –

He looked up to see he was still out of shooting range, even if tail shots were permitted.

GONG –

Gripped by panic, all he could do was run.

GONG –

The clock sounded its fourth chime. Maintaining his steady course, Whisker urged himself forward.

GONG –

The cats drew closer, their claws extended mercilessly.

GONG –

Furious Fur rose up like a shaggy, white monster, preparing to strike.

GONG –

The seventh chime of the clock announced to Whisker that time was almost up. Now was his moment to act.

GONG –

Using the last of his strength, he swung his tail in a wide arc and launched the ball high into the air.

GONG –

The cats skidded to a halt, their eyes raised to the heavens as the ball soared over their heads and across the field to the one player they had dismissed without a thought: Pete.

GONG –

The bony runt of a rat twirled unmarked on his pencil leg and, with his trademark roundhouse kick, sent the ball rocketing through the open mouth of the goal.

Whisker never heard the eleventh chime of the clock. The ear-splitting roar of the rent-a-crowd drowned out every other sound.

Somewhere in the chaotic celebrations a full-time

whistle was blown and Chatterbeak announced the Pie Rats as 'one-nil champions of Death Ball.'

The reception the Pie Rats received befitted a *ten-nil* performance. As the snarling, protesting cats followed the referee off the field, Pete was thrust onto Fred's shoulders and the bedazzled rat blew kisses to his adoring Athena. Horace held his broken racket attachment aloft like it was the real Trophy of Champions and Whisker found himself being smothered in hugs by Hera and Aphrodite. The two sisters appeared to have forgiven him for his past indiscretions and sang his praises for orchestrating the set play of the century: *The Double Decoy – Centre Steal with Roundhouse Twist.*

'Frankie and Pete, Frankie and Pete,' Whisker kept repeating as he squirmed away to the reserve bench. 'They're the real heroes.'

Hoping Ruby hadn't seen the sisters' gushing display of affection, Whisker was relieved to spot her on the far side of the field, fending off her own admirers: half a dozen love-struck hamsters all begging for a kiss. With a less-than-subtle response of, *'You'll get a boot up your backsides, you smelly little brats!'* Ruby stomped over to the Captain, still lying rigid on the bench.

Granny Rat and the Hermit stood calmly by his side, apparently unfazed by their son's current state of inactivity. Smudge perched on the Captain's chest like a miniature sentinel, guarding his master.

'He'll be right as rain, come tomorrow,' Granny Rat said, giving the Captain an affectionate pat on the cheek.

'Yes, yes,' the Hermit agreed, 'ready for the Sea Race.'

'What about the Stealth Raid?' Whisker asked in a whisper. 'Don't we have to pull that off tonight?'

'I'm sure you can manage without him,' Granny Rat said reassuringly. 'My nimble-footed husband has already loaded the cut-outs onto the *Apple Pie*, and the cart of pasties is hiding in the bushes near the fishing jetty in readiness for tonight's delivery. As far as I'm aware, no one suspects a thing. All you have to do is wait until dusk and then proceed with the plan. Touch the trophy and the championship is yours.'

There was a loud wheezing sound as Rat Bait staggered up to the small group, looking extremely rattled. All heads turned to him in surprise.

'We may have – a wee problem –' he panted.

While he tried to catch his breath, he pointed to the far bank of the dam, where Gustave stood in discussion with five of his sons.

'I saw several o' Gustave's lads arrivin' at the end o' the game,' he puffed. 'Their arms were overflowin' with supplies an' they were all talkin' at once 'bout the Blue Claw.'

'The Blue Claw,' Ruby gasped, grabbing a scissor sword from under the bench. 'Are they here?'

'Not 'ere,' Rat Bait said, with a shake of his head, 'but they've been spotted in Two Shillin's Cove, raidin' shops an' searchin' for a wanted felon o' some description. It's only a matter o' time before they extend their search up the hill. From what I could gather, the rabbits grabbed all the supplies they could carry an' raced back to the farm. The dock delivery's been cancelled an' I'd bet a parlour of pasties Gustave's about to make a big announcement.'

'Announcement?' Whisker said in confusion. 'What kind of announcement?'

Rat Bait pointed to the cloudless sky. 'It's a fine day for a sailin' race, don't ye think?'

Rat Bait's prediction was spot on. Within minutes, Baron Gustave moved to the centre of the dam and boomed into his bullhorn. 'Due to unforeseen circumstances, ze Sea Race vill commence at twelve o'clock *today.*'

There was a roar of support from the Cat Fish supporters, glad to have something to finally cheer about.

As Whisker studied the faces in the crowd, an intense feeling of panic spread through his body. He counted six of Gustave's sons scattered around the dam. He could hear the marmosets and the Penguin Pirates jabbering away behind him, but Sabre and his carnivorous crew were nowhere in sight.

The Velvet Wave, Whisker thought in horror. *With half the guards missing and the farm in a frenzy, it's the perfect time to mount a raid.*

Growing more anxious by the moment, he paused to reflect on the turn of events. The Pie Rats and Cat Fish were currently tied on two competition points. The cats had two Death Ball victories while the rats had three, edging them ahead for the first time during the games.

PIRATE CUP LEADER BOARD

DAY: 9   POINTS REMAINING: 2

PLACE	TEAM	POINTS	DEATH BALL VICTORIES
1ST	PIE RATS	2	3
2ND	CAT FISH	2	2
3RD	MARMOSETS	1	1
4TH	PENGUINS	1	0

With the Trojan Pasty plan now out of the question, the Pie Rats would have to win the Sea Race if the cats pulled off a stealth raid of their own. It seemed highly unlikely the rats could out-sail their competitors, especially with the Captain lying unconscious on a bench.

Whisker wondered if he was simply being paranoid.

The cats are probably lazing under an apple tree, licking their fur, he reasoned, turning his attention back to Gustave.

'... All participating crews must be assembled on ze wharf in thirty minutes,' the Baron announced. 'Ships are to remain in a moored position vith sails tightly furled until ze starting signal. Upon leaving ze river, crews vill make zeir vay through ze Crumbling Rock Islands. As zese vaters are currently uncharted, no maps vill be provided.'

Crumbling Rock Islands, Whisker repeated in his head. *Now why does that name sound so familiar?'*

He recalled sailing through the waters as a boy, following the wide Central Channel from southern Aladrya to Freeforia. The route was safe and easy to navigate, and few ships ever strayed into the rocky maze of islands to the north and south of the channel, in fear of being shipwrecked or buried alive by collapsing cliffs. Dangerous and inhospitable, no one had attempted to map the individual islands, and the whole place remained an uncharted mystery.

Although he couldn't quite place it, Whisker knew he had a more recent connection with the islands.

Did I overhear a conversation in the athletes' village? he thought. *Or was it something the fox said?* Unable to put his finger on it, he returned to Gustave's final instructions.

'Navigators may set zeir own courses,' the Baron said,

'but each ship is required to pass two checkpoints. Ze first is a cliff on ze northernmost island and ze second is a marker ship anchored to ze south of ze finish line.'

'And where exactly is the finish line?' squawked one of the penguins. 'Don't tell me it's an uncharted location, too.'

'Oh no, you'll have no trouble finding it,' Gustave grinned. 'It's none other zan ze desert island from ze Mystery Challenge. Ze first crew to reach its sandy shore and set off a flare vill receive one point, officially ending ze Centenary Games.'

'A fat lot of good one point will do us,' another penguin grumbled. 'The Cat Fish and the Pie Rats are the only teams that can still win the Cup.'

'True,' Gustave considered, 'but you can still have an impact on vhich team vins.'

'Great goats gobbling gumboots!' King Marvownion exclaimed, almost losing his crown. 'A flea-ridden rat on a victory podium is one thing, but there's no way I'm letting those cheating cats claim the trophy. It would be an abomination.' He turned to the Pie Rats. 'The Royal Court of the Marmosets are at your service.'

Before any of the rats could respond, a fairy penguin stepped forward and saluted them with a scorched flipper.

'Count us in, too,' he piped. 'The Cat Fish have used us for target practice one too many times.'

'Hear, hear,' agreed the rest of his crew. 'No more barbecued penguins!'

'Very well,' Pete said cautiously. 'We have ourselves an alliance. I can't guarantee success, mind you, but with three ships against one, we've at least got a fighting chance.'

The next fifteen minutes rushed by in a blur. There were hurried goodbyes to Mr Tribble and the twins, forced to return to school before the home-time bell. Next came a tirade of abuse from Granny Rat about the unkempt state of the *Apple Pie* and, lastly, a heated debate broke out about who should command the ship while the Captain lay concussed in his cabin. Pete won in the end, mainly due to his superior navigational knowledge and the number of six-syllable words he threw into the argument.

With the leadership sorted, the crew got straight to work, preparing the ship for the race.

As Whisker scampered up the rigging to make his final adjustments to the sails, he was relieved to see six cats skulking around the deck of the *Silver Sardine*. Climbing higher, he saw an empty fishing jetty in the distance.

They weren't raiding the Velvet Wave after all, he thought, relaxing his tail. *Gustave's sons must have moved the ship after the Blue Claw sighting.*

He hurried down the rope ladder to join Rat Bait and the rest of the crew, who had gathered around Pete.

'Our course will be roughly triangular in shape,' Pete explained, scratching three lines on the deck with his pencil leg. 'We'll circumnavigate the northern group of islands, staying well clear of the cliffs, and then sail back through the Central Channel. It's the longest route, but it's also the safest and we can utilise the kite sail for the downwind sections.'

'What about the other crews?' Horace asked. 'Which route will they choose?'

'The same as us if their heads are screwed on,' Pete replied. 'The *Silver Sardine* and the *Arctic Wind* are built for open-sea sailing – not for manoeuvring through tight passages; and *HMS Majesty* is bigger than both of them. Remember, the marmosets and the penguins are on our

233

side. A win for one of them equals a win for us.'

'Them penguins be yer best hope,' Rat Bait remarked. 'I know the *Arctic Wind* back-to-front from me years as a ship repairer an' I've no doubt she'll give the *Sardine* a run for her money. She might not look as flashy as the *Majesty*, but this ain't no beauty pageant.'

Whisker looked up at his own vessel, the humble *Apple Pie*. Her tarnished cutlery masts and tattered clothing sails were junk compared to the marmosets' gold-plated galleon and the cats' silver speedster. But she had saved them time and time again and, to Whisker, that made her priceless.

'Good luck to ye, Whisker,' Rat Bait said, giving him a friendly slap on the shoulder. 'I'll be waitin' on the finish line with a barrel o' berry juice to celebrate yer victory.'

With a cheeky wink, he scampered down the gangplank to where Granny Rat and the Hermit sat waiting in the *Golden Anchor*. Due to the imminent threat of the Blue Claw, Gustave had ordered for a full-scale evacuation of the farm. Not only were the four competing pirate ships leaving, but also the remaining spectator vessels.

Baron Gustave stood at the bow of a small mahogany passenger ship and gave the one-minute warning. Horace's sisters and parents waved enthusiastically from a crowded ferry as the Pie Rats prepared to cast off.

Whisker took his position on the wharf next to Fred, his paws gripping a rope in readiness. Further along the wharf he could see two members from the other three crews standing beside their own ships.

Cleopatra returned his gaze with a confident smirk, her green eyes gleaming with greedy ambition.

The final event was about to begin – winner takes all.

TWENTY-THREE

Crumbling Rock Islands

Gustave's shout of 'Let the race begin!' brought the entire wharf to life. Fingers and flippers moved like lightning. Boards echoed under stomping feet. With shaking paws, Whisker began unravelling his rope from the bollard.

One loop … two loops … three loops. Done!

Without looking up, he hurled the rope onto the deck and bounded up the gangplank. Fred thundered after him, dragging the heavy plank aboard.

'All clear!' he boomed.

Above him, Whisker saw the mainsail and foresail already filling with air.

'Sails are out,' Ruby shouted as the underpants jib sail cascaded open in the wind. 'Get ready to race.'

Whisker braced himself for the first jolting movement.

Nothing happened. The *Apple Pie* remained stationary on the wharf.

'What the flaming rat's tail is going on?' Pete hollered from the helm. 'We're supposed to be sailing, not sitting!'

Whisker rushed over to the starboard side bulwark, hoping he hadn't missed a rope. He leant over the edge and ran his eye along the hull.

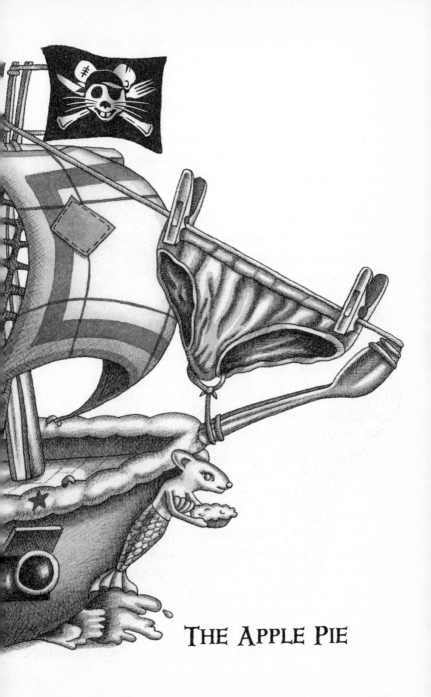

THE APPLE PIE

There was nothing connecting the hull with the wharf, but the ship still wasn't moving.

'Check the anchor,' he cried over his shoulder.

There was a clunking sound as Fred picked up a large metal object from the deck.

'Anchors away,' he said, perplexed.

Pete pounded the wheel in frustration. The rest of the crew scampered around the deck, laying blame and trying to figure out what had gone wrong.

Ahead of them, the other vessels had left the wharf and were making their way into the centre of the river. Tussling for pole position were *HMS Majesty* and the *Silver Sardine*.

Cursing under his breath, Whisker scurried to the bow of the ship, hoping the Mer-Mouse was simply snagged on a bulrush. As he surveyed the clear water, he was confronted by a loud commotion coming from the *Arctic Wind*.

The ship was a short distance away and moving at a snail's pace. Several of the penguins were squawking loudly and pointing into the air. Whisker followed the direction of their flippers to a huge white sail, suspended from the mainmast. In the centre of the sail was an enormous banana-shaped hole. The escaping wind whistled through the gap.

'Shiver me scissors!' Horace gasped, rushing up behind Whisker. 'That's taken the wind out of their sails.'

'It's worse than that,' Whisker said, pulling away from the golden figurehead, 'it's taken them out of the race. Our greatest ally has just fallen victim to sabotage and, judging by the mess we're in, so have we.'

'Rotten pies to sabotage!' Horace exclaimed, following

Whisker along the starboard bulwark. 'So who do you think did it? The marmosets? They love bananas.'

'If only,' Whisker replied gravely. 'Whoever did this wants us to think it was the marmosets.'

'Oh,' Horace gulped. 'That sounds like Sabre's handiwork.'

'Exactly,' Whisker said. 'The Cat Fish disappeared straight after the Death Ball final and there's no prize for guessing where they went.'

'Can we prove it was them?' Horace asked, wishfully.

'I doubt it,' Whisker said, stopping to examine a partly-shut cannon hatch. 'But I think I've discovered our snag. Look!'

He pointed to the bottom of the hatch, where a taut length of rope extended down the side of the hull and disappeared into the water. It was a similar ochre colour to the paintwork on the ship, making it almost impossible to spot.

With a sharp whistle from Horace, the hatch burst open and the cauliflower-shaped chef's hat of Fred popped out. Clutching the rope in both paws, he began hauling it into the ship.

Whisker almost tumbled overboard as the *Apple Pie* suddenly lurched forward. A moment later, a large banana-shaped anchor appeared at the end of the rope.

'We're off and running,' Pete hollered from the helm. 'All paws on deck. We've got a race to win!'

As the *Apple Pie* left the safety of the secluded Hawk River and sailed into the bustling cove, Whisker realised there was more than just victory to consider. There was also survival. The Pie Rats had lost their entire arsenal of cannon pies in the Dagger Island raid, leaving them totally defenceless.

Whisker could already hear the cannons firing from the wooden watchtowers along the wharf, as the procession of pirate ships and spectator vessels made their way past the fortified town.

At the front of the convoy, the Cat Fish returned fire with a wave of flaming fur-balls. The speeding projectiles raced through the air like meteors, exploding on impact and sending panicked crabs scuttling from the burning buildings. For the first time in his life, Whisker was thankful the cats were such excellent shots.

Continuing their escape through the cove, Whisker noticed the unmistakable outline of a Claw-of-War ship, docked on the western corner of the wharf. The sight of her claw-shaped battering ram sent a shiver down his tail.

As he studied the vessel more closely, he realised her twelve mighty sails were tightly furled, her oars were stowed and her hull was secured to the wharf by dozens of thick mooring ropes. Even her cannon hatches were fastened shut. Although the Claw-of-War was in no position to mount a quick pursuit, Whisker knew that once she finally got moving, she had the speed to outrun any ship.

Taking no chances, the Cat Fish sent a second round of flaming fur-balls hurtling towards the wharf. The deck of the Claw-of-War erupted in flames, as the fur-balls hit their target, and in seconds the entire vessel was ablaze – masts, battering ram and all. The crabs scattered like ants, frantically scooping up buckets of seawater to quell the ravaging flames. Breathing a sigh of relief, Whisker took his last look at Two Shillings Cove and prepared to enter the wide, open sea.

Firmly entrenched in third place, several minutes behind the other competitors, the *Apple Pie* rounded the coast of Aladrya and headed north-east. One by one, the spectator vessels peeled off towards the desert island, leaving the three pirate ships sailing along the western outskirts of the Crumbling Rock Islands. The *Arctic Wind*, almost out of sight behind the *Apple Pie*, made an ungracious exit from the race and limped to shore.

A strong eastern headwind forced the Pie Rats to rethink their kite sail strategy, and they had no choice but to tack in short legs rather than sailing in a continuous straight line. The tight manoeuvring and constant change of direction meant their bulky downwind sail would be more of a hindrance than a help, and the Eagle remained tightly stowed in a corner of the navigation room.

Despite their best efforts, the rats lost considerable ground as they made their way towards the northernmost point of the race. Their two-masted brig was considerably slower in open waters than the three-masted ships of their competitors, and the Captain's sailing expertise was sorely missed. Smudge spent much of his time flying below, hoping the Captain would suddenly awaken with a clear head and a brilliant plan.

But the Captain didn't wake up, and when the Pie Rats reached the first checkpoint, the other teams had already disappeared behind the curving cliffs to the east.

Whisker saw Chatterbeak perched on top of a windswept cliff, flapping his blue-and-yellow wings excitedly.

'Caw, caw,' he squawked. 'Welcome to checkpoint number one. Please proceed with caution and watch out for falling rocks – Oh, and in case you were wondering, you're officially in last place.'

'Marvellous,' Pete muttered from behind the wheel. 'And here I was thinking we were winning.'

Hoping for a clearer picture of the situation, Whisker called out, 'Excuse me, Chatterbeak, exactly how far behind are we?'

Chatterbeak tilted his head to one side, considering his answer.

'You're roughly five minutes behind *HMS Majesty*,' he chirped. 'And thirty minutes behind the *Silver Sardine*.'

'Thirty minutes!' Ruby exploded. 'Are you serious? There's no way we can catch the Cat Fish with a thirty minute head start. Not even the marmosets can.'

Chatterbeak flapped his wings and rose into the air. 'Caw, caw,' he squawked, flying in circles around the cliff top. 'You could always take the short cut ...' And with a final squawk he disappeared over the island.

'Short cut?' Horace exclaimed. 'What's he talking about?'

Pete let out a long groan. 'I believe our bird-brained friend is suggesting we take the *scenic route* through the islands.'

'Oh,' Fred sighed. 'Is it pretty?'

'Of course it's not pretty, you delusional day-tripper!' Pete snapped. 'It's filled with dead-end passages, hull-splitting waves and fifty metre cliffs that collapse on your head with the slightest puff of wind.'

'Isn't that a bit over the top, Pete?' Whisker ventured. 'I mean, one of the passages might continue all the way through.'

'And how would you know that?' Pete shot back. 'The islands are uncharted so unless you've been there ...'

'No,' Whisker conceded. 'I haven't been there. It's just

that …' he lowered the rope he was holding and closed his eyes. 'It's just that when I concentrate hard enough, I can picture the islands – right down to the very last detail. I can't explain it, but I'm convinced I've seen them before.'

'You have!' Ruby shouted, leaping off the rigging in excitement. 'We all have. Don't you see? It's so obvious.'

'Is it?' Horace shrugged.

'Yes!' Ruby cried. 'And we should have thought of it earlier – page six hundred and sixty.'

Without further explanation, she sprinted across the deck and disappeared into the navigation room.

Fred and Horace exchanged blank looks.

Ruby emerged a moment later, clutching the Book of Knowledge in her arms.

'Of course!' Whisker gasped, suddenly remembering where he'd seen the islands. 'There's a map near the outrigger page. We saw it on the desert island.'

Ruby raced up the stairs to the helm, with Whisker and Horace hot on her heels. She balanced the book on the wooden balustrade and opened to a page two-thirds of the way through. The bright afternoon sun began to work its magic. As the sun-reactive ink grew clear, Whisker noticed the number *715* on the bottom of the page. The rest of the paper was blank apart from one line of text:

Only in defeat do we really see clearly.

'Hardly motivational,' Horace muttered, as Ruby began flipping the pages back to *660*. 'I'll take *blind victory* any day.'

THE
CRUMBLING ROCK ISLANDS
A Bird's Eye View

ALADRYA

DAGGER ISLAND

ROCKY ISLAND

DESERT ISLAND

MERMAID ISLAND

Fishtail Passage

Rock Arch

Wrong Turn Passage

To Freeforia

CENTRAL CHANNEL

N
W   E
S

Anso's map of the Crumbling Rock Islands (subtitled *A Bird's Eye View*) was nothing short of spectacular. Where other maps of the region showed two shapeless blobs for the northern and southern groups of islands, this map revealed every curve, cliff and crag.

It only took Whisker a moment to find what he was looking for.

'There!' he exclaimed, pointing to a passage weaving its way through the northern islands. '*Fishtail Passage*. It begins at the tail of Mermaid Island, a short distance from our current location, then passes under the Rock Arch, continuing all the way to the Central Channel –'

'– Saving us at least half-an-hour of sailing,' Horace chimed in.

'Now hang on a minute,' Ruby said, tapping the map with her fingernail. 'I'm all for discussing our options, but we don't even know what the wind will be like in there.'

Whisker shook his head, refusing to be swayed. He knew how much was at stake, and there was no way he was letting anyone derail his plan.

'Calm or cyclonic,' he said, 'we have no other choice.'

'Says who?' Ruby huffed. 'As far as I can see, there's a whole ocean of choices out there. And most of them don't lead to shipwrecks –'

'That's enough, both of you,' Pete snapped, cutting Ruby short. 'I love a good argument as much as the next quartermaster, but this isn't getting us anywhere. Fishtail Passage will appear on our starboard side at any moment, so you'd better get those sails into position.'

Ruby folded her arms defiantly. 'So that's it? You're simply going to steer us into the islands without a proper plan of action, and we're expected to obey.'

'No,' Pete replied, stepping away from the wheel. 'I'm not going to steer you anywhere. Whisker is.'

'What?' Ruby gasped.

'You heard me,' Pete snorted, hobbling towards the stairs. 'I'm handing full navigational control to our headstrong apprentice. He needs to pass his sailing test sooner or later, and I for one don't want to be held responsible for crashing into a cliff when the Captain wakes up.'

Oh great, Whisker thought, grabbing the freely-spinning wheel. *I'm the saviour and the scapegoat at the same time.*

Ruby stood her ground, ready to mount a challenge, but Pete simply took her by the arm and sniffled, 'Give me a paw down the stairs, will you?'

Reluctantly, Ruby descended to the deck with Pete, leaving Horace clutching the Book of Knowledge and Whisker attempting to sail into the narrow mouth of the passage.

'I'd offer to navigate,' Horace said, placing the book gently on the ground, 'but I get my lefts and rights mixed up when I'm stressed.'

'You're stressed?' Whisker exclaimed, his tail coiling around the base of the wheel. 'What about me? I'm the one about to collide with a cliff …'

Before long, the open ocean had disappeared and the Pie Rats were surrounded by high walls of rock. Not a shred of vegetation grew on their jagged faces and, with nothing to distinguish one cliff from the next, Whisker realised how easy it would be to get lost in the maze of passages without a map. The occasional rock plummeted from the weather-beaten heights, splashing into the swirling water below. Reminded of the rock-throwing Tasmanian devils on the Island of Kings, Whisker steered the *Apple Pie* into the very centre of the passage.

The wind dropped considerably as the ship rounded a blind bend and the passage divided into two. The light breeze was ideal for smooth sailing, but not for catch-up racing.

Taking the northern branch of the passage, Whisker headed in the direction of the Rock Arch. The gaping archway was still out of sight behind a rocky outcrop, but he had a fair idea of what to expect.

The arch had been formed by the ocean. Over time the crashing waves and swirling seas had carved out a hollow at the base of the cliff, large enough to sail through. Whisker's only hope was that the arch could accommodate the mainmast, the tallest part of the ship.

As the *Apple Pie* sailed around the outcrop and the approaching waters began to appear, Whisker heard a deep groan from the front of the ship. He looked down to see Fred dangling over the bowsprit, surveying the path ahead.

A stream of equally alarming responses spread down the deck as the other crew members witnessed what Fred had seen.

Finally, as the rear of the ship cleared the outcrop, Whisker saw the horror that awaited him. Directly ahead, where the Rock Arch once stood, lay a collapsed pile of rubble. Huge shards of stone rose from the indigo water, like monstrous knife blades, blocking the entire passage.

Anso's shortcut had just become a dead-end.

TWENTY-FOUR

Wrong Turns

Mortified at what he was witnessing, Whisker stared at the collapsed arch and let out a pathetic whimper. He waited for the inevitable taunt of 'I told you so' from one of his crewmates, but all he got was a sympathetic 'There's always next time,' from Horace.

Whisker knew there wasn't going to be a next time – not for the Pie Rats – not for his family. Still, he couldn't quite bring himself to turn the ship around just yet. Paws firmly planted on the ship's wheel, he remained locked on a collision course with the ruined arch. As long as he kept moving forward, he wasn't truly giving up.

He looked down at Ruby, peering over the starboard side bulwark and he wondered why she wasn't hurling insults at him. He knew he deserved it, whatever she had to say. He'd been a liar, a choker and a sore loser – and that was before the Sea Race. Since then, his actions had only served to push her away further. Two weeks ago they were hanging off a precipice together. Now, there was a precipice between them.

As if sensing she was being watched, Ruby turned from the ocean and looked at him with one of her impossible-to-read expressions.

'If we've all finished moping,' she said flatly, 'I think I've found us a way out of here.'

'Yeah,' Horace murmured. 'It's called the *way in.*'

Ruby rolled her eye and pointed to a line of sea foam on the surface of the water.

'That foam was on our port side a moment ago,' she stated, 'and now it's on our starboard side. We haven't changed course, which means something is carrying it along.'

'Not the wind,' Horace pronounced. 'It's blowing in the wrong direction.'

Beginning to understand, Whisker released his tight grip on the wheel and felt the polished surface of the wood slide freely through his fingers. A tiny spark of hope flickered inside him.

'There's a current,' he said. 'Directly beneath us. I can feel it pulling on the rudder.'

'And it's moving across the passage,' Pete observed, his pink eyes fixed on the foam. 'The water must have found another way through the rocks after the arch collapsed.'

'So where's it headed now?' Horace asked.

'Wrong Turn Passage, I'm guessing,' Ruby replied dryly. 'The only other route through these islands.'

'Sounds delightful,' Horace gulped.

Whisker glanced down at the map, hoping Ruby's prediction was right.

'The tail of Mermaid Island barely touches the cliff near the Rock Arch,' he pointed out. 'That could be the weak spot.'

'There's only one way to find out,' Ruby said, scrambling up the rigging. 'All eyes on that cliff!'

Heeding Ruby's command, Fred swept his powerful eye

in a wide arc across the cliff face then locked on a shadowy section of rock covered with dried seaweed.

'There,' he grunted, pointing to the spot with his oversized paw.

It took Whisker a moment to realise what Fred had discovered, but as the *Apple Pie* moved closer towards the collapsed arch he saw a narrow crevice between the two islands. Barely the width of the *Apple Pie,* the gap extended upwards to the very top of the cliffs and downwards into the ocean. Water gushed through the centre of the crevice like rainwater in a drainpipe, splashing into the afternoon sunlight on the opposite side.

Whisker swung the *Apple Pie* a full ninety degrees, facing it directly into the short passage. He knew that a thorough safety assessment was in order, but the time for caution was gone.

'Hold on!' he shouted as the current took hold. 'We're going in.'

The sickening screech of wood grating against stone reverberated around the surrounding cliffs as the hull scraped through the tight gap.

Whisker held his breath, hoping the *Apple Pie* wasn't about to get stuck in the crevice like a cork in an Apple Fizz bottle. In seconds, the ship was sliding out the other side.

Assessing the damage to be no more than 'superficial paint scrapes,' Whisker wasted no time in orchestrating his next audacious move. 'Ready the Eagle,' he commanded.

'Don't be a dodo,' Pete shot back. 'You can't use a kite sail in here.'

'It won't be in here,' Whisker retorted. 'The sail will be flying up there.' He pointed high into the vivid blue sky. 'We all know these passages are too sheltered to generate any decent wind gusts, but if we can harness the power of an overhead wind, we might still have a chance.'

Pete screwed up his nose. 'Alright, bring out the bird. But if we all suffer horrible deaths on the rocks, I'm holding you personally responsible.'

With the added pressure of the crew's lives in his hands, Whisker watched as the huge kite was retrieved from the navigation room and unfolded on the deck. Four long ropes were attached to the corners of the sail and fastened to fixing points along the bulwark.

'Prepare to launch around the next bend,' Whisker ordered.

Fred scaled the rigging, clutching the top edge of the kite sail in one paw. The others took their positions at the foot of the masts, waiting for Whisker's signal.

The surface of the water was alive with choppy waves as the wind found its way into the passage. Fred had only just reached the top of the rigging when the sail in his paws began to flap wildly.

'Hold steady!' Whisker shouted.

Fred waited, hanging on for dear life in the howling wind, as Whisker spun the wheel around and around.

The moment the *Apple Pie* cleared the bend, the Eagle expanded with air and Fred released his grip. The golden bird rose steadily above the cliffs and soared majestically into the cloud-scattered sky.

The pull on the ship was instantaneous. The bow of the *Apple Pie* lurched through the water like a shark on the hunt. The Pie Rats were no longer cruising. They were now racing.

The explosive speed of the *Apple Pie* brought a whole new set of challenges for Whisker. Dead-end passages became potential crash sites. Submerged rocks were shipwrecks waiting to happen.

Following a direct, downwind course through the islands, Whisker held steady, steering with confidence and resolve.

Will we emerge in the lead? he wondered, *or will it be a mad dash to the finish line?*

He wanted to believe they could still win.

He *had* to believe they could still win.

From time to time, the shadows of the cliffs would creep across the deck of the ship, inching their way towards the open book. Whisker would hurriedly memorise the map before it vanished into shadowy blankness, only to reappear again with the next ray of sunlight.

The shadows grew longer. The sun dropped lower.

And then, just when the sun appeared to have set behind the high cliffs of rock, it appeared directly in front of them, shining like a golden orb through the open end of the passage. Whisker felt the blood pumping through his tail. His heart began to race.

'Fred!' he shouted, his voice edged with nervous excitement. 'What can you see?'

It took a moment for the *Apple Pie* to reach open water, and by that time, Whisker was too busy staring through his spyglass to even hear Fred's response.

To the south, trawling through the Central Channel and well out of contention, was HMS Majesty. To the west, radiant and terrifying, sailed the *Silver Sardine*. Amber sunlight sparkled off its glistening hull as it rounded the marker ship. A stone's throw to the north lay the sandy shores of the desert island.

Whisker's heart sank. He didn't need a navigation degree to know that, even with a high-flying Eagle sail, the *Apple Pie* would never catch up. The Cat Fish were on the home strait and the rats would be lucky to reach the purple-sailed marker ship before the cats skulked onto the beach to claim their prize.

Whisker knew that only a miracle could win them the race, and true miracles were the stuff of bedtime stories.

Think, he told himself, fighting back a wave of despair. *There's got to be a solution. There always is.*

Focusing his mind, he tried to come up with something – anything to stop the Cat Fish from winning.

A blue whale swallowing the Silver Sardine whole?

No. That's never going to happen.

A freak tidal wave throwing the cats off course?

Even more remote …

Hidden sandbars? No.

Whirlpools? No.

Lightning storms? No, no, no!

Nothing he could think of was ever going to happen.

With one last desperate hope, he closed his eyes and let his memories take over.

At first he saw nothing. Then, as the darkness of his mind began to close in, he pictured a ship with sails as black as the night, appearing in deathly silence …

The Black Shadow.

The haunting ship had appeared to him twice – always at sunset – somewhere close to his current location.

Could it appear to him again?

He felt an icy chill run through his tail. His fingers turned white on the wheel.

Be careful what you wish for …

Fighting back his terror, he turned his spyglass to the horizon and willed the ship to appear.

TWENTY-FIVE

One Winner

After what seemed like an eternity of staring into nothingness, dreading what he might actually find, Whisker was pulled from his trance by the sound of someone calling his name.

'…Whisker. Whisker.'

Immediately, all hopes of the *Black Shadow* were swept from his mind. He felt his tail collapse on the deck.

It isn't coming, he told himself, embracing reality. *It never was.*

He lowered the spyglass to see Ruby standing next to him on the helm. The sun was setting behind her, bathing the edges of her face and ears in a soft, golden light. She was neither angry nor upset, but the look of resignation she gave Whisker told him that the Cat Fish were destined for victory.

'We're not going to win this race, are we?' he said quietly.

'No,' she said, unable to hide the relief on her face. 'The games are over.'

Whisker nodded. He knew exactly what games she was referring to: not the games between competitors where winners were showered with gold but the games between friends where there were no winners.

Despite the bitter disappointment Whisker felt at losing the answer he so desperately sought, a small part of him felt relieved, too. He was no longer bound to the fox. With the trophy out of the equation, he could finally stop lying and he could finally be himself again – not a scoundrel with something to hide but a friend with everything to share.

The Pie Rats are all I've got now, he told himself. *And Ruby is one of them.*

Hoping he could salvage something from the wreckage of their relationship, Whisker decided to come clean.

'Ruby,' he said, mustering the courage, 'I've got something I want to tell you.'

'Okay,' she said, smiling. 'But can it wait until we reach the island? The trophy might be out of our grasp, but there's a pawful of loyal spectators who deserve a spectacular fin–'

She faulted midsentence, losing her train of thought. Across from her, Whisker's eyes had grown to the size of pie platters.

'Whisker, what is it?' she gasped.

'Y-your words,' Whisker stammered, his jaw gaping open. *'Out of our grasp …* It's not over. Don't you see?'

'See what?' Ruby frowned.

Whisker pointed to the blank book, lying face up in the shadows. 'Remember what Anso said? *Only in defeat do we really see clearly.* We were so obsessed with winning the Sea Race that we failed to see the real goal: *winning the championship.'*

Taking a deep breath, he raised the spyglass to his eye and swivelled it towards the desert island. The *Silver*

Sardine was approaching the sandy coastline but it was yet to pass through the line of breakers.

'Good,' he said to himself, 'We've still got time.'

'Time for what?' Ruby gasped. 'You're not making any sense.'

Without a response, Whisker turned the spyglass to the vessel closest to him: the purple-sailed marker ship.

Against the darkening ocean he saw the unmistakable flicker of violet flames illuminating the ship's three masts.

Whisker smiled to himself. The marker ship was no ordinary ship.

Out of our grasp? Whisker asked himself, fixing his sights on the trophy room of the *Velvet Wave. Or close enough to touch?*

He lowered the spyglass and looked up at the Eagle sail. The huge, rectangular kite hovered above the starboard side of the *Apple Pie*. Its four ropes creaked and strained as the strong wind threatened to tear the fabric away.

'Ruby,' Whisker said, finally addressing his confused companion. 'Is your bow still on board?'

'Yes,' Ruby said. 'And I've got a quiver of silver arrows in the navigation room – but, Whisker, what do you want them for?'

'You'll see,' Whisker said with urgency. 'But first, I need you to do exactly what I say.'

Several minutes later, seven lavishly dressed bunnies paraded up the stairs of the *Apple Pie* and onto the twilit deck. With Fred's gentle assistance, they shuffled to the bow of the ship, oohing and aahing and making wooden waving gestures with their paws. Some wore scarves, some wore luxurious coats. All of them were smiling.

One by one, they formed a tight row along the bulwark, staring blankly at the approaching ship.

The sight of the beautiful damsels sent the crew of the *Velvet Wave* into a frenzy. Dropping their paint-pellet rifles, they rushed to the port side of the ship and began wolf-whistling and twitching their ears uncontrollably.

'Well hello, ladies!' hollered the tallest rabbit. 'Welcome to checkpoint number two.'

'All my Easters have come at once,' cried a plump rabbit with pronounced front teeth. 'Seven beautiful bunnies and they're staring straight at me.'

'What heavenly burrow did you hop out of?' asked the smallest rabbit dreamily.

'Oh, it was no burrow,' came a high pitched response. 'We were shipwrecked on a barren island without so much as a carrot to nibble on. If it wasn't for these lovely rats, well, I'm sure you can imagine what would have happened …'

'Oooh no!' cried the entire crew of the *Velvet Wave*. 'It's a miracle you survived.'

Whisker chuckled to himself and pretended to adjust the foresail. From his elevated position halfway up the rigging he could see what Gustave's love-struck sons couldn't: Horace and Ruby crouching behind seven painted Frankie cut-outs, while Smudge moved their paws with pieces of string.

Horace was responsible for most of the bunnies' squeaky voices, though the occasional comment from Ruby stopped him from going completely overboard. The green-eyed sharpshooter waited patiently with a loaded bow in her paws and a silver arrow aimed unnervingly at

Whisker's left foot.

Glad to be on friendly terms with her again, Whisker wrapped his fingers around a rope of the kite sail and ran his eye up the tense, quivering line. The dark shape of the Eagle hovered silently above the *Velvet Wave*.

'A little to your starboard side,' Whisker mouthed to Pete behind the wheel.

'Aye,' Pete sniffled, giving the wheel a subtle spin.

As the *Apple Pie* slowly righted its course, Whisker recalled the words of Baron Gustave from the opening ceremony: *Ze first team zat can touch ze trophy, before ze end of ze last event vill receive one bonus point.*

In the fading light, Whisker could barely make out the *Silver Sardine* in the dark haze of sea spray that surrounded the desert island, but he knew that the cats were only minutes from the shore.

Now comes the real race, Whisker told himself, gripping the rope tightly. He knew his plan was reckless and bordering on insane, but that was exactly what made it so brilliant – the rabbits would never see it coming.

The bow of the *Apple Pie* drew level with the stern of the *Velvet Wave* and, with the Eagle flying directly above the trophy room, Whisker made his move.

Wrapping his legs around the course rope, he let out a sharp wolf-whistle. The sound had barely left his lips when Ruby released the string of her bow, sending a silver arrow whizzing through the air. With pin-point accuracy, the arrowhead sliced through the rope beneath Whisker's feet, severing it in two.

The sudden release of tension on the rope of the Eagle sail catapulted him upwards. All he could do was hold on as his body was jerked high into the air and then began curving down in a sweeping arc towards the trophy room.

The wind howled in his ears. The salty air stung his eyes. In the blur that surrounded him, he glimpsed the awakening figure of the Captain staring through a cabin window, he saw the rabbits raise their bewildered faces to the sky, and he felt the rope shake violently in his paws as the Eagle lost control in the wind.

Unable to maintain his grip, he began to fall.

For a moment he was bathed in a sea of purple light. Then he was tumbling through the open roof of the trophy room, clawing at crimson curtains and crashing onto a velvet covered pedestal.

With his head spinning and his eyes clouded with tears, he blindly threw himself forward, stretching out his rope-burned paws as six rifle-carrying rabbits stormed into the room.

They took one look at him, lying in the centre of the room and trained their sights on his twisted torso.

Not daring to breathe, Whisker waited for the purple projectiles to pepper his body, but the rabbits merely stared at him with bemused interest.

Exhaling in relief, Whisker looked down to see his fingers resting on a line of jewels at the base of an enormous gold trophy. The metal was warm, the jewels smooth under his grazed skin.

'Nice touch,' said one of the rabbits, lowering his rifle. 'It's yours for the keeping, you know. That little stunt just won you the championship.'

Whisker wiped his eyes with the back of his paw and looked up at the glittering object. Violet flames danced over the sides of its ornate rim, each tongue of fire reflected in the edges of two crossed torches and an engraved skull.

It was truly magnificent. It was breathtaking. And, best of all, it was *his*.

Deep down inside, he knew what the future held for the coveted cup, but right now, all he wanted to do was bask in its glory. It was a trophy made for champions and he was a champion. He had outwitted the rabbits and conquered the cats. And he had done it in true Pie Rat style – he had won by a whisker.

Through the open door of the trophy room, Whisker could see the orange glow of a signal flare rising into the dusk sky. The Cat Fish had reached the beach first but there could only be one winner.

They can have their Sea Race, he told himself, *I've got the Trophy of Champions.*

25TH PIRATE CUP		FINAL TEAM SCORES	
PLACE	TEAM	POINTS	DEATH BALL VICTORIES
1ST	PiE RATS	3	3
2ND	CAT FiSH	3	2
3RD	MARMOSETS	1	1
4TH	PENGUiNS	1	0

TWENTY-SIX

The Trophy of Champions

The next thirty minutes of Whisker's life were nothing short of surreal.

The flaming trophy was carried onto the *Apple Pie*, where Horace smothered it in wet, slobbery kisses. Fred began a celebratory rendition of the Pie Rats' battle cry: '*We are the dreaded Pie Rats and we are the cham-pie-ons,*' while Smudge buzzed along with his wings.

As promised, Pete awarded Whisker a pass on his sailing test (although the word *unconventional* was used repeatedly in the announcement).

In the midst of the excitement, Ruby helped the dazed Captain onto the deck and tried to explain *what in Ratbeard's name was going on*.

The rabbits, heartbroken to learn their beautiful bunnies were simply dolled-up billboards in expensive clothing, used a lantern to signal the news of the Stealth Raid to the island.

Whisker wished he could have seen the look on Sabre's face the moment the message arrived, but by the time the Pie Rats pulled their rowboat onto the sandy beach, the Cat Fish had finished any protesting and were nowhere in sight.

It seemed that every other animal on the island wanted to join in the victory celebrations, and the entire shore was teeming with Sea-Dog-turned-Cat-Fish-turned-Pie-Rat supporters, cheering and clapping and stomping their feet.

'Well done, *Whisker*,' Granny Rat applauded, using his real name for the first time. 'My husband was right. You're not such a spineless worm after all.'

'Yes, yes,' the Hermit gabbled. 'No worms here.'

'Thanks, Coach,' Whisker said, smiling politely as his tail writhed like a worm behind him.

Papa Niko and Mama Kolina began offering their congratulations, but were cut short by a loud squawk from Chatterbeak, calling everyone to attention. When the crowd was silent, Baron Gustave commenced his official closing speech. After a few token words, he presented the Pie Rats with three chests of gold and six gold medals engraved with the words *25th Pirate Cup Champions*.

'Argh me pastries, these things are heavy!' Horace exclaimed as Gustave placed the medal around his neck.

'What did you expect?' Hera muttered from the crowd. 'They're made from gold, not sea sponges …'

'That's true,' Athena added, tipping her glasses for a better look. 'Although sea sponges can be extremely heavy when they're holding water.'

'Put a sock in it, Miss Science,' Aphrodite snorted. 'Whoever heard of anyone wearing a wet sea sponge? They're so unflattering!'

'Here we go again,' Horace groaned to Whisker. 'Even world champions have to deal with annoying family members. Next they'll be wanting to wear our medals.'

'Oh, yeah, sure …' Whisker responded half-heartedly.

At the mention of the word *family*, his attention had shifted from the ceremony to the daunting task that still lay ahead. His medal could have been made out of tin and worn by every member of the Cat Fish crew for all he cared. All that mattered was finding his family. But that required the trophy, and smuggling the priceless object off the island seemed almost as hard as winning it in the first place.

The moment Chatterbeak extinguished the trophy's purple flames, a swarm of star-struck spectators flocked to have their portraits drawn with it. Some held the trophy aloft like they were the champions. Others (like Horace's sisters) wrapped their arms around the glorious object and refused to let go.

Whisker watched patiently from the shadows – a thief in the night, his eyes never leaving the trophy.

As darkness set in, small campfires were lit around the island. Most were quickly abandoned in favour of the roaring bonfire in the centre of a jungle clearing.

In contrast to Whisker's pensive mood, the Pie Rats were the happiest they had been in a long, long time. Pete danced with Athena around the fire, twirling on his pencil leg, while Granny Rat and the Hermit skipped youthfully behind them. Horace, Papa Niko and Fred relived their Death Ball victory with the help of a small coconut and two palm trees. The Captain swapped tales with his fellow captains King Marvownion, Baron Gustave and the entire penguin crew (who all claimed to be captain of the *Arctic Wind*). Athena and Hera wore Horace's and Fred's medals and posed for a sketch artist, while Mama Kolina stirred a large pot of soup in the coals of the fire. Above her, Smudge perched on the tip of a palm frond, taking in the glorious spectacle.

Further from the clearing, Whisker heard the rambling chorus of a sea shanty as Rat Bait rolled a large barrel through the bushes.

That left Ruby.

Whisker didn't have to wait long to find out where she was.

'Howdy, stranger,' came an abrupt voice from behind him.

Taken by surprise, Whisker spun around to see Ruby standing a few feet away.

'H-hi,' he squeaked.

'Everything alright?' she asked suspiciously.

'Oh – yeah,' Whisker gabbled. 'Everything's … fine.'

Ruby took a step towards him, clearly unconvinced.

'Look, Whisker,' she began, 'I don't know what's been going on lately, but you said you had something important to tell me on the ship. If you still want to talk, I'm all ears.'

Whisker's bottom lip quivered. Of course he wanted to talk. He wanted to free himself from the lie and tell Ruby everything: his encounter with the fox; the secret deal; his plan to steal the trophy.

But he couldn't.

Not now. Not with the trophy in his possession, not with his family's life at stake. And definitely not with two dozen furry ears listening to every word he said. As a member of the winning team, he was bound to attract some form of attention, but he couldn't shake the sick feeling that any one of the weasels, ferrets or meerkats skulking around the bonfire could be spying for the fox.

It was a risk he wasn't prepared to take. The fox had demanded secrecy and Whisker knew he had to hold his tongue.

He stood there like a statue without uttering a word.

'So we're back to the silent treatment, are we?' Ruby asked after a long, awkward pause.

Fighting hard to avoid Ruby's piercing stare, Whisker pretended to be distracted by Rat Bait. The jolly sailor was pushing his barrel into the clearing and singing loudly:

A barrel full of berry juice, sour as a plum.
Yo ho, ho and the night be young!
A toast from the trophy be my idea o' fun.
Yo ho, ho and the night be young!

When Rat Bait reached the foot of the enormous cup, he turned the barrel on its end and clambered up.

'Well I'll be a chimney sweep!' he exclaimed, peering over the broad rim of the trophy. 'There's more ash in this wee vessel than a blacksmith's fireplace!' He held up a soot-covered finger. 'I don't suppose anyone's got a scrubbin' brush?'

Whisker's tail twinged. This was the invitation he'd been waiting for.

Without hesitation, he leapt out of the shadows.

'I'll clean it for you, Rat Bait,' he piped. Then not wanting to sound overly enthusiastic in front of Ruby, he added, 'I mean, it wouldn't be right to have an ash-tainted victory toast.'

'That be mighty kind o' you, Master Whisker,' Rat Bait said. 'But no one expects the tournament champion to be gettin' his paws dirty on celebration night.'

'It's fine, honestly,' Whisker said, scrambling over to the trophy. 'I'm not really much of a *celebrator*.' He could feel Ruby's eye boring a hole in his back, but resisted the urge to turn around and explain himself. As much as it pained him to leave things on a sour note, he knew there was no other option. Ruby could see straight through him. A single word would give his intentions away.

He heard a frustrated 'Hmph' as Ruby finally ran out of patience and stomped off to join the Death Ball re-enactment.

Whisker climbed up beside Rat Bait.

'If you ask me,' he said, peering at the blackened insides of the cup, 'a dash of salt water is the key. The beach isn't far from here and I can use the sand as an abrasive cleaner.'

Rat Bait looked hesitant.

'Don't worry,' Whisker reassured him, 'I've had plenty of experience scrubbing pots in the galley, and I'll have the trophy back to you before you've even popped the cork.'

'Oh, all right,' Rat Bait conceded, climbing down from the barrel. 'Yer a trustworthy lad an' charcoal-flavoured berry juice is hardly me drink o' choice.'

Whisker tried to smile, but the pang of guilt in his stomach made it almost impossible. Rat Bait was yet another companion he was about to betray. He'd grown fond of the old rogue over the course of the games and the thought of breaking his trust now pained Whisker almost as much as stealing the trophy itself.

This is the way it has to be, Whisker repeated in his mind. *You already know that.*

Pushing his guilt aside, he removed the medal from his neck and placed it over Rat Bait's head, hoping, in some small way, it would atone for his actions.

'What's this?' Rat Bait exclaimed, looking down at the golden object.

'It's … a thank you present for helping us win the championship,' Whisker replied cagily.

Rat Bait shook his head.

'I can't accept this,' he said, beginning to remove the medal. 'It belongs to ye.'

'Then it's mine to give away,' Whisker said, placing his paw on Rat Bait's forearm.

'I still can't accept it,' Rat Bait said, brushing Whisker aside. 'This medal be made for a champion, not for a lousy Head o' Security.'

'You're not *lousy*,' Whisker objected. 'If it wasn't for your tip-offs, we would have been out of the contest days ago.' He took a deep breath. 'Look, if you won't accept the medal, at least hold on to it until I return from the beach. Pete would pickle me in pineapple juice if I lost it in the surf.'

Rat Bait gave a long sigh and let the medal drop onto his chest. 'Very well, I'll keep it safe 'til ye return. Now be off with ye, young scallywag. Me throat be growin' dryer by the minute!'

Taking his cue, Whisker leapt down from the barrel, wrapping his paws and tail around the trophy. The golden cup was nearly as tall as he was and Whisker was barely able to raise it off the ground. After several struggling steps, he realised he'd never navigate past the dozen or so curious spectators blocking his path.

Fortunately, Rat Bait's cry of 'So, who's first in line for a drink?' had them scurrying out of the way in an instant.

With the rest of his companions distracted by the celebrations, Whisker made his way past a silver bow and a quiver of arrows propped up against a tree and slowly disappeared into the jungle.

He glanced over his shoulder, half expecting to see Ruby skulking after him or at least aiming an arrow in his direction, but she was nowhere in sight.

The voices of jolly revellers grew fainter as he continued through the lush undergrowth. In utter silence, he reached a small campfire at the crest of a sand dune overlooking the beach. Whoever had made the fire had long since joined the festivities in the centre of the island. All that was left was a charcoaled branch and a pile of glowing coals.

Staring down at the smoking remains, Whisker realised he'd come to a crossroad. Behind him lay the bizarre, unpredictable world of the Pie Rats – a world he had come to know and love. Ahead of him lay the answer he so desperately sought: *Where is my family?*

For the first time, he realised that there was no going back. Once he made his decision he was on his own.

As he watched the smoke coiling around the coals, the words of the Pie Rat code drifted into his mind: *Loyalty before all else, even pies …*

Even trophies, he told himself. *Even families …*

He knew the consequences of his actions. He was about to become a traitor, and traitors had no place on a Pie Rat ship.

Never again would he stand with his fellow crew members and raise his scissor sword high. Never again would he laugh at one of Horace's one-liners or gobble down a slice of Fred's piping hot berry pies. And never again would he blush bright red when Ruby walked into the room.

Whisker knew he would miss her the most.

He missed her already.

How he wished things could be different. Overcome with a deep feeling of helplessness, he sank to his knees, his paws sliding despairingly down the sides of the trophy.

It was almost too much to bear.

Why am I cursed with this burden? he asked himself. *Why does it have to be this way?*

Six weeks ago he was a happy-go-lucky circus rat with a family and a future, and now he was sitting on a beach with a golden trophy, facing a decision that could leave him with nothing. It pained him to think about it, but deep down inside he knew that his family might already be dead.

Trying to dispel the dark thoughts from his mind, he raised his eyes to the moonlit sea. The glowing ball of white hovered over the waves like an enormous lantern, its crater-covered face an almost perfect sphere.

In the radiant light, Whisker could see everything: the foaming white caps of the breaking waves; the silver-lined edges of cottonwool clouds; the line of small spectator vessels running along the sandy beach. And, in the midst of it all, he saw the fleeting silhouette of a cat disappearing into the Pie Rats' rowboat.

Whisker froze.

Was he imagining things? He rubbed his weary eyes and looked again. The beach was deserted.

Puzzled, he continued to stare, praying the smoke of the fire would conceal his whereabouts as several more cats materialised out of the darkness and converged on the rowboat. In seconds, they had leapt over the side of the small vessel and vanished from sight.

Whisker stifled a cry. The Cat Fish were setting an ambush.

For nine days, the protective rules of the Pirate Cup had kept the Pie Rats safe, but with the games officially over, the cutthroat laws of piracy once again reigned supreme.

Steal or be stolen from. Kill or be killed.

Whisker had no idea if the cats had followed him from the bonfire or whether their timing was purely coincidental, but he knew for certain they had come for the trophy and they'd stop at nothing to get it.

He was faced with a terrible dilemma: *What to do next?*

If he warned his friends he would lose his one chance to escape. But if he didn't …

He let out a low groan. Every option seemed like the wrong one and he was running out of time – fast.

The options are right in front of you, he told himself. *You have to choose.*

But he knew it was never going to be that simple.

And so, with a whirlwind of emotions, he took his last look at the fire, wrapped his grey-hooded cloak around him and made his decision.

TWENTY-SEVEN

The Answer

The *Golden Anchor* glided effortlessly through the calm water of the Hawk River, barely leaving a wake. Its lone passenger fixed his eyes on a small fishing jetty and steered the vessel to shore.

It was late in the evening and his journey was nearing its end. He had sailed undetected past the blackened watch towers of the cove and slipped silently into the mouth of the river. As hoped, the tired crabs had been too busy repairing the wharf to notice one, small sailing boat returning to the scene of the crime.

On arriving at the fishing jetty, he secured the vessel to a sturdy pylon and hauled the golden trophy onto dry land. In the pale moonlight, he had no trouble locating the cart of Trojan pasties hiding in the nearby bushes. Using his sword as a lever, he prized open a pasty like a clam shell and began removing great chunks of sticky filling. Despite the enormous size of the pasty, it took some gentle manoeuvring before he finally fit the trophy inside the crust.

Resealing the pasty, he wrapped his greasy paws around the handle of the cart and began lugging his precious cargo up the steep path to the Fish 'n Ships Inn.

The Inn was alive with music and laughter, the open windows of the restaurant revealing a bustling bar and a crowded dance floor.

Ignoring the late night festivities, the hooded cart-bearer followed the gangplank to the swinging saloon doors. He was met by a familiar looking mink in a black and white apron.

'Good evening, Sir,' she said politely. 'My name is Delores. Welcome to the Fish 'n Ships Inn.'

'Evening,' he mumbled, keeping his head bent low.

She stared at him with a puzzled look on her face before letting out a small gasp.

'Whisker!' she exclaimed. 'Is that you? I almost didn't recognise you under that hood. Have you come to visit Mr B again?'

Whisker raised his head and looked at Delores in confusion. *'Mr B?'*

'Yes,' she said. 'Mr Belorio.'

'Oh,' Whisker said, finally understanding. *'Frankie.* Yes – of course.'

Delores pointed to a pasty protruding from the top of the cart.

'I see you've brought some midnight munchies with you,' she laughed. 'I hope you're hungry.'

'They're Frankie's favourite,' Whisker said, playing along.

'Well, we'd best not keep him waiting then,' Delores said, ushering Whisker into the foyer. 'Mr Belorio is staying in the penthouse suite of the eastern tower. The stairs are located at the end of the first corridor, past the high rollers' room.' She gave him a small curtsy. 'Can I assist you with anything else tonight?'

'No – thank you, Delores,' Whisker said, stepping into

the corridor. 'You've told me everything I need to know.'

The sounds of the restaurant faded to silence as Whisker tip-toed down the lantern-lit corridor. Only the sound of the cart's rubber wheels broke the eerie stillness.

… Squeak … squeak … squeak …

He passed a door marked *Two Up* and another labelled *Blackjack,* and, before he knew it, he was facing a carved oak door with the words *High Rollers' Room* painted in thick gold letters.

This is it, he thought, drawing a breath. *This is where my search ends.* He raised his arm to the door, but a sick feeling of dread seemed to paralyse his fingers.

Can you really trust the fox to keep his word? he asked himself. Forcing himself to be brave, he placed his paw on the brass handle and opened the door.

The only light of the room came from a stumpy candle in the centre of the card table, its smouldering wick clearly struggling to stay alight. Wax oozed over its sides, pooling on the lush felt below. A solitary figure sat at the table, clutching a deck of cards. His black trench coat disappeared into the deep shadows of the room. His orange eyes glowed like coals in the flickering candlelight as he stared unblinking at Whisker.

'I trust you've brought my *trinket,*' the fox stated casually, without a word of introduction, as if expecting his guest.

'Yes,' Whisker said, pulling the cart inside.

The fox shot a quick glance at the pasties and then shifted his attention to the open doorway.

'And who else is with you?' he asked suspiciously.

'No one,' Whisker said, hurriedly closing the door. 'I kept your secret – as promised.'

The fox locked eyes with Whisker, studying him closely. 'Really?'

Whisker held his gaze, not daring to look away.

After a tense moment, the edges of the fox's mouth curved into a satisfied smile.

'Very well,' he said, rising from his chair. 'Now show me the trophy.'

The fox watched attentively as Whisker broke open the pasty and began removing the vegetable-covered trophy. Using his sleeve as a rag, he wiped the parsnip and turnip filling off its surface and placed the sticky object on the edge of the table.

A look of greedy delight flashed across the fox's face.

'It appears the pirating world has a new champion,' he mused, placing the deck of cards in front of him.

Whisker stared down at the top card.

Ace of Diamonds, he gasped. *The fox's lucky suit.*

The fox stepped eagerly towards the trophy, his paw twitching on the diamond hilt of his sword.

Whisker suddenly felt ill.

'A-and what about my answer?' he stammered. 'I've kept my end of the bargain.'

'Oh, yes,' the fox said, with a mock sigh. 'Your poor lost sister. I'd almost forgotten about her.'

A spark of anger flashed inside Whisker.

'What have you done with her?' he burst out. 'If you've touched a hair on her head –'

The fox's eyes narrowed.

'How dare you,' he snarled, his fingers tightening on the handle of his sword. 'I'm a trader, not a monster.' He took a step towards Whisker and spat, 'Dead rats are worth nothing to me – don't you forget it!'

Whisker cowered back, panting for breath, the fox's words echoing in his head. *Dead rats are worth nothing ...*

'So – she's – alive?' he gasped.

The fox stared at Whisker, unmoved. For a moment he said nothing. Then he answered with a single word, 'Yes.'

Whisker's heart almost burst from his chest.

Anna was alive!

'W-where can I find her?' he cried, yearning to know more.

'On a mountain,' the fox said in a flat, expressionless tone. 'She's found a new home with a family of birds. They love rats dearly.' His lips formed a thin smile. 'Your sister was a little undernourished for their liking, but I'm sure with a few mountain berries she'll be as plump as a pig in no time ...'

Whisker struggled to process everything he was hearing. *Mountains ... berries ... birds ...* All he knew was that his sister was alive.

'And what about my parents?' he asked excitedly. 'Are they alive, too?'

'Your parents?' The fox repeated, a cruel smirk creeping across his face. 'I recall our deal was for one answer, not two.'

'What?' Whisker gasped, his stomach twisting into a knot. 'But that's not fair ... y-you've got to tell me. Please –'

'A deal is a deal,' the fox snarled, pushing past Whisker to the trophy.

In anger and desperation, Whisker moved his paw to the handle of his scissor sword. 'Tell me where they are or I'll-I'll ...'

'You'll what?' the fox hissed, scooping up the trophy in his arms. 'Stab me with a broken piece of stationery? I think not!' He stepped backwards, raising the trophy like a shield. 'I'd love to stay and fight, dear apprentice, but both of us should really be getting a move on. And I thought rats had good hearing ...'

Whisker shot a terrified glance at the open window. The unmistakable scuttle of crabs echoed from the balcony beyond.

'The Blue Claw,' he gasped.

By the time Whisker had found his legs and turned to flee, the fox was already disappearing out the door.

Panic-stricken, Whisker hurtled over the hollow crust of the pasty and sprinted for the closing door.

With a rumbling *THUD-D-D*, the door slammed shut in his face.

Frantically, he lunged for the door knob. There was a soft *click* from the other side and Whisker knew his fate was sealed.

Trapped in a room with nowhere to hide, he did the only thing he could think of: he drew his sword, steadied his nerves and sprinted for the window.

The Blue Claw converged from both ends of the long balcony, their powerful claws snapping wildly. They reached the high rollers' room as the cloaked body of Whisker hurtled through the window. With a panicked squeak he cleared the balcony and plunged head first into a fish-shaped topiary tree.

The leafy foliage broke his fall, but the branches left him stinging and sore.

With no time to examine his wounds, he scrambled down the tail of the giant green fish, landing on the dew-covered grass.

Desperately, he scanned the moonlit courtyard for an

escape route. He was surrounded on all four sides by solid brick walls. Above him, the two huge towers of the inn rose high into the air. In the centre of the courtyard stood the glorious stone fountain. Water squirted from the mouths of three enormous fish, splashing playfully into the pool below. Pale moonlight reflected off the rippling surface of the water, bringing the entire courtyard to life.

As beautiful as the fountain was at night, it was the wrought iron door in the centre of the northern wall that caught Whisker's attention.

Ignoring the shouts of the watching crabs, he scurried across the courtyard towards his only exit. He had barely reached the fountain when the door burst open and a swarm of angry crustaceans surged through. Led by a gigantic blue soldier crab, they fanned out in a wide arc.

Outnumbered fifty-to-one, Whisker stumbled backwards into the pool, splashing through the shallow water towards the closest stone fish.

The crabs continued their advance, moving in an unbroken ring, their claws open and their eyestalks twitching in anticipation. Reaching the pool, they began to swim.

Whisker stowed his sword and climbed. Using the strength in his arms, he pulled himself up the stone scales of the fish until he reached the very top of the waterspout. Icy water splashed over his hooded cloak, soaking him to the bone. His chest heaved as he gulped in great breaths of air.

He looked down to see the leader of the crabs hauling himself onto a ledge at the base of the fish. He was broad-shelled and powerful, sporting the biggest claws Whisker had ever seen. The lightning-bolt tattoos on either claw revealed his unmistakable identity: General Thunderclaw, the most feared officer in the Aladryan Navy.

Thunderclaw let out a sharp whistle and a mottled blue soldier crab wearing a monocle appeared on the edge of the pool. In his undersized claw he clutched a tightly rolled scroll.

Whisker instantly recognised the crab as the clerk from Prison Island.

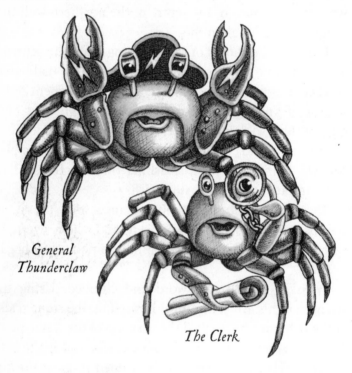

General
Thunderclaw

The Clerk

'Is that our suspect?' Thunderclaw asked, raising a claw in Whisker's direction.

The clerk unrolled the scroll to reveal a crumpled poster. In its centre was a portrait of a scruffy-looking rodent wearing a grey hooded cloak.

WANTED
DEAD OR ALIVE

HOODED MOUSE BANDIT
1OO GOLD PIECES
REWARD

Whisker glanced down at his soggy, grey traveller's cloak and he wished he'd worn his tacky palm tree tourist shirt instead.

'It's our mouse, alright,' the clerk acknowledged, peering through his monocle. 'We've been on his trail for several weeks.'

'Then it's high time we brought him into custody,' Thunderclaw roared. 'You know the drill. Dead or alive – but preferably dead!'

With a great cheer, the crabs converged.

TWENTY-EIGHT

Flight

Whisker never dreamed his life would end this way – all alone, on the wrong side of the law, but as the hostile crabs surged up the sides of the fountain, three little words gave him hope.

Hold on, Whisker.

The words seemed to be carried on the wind, barely louder than a whisper.

In confusion, he looked down, his head spinning, water blurring his eyes. The crabs were right below him, snapping their claws and taking wild swipes at his toes. But as hard as they tried, they couldn't quite reach him.

Mystified, he continued to stare as the bodies of the crabs shrank smaller and smaller. Then, to his amazement he saw that he was no longer standing on the fountain. He was floating in mid-air, high above the courtyard.

Am I dead? he thought, trying to move his arms and legs. A sharp, stabbing pain in his shoulder gave him the answer.

'Caw, caw,' squawked a familiar voice. 'Stop your squirming or I'll drop you!'

'Chatterbeak?' Whisker exclaimed, looking up at the shadowy mass of feathers above him. 'Is that you?'

'Keep your voice down,' the bird cooed. 'I don't want

my beak featured on the next wanted poster.'

'But-but what are you doing here?' Whisker gasped.

'I thought that was obvious,' came a second voice from above. 'He's rescuing you.'

'*Ruby?*' Whisker gasped.

'And me,' Horace called down to him. 'There's room for two on this flying taxi.'

'Skraww, skraww!' Chatterbeak shrilled, gliding past the turret of the eastern tower. 'Prepare for landing!'

Whisker had just enough time to glimpse the circular balcony of the penthouse before Chatterbeak released his talons and he was somersaulting through the open door.

'Ouch,' he groaned, landing in a soggy heap at the foot of a luxurious four-poster bed.

Frankie Belorio, dressed in a pair of gold-thread pyjamas, rushed over and helped him to his feet. Smudge buzzed in circles around his head.

'Evenin', Whisker,' Frankie said in a matter-of-fact voice.

Smudge pointed vigorously to the open French doors. Sensing he was not out of danger yet, Whisker drew his sword and turned to see Ruby storming into the room. Behind her, Horace was still clambering off Chatterbeak.

'You've got some explaining to do, apprentice,' she hissed, striding up to him.

Before Whisker could stop her, she had thrown her arms around his neck and was hugging him tightly. Speechless, Whisker dropped his sword and hugged her back.

'I'm still angry with you,' she said, her voice quivering with emotion. 'And I haven't forgotten you're a lying scumbag.'

'I know,' Whisker said, smiling through his pain. 'It's good to see you too, Ruby.'

Ruby released him from her embrace and pointed to a crumpled scrap of paper lying on a bedside table. Large words were scrawled across its yellowed surface in campfire charcoal.

> DEAR RUBY,
> I HAVE GONE AWAY.
> I CAN'T SAY WHERE AND I
> CAN'T SAY WHY BUT I WANT
> YOU TO KNOW THAT I'M
> SORRY - FOR EVERYTHING.
>
> WHISKER
>
> P.S. THE CAT FISH ARE
> HIDING IN THE ROWBOAT.

'I found your note in my quiver of arrows,' Ruby said, picking up the paper. 'Something told me you needed our help.'

'Isn't that the truth!' Horace called out.

'What about the cats …?' Whisker began.

Ruby flashed him a mischievous grin. 'Still dozing in the bottom of our rowboat. The Captain thought it would be safer if we took their boat instead. As you can see, Horace and I found a swifter way to reach you.'

'Fred wanted to come, too,' Horace added, 'but our fine feathered friend imposed some weight restrictions.'

Chatterbeak shook his tail feathers defensively. 'Caw, caw! I'm not a flying packhorse!'

Whisker was still puzzled about one thing.

'How did you know *where* to find me?' he asked.

'The clue on your note was a dead giveaway,' Ruby replied.

'Clue?' Whisker said, dumfounded. 'What clue?'

Ruby flipped the scrap of paper over to reveal a detailed map of a deserted farm and a ship-shaped inn.

'Gustave's Plan B,' Whisker said, feeling slightly stupid. 'It was the only paper I had.'

'A fortunate coincidence,' Ruby quipped. 'We already knew that something strange happened to you in the inn – something you couldn't tell any of us.'

'And when we spotted the fish-shaped topiary trees from the air, it seemed like the logical place to find you,' Horace added. 'Frankie even offered up his penthouse suite for our stakeout.'

'Thanks, Frankie,' Whisker said gratefully. 'I'm sorry to drag you into this mess.'

'Oh, don't apologise,' Frankie said cheerfully. 'I'm rather enjoyin' all the excitement. It's not every day a band of trophy-winning desperados show up on my balcony!'

Whisker felt a sudden pang of guilt.

'A-about the trophy,' he began, shuffling uncomfortably from foot to foot. 'It's, well … gone.' He shot a wary glance in Ruby's direction, expecting a scathing remark or a word of rebuke but Ruby simply pursed her lips and shrugged.

'Never mind, Whisker,' Horace said, pointing his hook at a large hole in his companion's cloak. 'We've still got the prize money, and judging by the state you're in, the trophy was more trouble than it was worth.'

Whisker felt an enormous weight lift off his shoulders.

But before he could say anything, there was a loud commotion from the balcony.

'Skraww, skraww!' Chatterbeak screeched, extending his neck over the railing. 'Don't look now, but more trouble is on its way.'

Horace rushed to the edge of the balcony and peered below.

'The Blue Claw,' he gasped. 'Hundreds of them! And they're headed for the tower.'

Ruby frowned. 'I don't know what kind of mess you're in, Whisker, but it's high time we got an explanation.'

Taking a deep breath, Whisker began to retell the events that led him to the courtyard, starting with his dance floor disappearance. A satisfied smile crept across Ruby's face on hearing the words 'abandoned' and 'Hera' in the same sentence, but her joy was soon replaced by a deep look of concern when Whisker recalled his dramatic encounter with the fox. Horace stared wide-eyed, his mouth hung open in disbelief.

The sound of scuttling grew louder as the story continued. '... And I don't know what happened to my parents,' Whisker gabbled, speaking at a frantic pace, 'but the fox said my sister was alive and living with a family of birds on a mountain –'

Chatterbeak let out a startled *SQUAWK!*

'Pluck my tail feathers and roast me for Thanksgiving!' he screeched. 'Do you hear what you're saying? Those birds are not some berry-loving budgerigars. They're the dreaded birds of *Cloud Mountain.*'

Whisker felt himself turning white with terror.

How could I be so blind? he thought.

He'd read about the famous mountain in the Book of

Knowledge and the words were still fresh in his mind.

... Cloud Mountain is home to four species of birds: the hawk, the raven, the peregrine falcon and the golden eagle. These species are often described as hunters or ...

'*... birds of prey.*'

With a stabbing pain in his heart, Whisker understood the true meaning of the fox's last words.

There was no friendly family looking after his sister. There was only a flock of vicious predators with dinner on their minds. The birds were hunters and his sister was their prey.

'We've got to do something,' he cried, struggling to hold back the tears.

'If it's not already too late,' Ruby said gravely.

'Time, time,' Chatterbeak prattled. 'There's still time.'

'Time for what?' Whisker quavered.

Chatterbeak raised his right wing and pointed to the waxing moon.

'The first full moon of autumn,' he chirped. 'Every year the mountain birds hold a mighty feast to herald the coming of winter. It's no secret their favourite food is *live rodent.*' He lowered his wing and continued sorrowfully, 'Coo, coo. Your sister's not the first poor creature they've ensnared for their celebration.'

Whisker stared up at the moon. Only a thin sliver of its surface still lay in darkness.

'How long do we have?' he asked.

Chatterbeak studied the glowing sphere carefully.

'Three nights till full moon,' he trilled.

'Do you think we can reach her in time?' Whisker asked, hopefully.

Horace looked sullen. 'It's a six day hike to Cloud

Mountain.'

'Who said anything about hiking?' Ruby said, raising an eyebrow at Chatterbeak.

Chatterbeak stuck his head under his wing.

'Leave me out of this,' he clucked. 'Birds of prey don't take kindly to aerial intruders.'

'Have a heart, you selfish swan!' Horace snapped, prodding the parrot with his hook. 'There's an innocent life at –'

CRASH! A mighty tremor shook the penthouse. Splinters of wood flew across the room as a lightning-branded claw broke through the stairwell door.

Startled into action, Chatterbeak leapt onto the balcony, flapping his blue and yellow wings vigorously.

'Madness, madness!' he screeched. 'You rats will be the death of me. Now climb on board before I change my mind.'

Without hesitation, Whisker leapt onto Chatterbeak's back. Ruby scrambled up behind him.

'You're on the bottom, pipsqueak,' Chatterbeak squawked, snatching up Horace in his talons.

'What about Frankie?' Whisker gasped.

'He'll be fine,' Ruby hissed, wrapping her arms around Whisker's waist. 'Now, hold on tight and don't let go.'

Whisker dug his fingers into the soft, blue plumage of Chatterbeak's neck and locked his knees into place.

'Tell the Captain where to find us,' Ruby called out to Smudge. 'And ask him to bring reinforcements.'

Smudge buzzed his wings in acknowledgement and flew off towards the ocean. With a high-pitched *COOOEEE,* Chatterbeak launched himself into the air.

Whisker caught a final glimpse of Frankie Belorio collapsing into a padded chair before the crabs flooded into the room.

'Thank goodness you arrived in time!' Frankie exclaimed. 'Those dirty rats took me hostage and threatened to turn me into a pie …'

Safe at last in the windy heights of the sky, Whisker let out a sigh of relief. His body was wracked with pain, but his spirit remained strong.

His sister was alive, and she needed his help.

He felt the warmth of Ruby's arms pressing against his cloak, and knew he wasn't alone.

Together, they had won the Trophy of Champions, and together, they could save his sister from the birds of Cloud Mountain.

As the moonlight spilled onto the glassy ocean far below, Whisker saw the outline of a shadowy black ship.

The Black Shadow, he thought with a shiver. *A bad omen or something far worse?*

Turning away, he fixed his eyes on the snow-capped mountains to the north. As the first light of dawn appeared on the horizon, he let his troubled mind relax, safe in the knowledge that where he was going, no ship could ever follow him.

Book 5
Child of the Cloud

Deep in the heart of Aladrya stands a mighty mountain. Rising high above the clouds, its rocky crags and windswept cliffs are home to four species of birds.

With only three days left until the full moon feast, Whisker's rescue mission to save his sister hangs in the balance. Even if he can reach the mountain alive, he still has to out-fight and out-fly the dreaded birds of prey.

Discover more about the Pie Rats at:
www.pierats.com.au